IN THE DRIFT

IN THE DRIFT

Borto Milan

HEADLINE

First published in Great Britain in 1995
by HEADLINE BOOK PUBLISHING

10 9 8 7 6 5 4 3 2 1

British Library Cataloguing in Publication Data

Milan, Borto
In the Drift
I. Title
823 [F]

ISBN 0–7472–1282–1

Phototypeset by Intype, London
Printed and bound in Great Britain by
Mackays of Chatham PLC, Chatham, Kent

HEADLINE BOOK PUBLISHING
A division of Hodder Headline PLC
338 Euston Road
London NW1 3BH

'No man can save his brother's soul or pay his brother's debts'

MATTHEW ARNOLD

One

'What the hell was that?' Stutz exclaimed, as he jerked forward, twisting in his seat to look over at the park.

'Backfire. Maybe a kid with some firecrackers,' his partner answered lethargically.

Stutz glanced over at him.

Hal was seated behind the steering-wheel of the squad car, intently examining a young woman across the street.

The young woman was wearing a pair of very short Levi cut-offs and a T-shirt that ended well above the waistband of her shorts.

'Sure the hell sounded like shots.'

'C'mon, relax, would you. It's Sunday afternoon, nobody shoots anybody on a Sunday,' Hal drawled.

Stutz examined his partner closely, searching for a trace of amusement. It depressed him when he realized that the other man was completely serious.

'Maybe I should go take a look around.'

'Suit yourself.' His partner shrugged, never taking his eyes off the young woman.

Stutz let his gaze travel over to the park. The midday glare of the Florida sun didn't make it appear especially inviting. Sheltered somewhat inside the squad car from the heat and humidity, he found the thought of a quick walk through the park not a particularly appealing one.

Stutz surveyed the park, looking for any signs of trouble. There was an elderly woman, watching in maternal satisfaction as her poodle relieved itself at the base of the flag-pole, a couple of teenagers, sitting in the shade of a palm-tree, indolently rolling a

1

basketball between them, and two kids running round the duckpond. And that was it.

'So, you going to go look?' Hal asked, then quickly leaned forward and squinted through the windshield as the young woman crouched over to examine the interior of a shop.

'Nah, it's probably nothing,' Stutz muttered, following his partner's gaze, noticing the way the back of the woman's shorts rode up over the cleanly defined swell of her buttocks.

Two

Lisa Ryan, at eight, was five years older than her brother Ollie. She clung tightly to his hand as she hurried across the park. She tugged impatiently when Ollie became distracted by a butterfly. 'C'mon, Ollie,' she called impatiently, pulling him along beside her.

'Butterfly?'

'Not now, Ollie. Hurry up,' Lisa ordered, moving past the swing sets, past the monkey bars, and on towards the residential street that bordered the park.

Ollie stumbled along beside her, barely able to keep up with her longer strides.

Reaching the street, Lisa paused for a moment, then, spotting the squad car, quickly turned and dragged Ollie over to it.

She stepped up to the passenger side of the vehicle. 'Mister?' she said softly, then hesitated, not quite sure now what it was she wanted to say.

The man slowly turned to her.

Lisa met his gaze and glanced down at the pavement. She felt Ollie leaning against her thigh, and without thinking about it put her arm round his shoulder.

'What is it?' the policeman asked, smiling gently.

It was the smile that gave her the courage and, in a way that she didn't quite understand, started her crying. 'It's my daddy,' she said, through the surprising arrival of the tears.

'What about him? Did you lose him?' asked the man with a hint of amusement.

Lisa shook her head.

'C'mon, honey, what's wrong?' he asked. This time he opened the door and stepped out of the car.

3

Lisa took a step back, pulling Ollie along with her. She felt him ducking his head into her hip and his hand tugging at the back pant-leg of her jeans. She shook her head, wiped her eyes and said, 'He's over there.' She turned and pointed towards the center of the park.

The man glanced over to where she was pointing, then brought his gaze back to her face. He stooped down until his eyes were level with hers. 'What is it?' he asked, and this time there was a seriousness about his voice that frightened her.

Lisa tried not to. She didn't want to scare Ollie, but she couldn't help herself. She sobbed and a moment later heard Ollie begin to do the same. Hugging her brother tightly, she looked up at the police-man before her and said, 'He won't get up. My daddy fell down and now he won't get up.'

For Lisa and Ollie everything that happened afterwards was inex-plicable. The time passed in a blur of strange faces and hushed voices. It was worse for Lisa, for she had a vague idea of what had happened.

Whenever she thought about her father, she was filled with an overwhelming sense of foreboding. And what made this even worse was that she couldn't quite comprehend why she felt this way. She just wished he would come home to explain what was happening. But he never did, and this frightened her even more because she had begun to believe that maybe he would never come home again.

For Ollie it was much easier. He didn't have any idea of what was going on. The ride in the police car had occupied his imagination for almost two full days. He would ramble on about it, in his sometimes incoherently excited way, seemingly unaware of everything else that was happening.

It wasn't until the third day that he started to ask about Daddy. Lisa didn't know what to tell him and there wasn't anyone around to tell her what she should say. She rarely saw her mother over this period and when she did it was only for the briefest possible time. When these infrequent moments occurred, her mother would rush into their room to hug the two of them tightly and begin to cry. Her crying frightened Lisa even more.

Her Aunt Sis wasn't any better. Whenever she asked about her father Aunt Sis would only smile and say he'd gone away on a long trip and wouldn't be back for a while. But Lisa could tell by the worried expression behind Aunt Sis's eyes, that there was something more she wasn't saying.

By the third day she had begun to guess what this might be. It was a word that she had heard before, but it was also a word that was almost too big for her to understand. The word was dead. And when she thought about it, thought about it in conjunction with her father, it frightened her so much that she decided, in a very adult manner, that she simply would not think about it any more.

'So tell me what you did in the park, Lisa?' the policeman asked her.

It was a different policeman from the one four days ago. Lisa knew this, because this policeman wore a white shirt, and a tie.

'Did you play on the swings?'

Lisa nodded, remembering the way her father had pushed Ollie too high, and the funny way Ollie had clung to the ropes on each side of the seat. It had made both her and her father laugh, and after a while even Ollie had laughed too.

'Then what'd you do?'

'Then we went to look at the ducks,' Lisa told him, swinging her legs over the edge of the chair, wishing she were taller so she could reach the floor.

'Was there anybody else with you?'

'No.' She shook her head. 'Just me and Ollie and Daddy.'

'So after you watched the ducks what'd you do?'

'Daddy bought us cokes.'

The policeman nodded, waiting for her to go on, but she didn't know what else to tell him. All they'd done that day was to take their cokes over to the side of the pond and then they'd sat down to drink them. Ollie had started to make those noises through his straw and had peeked up at the two of them to see if they'd heard him. When Daddy had glared at him, not angry, but pretending to be angry, Ollie'd made more noises until Daddy had smiled. Ollie started laughing until coke had spurted out of his nose. Lisa'd taken one look at him, cried 'Gross', and had quickly turned away.

Remembering this now made her smile again.

'What's funny, Lisa?' the policeman asked her, but she knew she could never tell him about that and make him understand it. 'And then what did you do, after you drank your cokes?' he asked.

Lisa cringed. This was the part she didn't want to remember, the part that she'd decided never to remember again.

'C'mon, Lisa,' the policeman gently prompted. 'What happened next?'

Lisa twisted and glanced up at her mother standing beside her. Her mother touched her shoulder. 'Go ahead, honey, tell him what happened.'

'Then the firecracker went off and Daddy fell down. I didn't know what to do. Daddy wouldn't get up, so I went to get somebody to help me wake him up,' Lisa said quickly, thinking if she said it real fast, then it wouldn't count.

'When your daddy fell down, was there anybody else around?'

Lisa closed her eyes and thought about the duckpond. She remembered the way the ducks kept swimming in little circles, digging into the water with their orange beaks. She never saw them catch anything, but when they lifted their heads out of the water they always looked like they were swallowing something. She remembered asking her father what they had in their mouths, but he'd never answered her, he'd only shrugged and made a face. She'd always liked ducks. One Easter she'd gotten a real live one in her basket. She'd kept it out in the garage in a banana box. She'd put crumpled paper and rags in it so it was just like a little nest, and she'd fed it water and corn every day, right up until that one morning when she'd gone out and it was . . .

'Lisa? Lisa, did you see anybody else?' the man asked and Lisa turned and buried her face in her mother's leg. She could smell her mother's scent, feel the fabric of her dress against her cheek, and thought this is where I'm going to stay until everything's right again, until Daddy comes home and I can ask him about the ducks.

'Lisa?' her mother said softly, but Lisa only clung on more tightly.

'I'm sorry,' she heard Mommy say, and wondered if she'd made her mad.

A moment later her mother's hand came to rest on her shoulder, and Lisa knew that everything was all right.

'It's okay, I understand how difficult this must be for all of you,' the policeman said quietly.

Lisa peeked out at him from behind her mother's leg.

'Have you heard from the brother?' he asked a moment later and Lisa couldn't understand why he would ask something like that. Ollie was sitting right outside the door with Aunt Sis waiting for them. Of course they'd heard from Ollie. It was almost impossible not to hear from Ollie. He was always talking.

'No, not in a long time,' her mother answered.

Surprised by the sharpness of her tone, Lisa glanced up at her, forgetting for a moment that she was supposed to be hiding.

'If you do, I'd appreciate your letting us know.'

'I doubt there's any possibility of that happening. Eddie doesn't care one way or another about us, or his brother.'

Lisa felt her mother's hand tighten on her shoulder. She looked up at her curiously, trying to understand what she was talking about.

Who was Eddie?

Eddie wasn't her brother. Ollie was.

What did Mommy mean?

Three

When he closed his eyes, Edward Ryan could drift anywhere he wanted. He could trip back a few years to Mexico and almost taste the salt coming off the waves of the Pacific. The image would be so vivid that he could practically feel the hot sand scratching against his back and shoulders. Or, if he wanted, he could drift through his memories of Zella until he found one he wished to recreate; almost always it would be one of the earlier ones, before everything fell apart.

There was one he especially liked to bring back. It was when the two of them had found a vacant condominium swimming pool. After a more than liquid night, they had quickly and quietly undressed and slipped into the cool evening water. The small rectangle of shimmering blue light had rapidly become their own private world. Arms splayed out to either side of him, holding onto the edge of the pool, Ryan had watched as Zella had undressed and slowly lowered herself into the shallow end of the pool. Her long legs disappeared into the placid surface. The water rose to her knees, thighs, and to the silky patch of dark hair between her legs. Watching her, feeling his desire for her build, he had pushed himself beneath the water. Keeping his eyes open, he swam towards the blurred and hazy configurations of her body.

'Ryan, what the fuck you doing, man?'

The voice obliterated the image. Ryan opened his eyes and glanced across the room to see Fish looking at him curiously.

'Nothing,' he answered, shaking his head, clearing away the rest of the memory.

'Man, you looked out of it there for a while.'

'Just thinking.'

9

''Bout what?'

'Stuff. Just old stuff. Things that don't matter any more.'

'Sure one fuck of a lot of those.' Fish grinned.

Ryan agreed and reached for his beer. He killed it quickly and threw the empty on the floor. 'Let's get the fuck out of here,' he said, pushing himself to his feet and moved towards the door without waiting for Fish's response.

Ryan climbed onto his bike and started it up. The deep roar of the engine soothed him. He waited while Fish kick-started his bike, ignoring the other man's taunting smile.

'When you going to dump that gook piece of shit?' Fish asked, nodding towards Ryan's cycle.

Ryan shrugged, kicked into first gear and wheeled out of the lot. A moment later he heard Fish racing up beside him.

Cimarron's was the name of the bar. The lot was filled with Harleys. Ryan and Fish parked and climbed off their bikes.

'Man, when you going to get a hog?'

Ryan shrugged.

'Fucking jap bikes, man.' Fish shook his head in disgust. 'Ain't worth a shit.'

'It's all right.'

'You don't miss the Harley?' Fish wanted to know.

'Yeah, I miss it. But what the fuck am I supposed to do? Thing was totaled. This was the best I could do for the money.' Ryan paused as he lit a cigarette. 'I got eight large stashed. Another four, and I'll be riding something strong again.' He glanced over and held the other man's gaze. 'It was either this or a Ford Escort,' he said dryly.

Fish shuddered and started for the bar, where Ryan joined him a moment later.

The club was packed with the usual Saturday night crowd. Ryan wedged himself into the bar and ordered a beer, then turned to survey the room. He knew most of the people there. He spotted Fish over by the juke-box. He was standing beside two women seated at a table, trying to look like they belonged there. The women were the usual weekend secretarial types, looking for something a little rough.

Ryan turned back to the bar and picked up his beer.

'You still riding that thing?'

'Yeah.'

The bartender grimaced behind his beard and moved off to fill an order.

Ryan listened to the noise around him and leaned forward and closed his eyes. He tripped back to a ride he'd taken up the coast with Zella. The two of them had found a deserted beach, then parked and climbed down the embankment to the shore. Zella had disappeared behind the rocks, while Ryan had paused to examine the skeletal remains of a fish. He had straightened, then glanced around trying to find her. Suddenly she'd reappeared, stepping gingerly around the rocks, wearing only a pair of white shorts and swinging her halter top in her left hand. The sight of her beneath the glare of the sun. Her breasts, the smooth line of her stomach, dark hair swinging behind her . . .

'Got two.' Fish grinned, nodding towards the table by the juke-box. 'Come on over. You can have the blonde.'

Ryan turned to glance over at the women. He caught the blonde's eye, saw the anticipatory smile before she turned back to her companion.

'We'll juice them, then take them over to my crib.'

Ryan nodded and ordered another beer. When he got it, he went over to the table to join them.

'Where'd you get all these scars?' she asked, tracing her finger lightly across his chest and stomach.

'The wars.'

'Which ones?' She bent over and kissed one of the scars laced across his chest.

'What'd you say your name was?'

'Cindy,' she answered and moved her lips and hands across his stomach.

Ryan closed his eyes.

He woke up early, slipped from beneath the tangle of her arms and legs and quietly left the apartment. Outside he stretched hugely in the dawning light, then climbed onto his bike and started it up. He drove slowly along the deserted streets, enjoying the feel of the bike and the early morning Sunday sense of emptiness of the world.

Back at his apartment Ryan made coffee and climbed out onto his fire escape. The metal cage looked out at the alley three floors below. If he stood in one corner of the platform he could just see over the apartment building across from him. This vantage point gave him a view of the city.

He lit a cigarette and watched the city slowly wake. The sun shafted its first rays up the side of the building. Ryan felt them travel up his body, warming him as they climbed.

He slipped through his window to refill his coffee and was stopped by the sound of the phone. He debated for a moment, then, losing, went over and answered it.

An hour later, he tied his duffle-bag to the back of his bike and climbed on. Twenty minutes after that he hit the interstate and headed east. He figured he had a three- maybe four-day ride ahead of him, depending on how hard he pushed it.

He shifted in the seat until he found the position he wanted and settled in for the long ride. He let the road take him until it erased everything but the sound of the bike and the feel of the wind in his face. Whenever he was threatened by other thoughts – the voice on the phone, the memories it dredged up – he twisted the throttle and whipped the bike from lane to lane, until the feel of the road dragged him back to the present.

He rode steadily through the day and late into the night. Early the next morning he pulled over and slept on top of a picnic table at a travel stop. He woke to the curious stare of a young boy.

'Harold, leave the man alone.'

Both Ryan and the boy turned to the voice.

'C'mon, Harold. Get over here. Right now!' the man called, then, looking apprehensively at Ryan, added, 'Sorry about that. Hope he didn't bother you.'

Ryan pushed himself to a sitting position and glanced down at the boy. His wide-eyed glance traveled from Ryan to the cycle parked beside the picnic table, then back again to Ryan.

'Your dad's calling you.'

The boy nodded, turned quickly and raced over to his father, who grabbed him by the hand and, without a backward glance, dragged him towards the car.

Ryan watched them speed out of the lot. He ran a hand through his hair, brushing it back out of his face, then hunched forward and lit a cigarette. He pushed himself to his feet and stretched tightly, feeling the muscles pull in his arms and shoulders, then made his way over to the rest rooms. Once inside, he splashed water across his face and dried off, trying to avoid the bloodshot gaze staring back at him from the mirror.

He drove to the next exit and stopped at a Waffle House for breakfast. As he stepped inside, there was a moment's silence while the other customers took in his appearance. He ignored it and sat down at the counter.

He ordered coffee and bacon and eggs. He heard a voice behind him snicker, then disdainfully mutter something about Hell's Angels. Glancing in the mirror behind the counter, he saw three men seated in a booth, one of them looking his way.

Ryan lit a cigarette and sipped his coffee, ignoring the steady stream of comments coming from behind.

He finished his breakfast, threw some bills on the counter, rose and turned to the table behind him. 'You guys got a problem?'

'Nah, we're fine. Why? Something bothering you?' one of the men answered. The challenge was there for Ryan either to accept or ignore.

'Nothing bothering me at all.' Ryan shrugged, wiping his smile away as he leveled his gaze at the man. The other two quickly looked away.

Ryan stood beside the table, waiting. When nothing happened, he turned and went out to his bike. He wheeled out of the lot and hit the interstate.

Two days later, he was on the outskirts of the town. His leather jacket was tied to the back of his bike, along with his flannel shirt and duffle-bag. Down to a black T-shirt and jeans, the heat was still overwhelming. He felt sweat dripping along his back and across his ribs.

Entering the town, he noticed a small park surrounding a duck-pond and continued on. It took him another fifteen minutes before he located the street.

He drove slowly, examining the neat homes on each side of him.

He found the address he wanted, pulled into the driveway and parked. Swinging one leg up and resting it over the top of the bike, he sat for a moment, looking thoughtfully at the house before him. He took his time lighting a cigarette, wondering about his reception inside.

The front door suddenly burst open and two children flew out onto the front porch. A little boy, and a girl a few years older, stared down at him. The boy quickly moved towards the steps and started down the stairs.

'Ollie?' the girl called, but the boy ignored her and raced over to Ryan. He stopped a few feet away, excitedly eyeing both him and the motorcycle.

'Ollie, come back here right now.'

Ollie, without a backward glance, took a step closer to the bike. He started to reach out to touch it.

'Don't,' Ryan warned him. His voice startled the boy. He moved back fearfully. 'It's hot. You'll burn yourself,' Ryan explained gently.

'Ollie?'

Ollie glanced over at the girl, then back at Ryan. Suddenly he smiled and said, 'Ride.'

Ryan grinned back at him.

'What're you doing here, Eddie?' All three of them turned to look at the woman standing beside the door. 'You've no right to be here.'

'Mom?' the girl asked.

'You get back into the house. And you too, Ollie. Get inside right this minute.'

'Want a ride,' the boy whined.

'Ollie,' the woman threatened.

Ryan watched the little boy's face tighten up. He flipped his cigarette off to the side, then suddenly leaned over and picked up the boy and swung him up onto the seat in front of him. He held him tightly, feeling the excited heave of the kid's chest.

'Eddie,' the woman warned.

'Mommy, look at me,' the boy screamed, then crouched forward and gripped the handlebars. He began to make engine noises, glancing up excitedly at the woman and the girl on the porch.

Ryan kept his hands at the boy's side, holding him in place as he twisted and turned during his imaginary ride.

'Eddie,' the woman said softly, then, shaking her head wearily, turned and disappeared inside the house.

Ryan glanced at the girl and turned to the boy as he twisted in the seat to look up at him. 'Who're you?' he asked quizzically.

After a moment, Ryan smiled down at him and answered, 'I'm your Uncle Eddie.'

Four

There were two men in the room. The taller one, the one standing by the window, seemed to be in a constant state of motion. The other one, the one sitting at the conference table, appeared perfectly calm.

'I just think it was a mistake,' repeated the one at the window. His fingers tapped nervously on the sill.

'If it was, it's much too late to worry about it. It's done.'

'But, Jesus, why the hell wasn't I told?'

'There was no reason,' the man at the table answered soothingly.

The other man suddenly turned. In his right hand he held a pencil. He twirled it between his fingers. 'There was a reason, Richard. I'm a full partner in this venture and I should be aware of everything that's being considered.'

'There was no time, John.'

'There was plenty of time. All it would have taken to call me in on this would have been ten minutes.'

'We already knew what your answer would be. We took that into consideration before we decided on our course of action.'

'Jesus.' John shook his head in exasperation. 'You moved too fast. He wouldn't have said anything.'

'He might have.'

'And on that basis you decided to act?' John asked, now leaning over the table, staring across its surface at the other man.

'Yes. Are you forgetting what would happen to us if any of this were made public?'

'No.' John turned and strode across the room. He stepped over to the water cooler in the corner.

Richard watched him closely.

'I'm very much aware of the risks. I just feel that there are things that should be discussed, before any of us moves unilaterally.'

'John, that wasn't the case in this particular situation. We discussed this almost a week ago and we were all well aware of the possibility that this type of action might prove to be necessary.'

'He would not have said anything,' John repeated firmly.

'Neither I, nor any of the rest of us, was willing to take that risk.'

'It wouldn't have been a risk. I know . . .' John paused, then corrected himself, 'knew this man. He would not have done anything.'

'Well, be that as it may, it's done now, and there's nothing we can do about it other than try to minimize the risk.'

John suddenly grew still. 'What're you saying?'

After an appraising glance, Richard commented, 'He wasn't alone at the time.'

'Are you talking about the children?'

'Yes.'

'Richard, come on, they're only kids.'

'It's not a matter of age, as you should well know,' Richard said, then paused, allowing a moment for his words to take effect. 'It's a matter of what they saw, and what they're willing to say about what they witnessed.'

John crumpled the empty paper cup and threw it towards the garbage can.

'So far, our people have reported that neither child appears to have seen anything,' Richard said, watching as John turned round. His hopeful glance was so obvious that Richard took great pleasure in adding, 'but that's still inconclusive. We need to continue watching them, until we're absolutely sure that they won't suddenly remember some wayward bit of information that might threaten all of us.'

'And if they do?'

Richard smiled cruelly. 'Well, that will be a problem that we will most definitely have to rectify.'

'I don't want anything to do with that.'

Richard pushed himself to his feet. He took his time straightening his tie and suit coat. On his way to the side door of the office he commented, 'It's much too late for that, John. You're a full partner and you carry a full partner's responsibility for everything the group does.' He smiled, turned and exited the room.

John stepped over to the window. He looked down at the street below, bathed beneath the searing rays of the sun. The fingers of his right hand tapped anxiously against the sill.

The knock at the door startled him. He turned to see his secretary leaning in through the doorway. 'You have a call on line two.'

'Thank you, Linda.'

'Has Mr . . .'

'Yes,' John interrupted. 'He took the side door out.'

Linda nodded and closed the door behind her.

John went over to the telephone and hit the speaker button. 'Johnny.'

At the first intonation of the voice, John quickly picked up the phone and transferred the call to the receiver. 'What're you doing calling me here?'

'John, for Christ's sake, calm down.'

'After what's happened I think it's an unnecessary risk.'

'Johnny, come on. Who's going to know? And anyway, Richard suggested I give you a call. He figured you might need a little diversion this evening.'

John's hand grew clammy with equal amounts of anticipation and reluctance. 'What?' he managed to croak out, then listened to the laugh at the other end of the line.

'Who, might be a better question,' the voice responded.

John waited for him to go on, hating the excitement he felt building inside his body, but unable to do anything to stop it.

After he'd hung up he buzzed his secretary. 'Linda, cancel that dinner appointment I had this evening with Shefield from the Better Business Bureau.'

'Mr Caldwell, that will be the third time you've canceled,' Linda reminded him.

'Just do it, Linda.'

'Yes, sir.'

Later, seated behind his desk, John leaned back in his chair. He tapped his foot against the floor as he thought of some of the things he might be able to do later on that evening. The images that came to mind only increased his usual nervousness.

Boland Stutz sat nursing a beer at the chickee bar at the Beach Hotel. The bar was situated fifty feet from the Gulf of Mexico and commanded an unobstructed view of the water.

It was still a couple of hours before sunset and the occupancy of the bar reflected this fact. The locals were all toiling away at their jobs and wouldn't appear for another hour or so. The few guests staying at the hotel had retired to their rooms to shower and prepare themselves for their evening's adventures. Mid-June was not a month that many would think to vacation in Florida.

It was a time of the afternoon that Stutz treasured.

'Another one?'

'Yeah, what the hell,' Stutz shrugged, glancing across the bar at Judy.

'How come you're so down?'

'Bad couple of weeks.' Stutz shook his head wearily.

'Really?' Judy asked, leaning forward to rest her arms on top of the bar.

Stutz took a moment to admire her breasts, before he nodded and said, 'Yeah, seems like all the crazies have been coming out. I caught a domestic out in The Gate the other night. Some woman'd hammered her old man half to death with his tackle box. Guy was bleeding like a pig.'

'How come she was doing that?' Judy smiled, shaking her head in amused disbelief.

Stutz took a sip of his beer. 'Said he wouldn't take her out fishing on his boat any more.'

'It's the heat,' Judy offered. 'It makes everybody nuts.'

'Yeah,' Stutz sighed, 'I know, but it doesn't help any knowing that.'

She turned and went over to serve a waiter at the other end of the bar. Stutz watched as she bent forward to fill two glasses with ice, admiring her legs and the clean jut of her ass.

'I keep thinking about those two kids. I can't seem to get them out of my mind,' he said when she returned.

'The ones by the park?'

'Yeah. God, it was pathetic. Little girl was just standing there, hanging onto her little brother for dear life, telling me how her father fell down and wouldn't wake up. Shit,' Stutz exclaimed, then paused to finish off his Budweiser.

Judy quickly replaced it. 'That one's on me.'

Nodding his thanks to her Stutz continued, 'I didn't even know what was going on. If I had, I never would have made them show me where he was. Jesus, how the hell was I supposed to know somebody'd blown a hole right through the back of the guy's head.'

Judy leaned forward, a slight smile of anticipation on her face. 'Pretty bad?' she asked softly.

Stutz glanced over at her and saw the smile. 'A fucking nightmare.' He nodded, smiling back at her. He raised his beer, and carefully put it down in front of him. Studying it, refusing to meet her eye, he asked, 'What time you get off?' When he raised his eyes to hers, he watched her smile widen. It gave him the courage to add, 'Why don't we get something to eat and I'll tell you more about it.'

Stutz took her to a restaurant that fronted Siena bay. They were shown to a table overlooking the water and ordered margaritas and a dozen oysters on the half-shell. Slurping the lubricious shellfish he answered her questions, playing up the more violent aspects of his job. His exaggerations grew in direct proportion to her obvious excitement with the more gory details of his occupation.

Over the Snapper Rockefeller Stutz was in the process of describing an imaginary shoot-out with two Colombian drug dealers, deep in the Everglades, when he spotted the man stepping up to the bar. 'Who the hell is that?' he said, abruptly interrupting his own story.

Judy twisted in her seat. 'He looks like a fugitive from Hell's Angels.'

'You ever see him before?'

'No,' Judy shook her head, then added, 'He sure doesn't look like a tourist, though.'

'If he is, I hope he isn't traveling with a group,' Stutz commented dryly, earning him a laugh from his date.

He watched the man take a seat at the far corner of the bar. He was dressed in worn jeans and a black Harley T-shirt. The shirt was frayed at the arms and collar. His right biceps sported a multicolored tattoo. Stutz was too far away to make out the design. The biker's long brown hair was tied back in a pony-tail that hung down well below his shoulders. His face sported a thick growth of dark hair that looked more the product of negligence than any serious attempt at a beard.

Stutz examined him closely.

'Who you think he is?'

Stutz shrugged, noticing the way the man sat with his back to the wall, facing the rest of the restaurant and bar.

'You going to go question him?'

'About what?'

Judy shrugged. 'I don't know, being suspicious or something.'

Stutz noticed the brightness of her gaze and turned back to the man at the bar. For a moment he debated about walking over and talking to him. He knew it would probably be more than enough to lure her into his bed, but there was something about the way the guy held himself that stopped him.

He turned back to Judy and smiled. 'No reason to mess up a perfectly good dinner,' he said and saw disappointment in her glance. 'I tell you about that guy I caught coming out of The Buggy with the razor?' he quickly offered. Judy's excited smile let him know that the bait had been taken.

He launched into a lengthy account of the fictional episode and managed to drag it out through coffee and half-way to his car.

Later on, leaning back against the headboard watching her slip into the bathroom, he thought briefly about the face of the man he had seen in the bar.

Judy's sudden reappearance in the doorway quickly banished the thought. Naked, without a trace of self-consciousness, she stepped over to the side of the bed and smiled down at him. Stutz grinned back at her and wrapped his arms round her thighs.

Five

Lisa stared up at her bedroom ceiling, listening to Ollie make his engine noises from the other side of the room. 'Ollie, go to sleep,' she told him. The noises stopped for a moment, then began again. If anything, they seemed a little louder now. 'I'm going to tell Mom.'

'Where's Mommy?'

'Downstairs with Aunt Sis.'

'Where's Daddy?'

'Daddy went away,' Lisa answered, glancing across the dark bedroom. She caught a glimpse of the pale blur of her brother's face.

'Where?'

'Indiana.'

'Why?'

'Because.'

''Cause why?'

'Because he had to,' she told him, putting a note of finality into her voice.

Ollie was silent for a moment. Lisa heard him shifting beneath his sheets. 'When's Daddy coming home?'

'Soon.'

'Tuesday?'

'Maybe Tuesday,' Lisa told him, as she leaned forward and looked over at him. She saw him shift onto his side and curl up.

'I miss Daddy,' he said softly and was instantly asleep.

Lisa closed her eyes but opened them a few moments later. She wasn't at all tired. She thought about getting out her new Nancy Drew book but knew if she turned on the light it would only wake up Ollie, and then he would want her to read to him. She hated reading books to him that she was trying to read for herself. She could never concentrate when she was reading out loud. Somehow the words, once she spoke them out loud, just seemed to disappear somewhere. Whereas if she spoke them only to herself they stayed inside her head.

She heard Aunt Sis's voice coming from the kitchen and knew that she and her mother were sitting at the kitchen table drinking coffee and talking. Sometimes, over the last week, she had heard the sound of her mother crying. She had fallen asleep, more than once, listening to her mother's sobs. She knew she was crying because of her father but still wasn't sure how long it would go on.

Lisa had already accepted the fact that her father was never coming home again. It had been hard at first realizing that she was never going to go to the park with him again, or drive up to Disney World the way they did every Thanksgiving. But after almost seven days she had come to accept this and had even begun to wonder if maybe they still couldn't go to Disney World without him. It would be different, but it would still be all right, Lisa had reasoned.

She glanced over at her brother's sleeping form and wondered if he had any idea of what was going on. His questions earlier about their father had been more curiosity than anything else.

Ollie had quickly learned that whenever he asked about Daddy someone would give him something. Either a hug from their mother, or a cookie or candy bar from their Aunt Sis. At first she had resented this, but after seeing Ollie's gleeful smile she'd been unable to maintain her resentment. He was only three; how could he understand that Daddy was gone?

Saying that word surprised her.

Gone.

Where did he go, she wondered?

Was he somewhere with Daffy, her duck?

Was he watching her from heaven like Mrs Howard from next door said?

The questions troubled her and she had no one to answer them for her. Every time she tried to ask her mother or her aunt about them, they quickly shooed her out of the room. She knew they were only doing this because they didn't want to cry, but knowing that didn't help any. She wanted someone to tell her what was happening. Not just that Daddy was gone and wasn't coming back, but why he was gone and what had happened to him. So far there hadn't been anyone who would do that.

Thinking about this, she suddenly remembered the man on the motorcycle. He'd scared her at first. She'd heard the sound of it before anyone else and had raced through the house towards the front door, ignoring her mother's plea not to run. Along the way, Ollie had started to follow her.

Pushing her way out onto the porch and seeing the man sitting there on his motorcycle had startled her. She could still close her eyes and remember the way he had looked. He had seemed so big, sitting there with his leg resting on top of the bike. He'd been smoking a cigarette, something that both her mother and father had said was a dangerous thing to do. But the man on the motor-cycle had looked too dangerous to let a little thing like a cigarette bother him.

His hair had been even longer than hers and he'd worn it tied back in a pony-tail. And on his arm had been a bright blue-and-red tattoo. She'd wanted to look at it but was too afraid to go near him. Not Ollie, though. Stupid as he was, he'd just run right down the steps towards the man. She'd tried to call him back, but Ollie wouldn't listen. He never did when he got like that.

Lisa hadn't known what to do. She was torn between running back into the house and getting her mother, and wanting to stay outside to see what would happen next.

What would the man do when Ollie asked him for a ride? She'd known he was going to do that as soon as he raced down the steps.

She'd watched him reach out to touch the bike when the man suddenly told him not to. The sound of his voice had startled her as much as it had Ollie. She'd been all set to run into the house to get her mother when the man had told Ollie he'd get burned if he touched it. It was the voice that had stopped her. It had sounded so familiar. She had almost remembered where she'd heard it before when her mother had suddenly appeared behind her.

She'd turned quickly to stare up at her, hearing the strangeness in her tone. It was a voice that Lisa had always known. She knew when her mother was angry just by the way she spoke her name. She also knew when she was happy or sad. But her mother had sounded completely different from any other time she'd ever heard it. She'd stared up at her curiously, trying to decide what this new voice meant.

'Eddie,' she had called the man on the motorcycle. She knew him, Lisa had thought, finding this exciting, thinking maybe it would be all right if she went down to look at the man's tattoo.

Lisa had turned back to him just as he had reached down and swung Ollie up onto the seat in front of him. For a moment she had been filled with envy.

'I need to go talk to your mother,' the man had said softly to Ollie.

'Now?'

'Yeah, Ollie, right now.'

Lisa had watched as Ollie's lower lip started to push out into its usual pout. The man had suddenly reached up and put the tip of his finger right on Ollie's lower lip and rolled it down. Ollie had squealed deliriously and the man had lifted him high up off the bike and swung him down to the ground.

'Now you keep away from this, Ollie. It's hot and you'll burn yourself,' he had said, crouching down in front of Ollie to meet his eye.

Ollie had nodded solemnly. One finger started to rise to his nostril before he remembered and stopped.

The man had smiled, stood up and looked right at her. This time she had forced herself to meet his gaze. He was so strange looking that she couldn't understand how his voice could sound so much like her father's.

He took the steps two at a time until he was standing right in front of her. She had been aware of Ollie watching them, but was unable to pull her gaze up from her feet.

'Lisa,' the man had said softly, and she had looked up at him thinking he wanted something. But he had just smiled back at her and said her name again. A moment later he'd walked into the house.

Lisa had stepped over to the screen door, trying to listen to what he would say to her mother, but her Aunt Sis had quickly appeared in the doorway and warned both of them to keep away from the bike, and then she had turned and closed the door, shutting off the noises from inside.

'Uncle Eddie,' Ollie had said, grinning up at her, and turned to look at the motorcycle in front of him.

'Ollie, don't,' she had warned him. He had glanced up at her over his shoulder. 'Don't,' she'd said again, watching his lower lip start to come out and remembering the way the stranger had touched it with his finger. For some reason the memory had made her smile.

Even now, thinking about it made her smile again. She turned over on her stomach and rested her head on her arms, wondering where the man was right now. Was he going to come back?

She closed her eyes, thinking about her first sight of the gleaming motorcycle and the man seated on it. She remembered the tattoo and was disappointed that she'd been so nervous about being so close to him that she'd forgotten to look at it. She hoped he would come back again. She'd like to see his tattoo.

She slept and dreamt about being on the motorcycle, going faster than she'd ever gone before, faster even than the Twirly Bird at Disney World. The sudden sound of firecrackers jerked her awake. For a moment, in the silence of the dark room, she didn't know where she was.

'Daddy,' she called, then turned on her side and slipped back into sleep.

Six

Ryan sipped his beer and waited. He was used to the curious glances directed his way. Looking the way he did, he had expected them, and in truth had hoped this would happen. For the time being, he wanted to be noticed. The biker look, while not completely accepted on the west coast, was as least tolerated. Here, in this small conservative corner of south-west Florida, it was too much of an anomaly to go unnoticed.

On his second beer, he became aware of the gazes leveled his way from a couple seated at a water table. The woman's glance was a familiar one. He discounted it and concentrated on her companion's. For a moment he caught the man's eye. In that instant he knew he was a cop. It was a survival sense that Ryan had picked up over his years on the road.

He broke away from the other's eyes and lit a cigarette. He was just stubbing it out when he saw Charlie step through the front door. Ryan watched as he scanned the bar. His eyes drifted by him, then darted back. A moment later a smile broke across the other man's face as he started towards him.

Ryan rose from his stool and offered his hand.

'Jesus Christ, Edward. What the hell've you been doing?' Charlie said, enthusiastically gripping his hand and surveying him from head to toe. 'You look like something out of biker hell.'

'You think so?'

Charlie shook his head in feigned disgust and turned to the bartender. He ordered another beer for Ryan and a gin and tonic for himself. Once settled with his drink, he said, 'I'm sorry about Neal.'

'Yeah.' Ryan nodded.

'Did anybody else call you?'

29

'No, only you.'

'Maggie didn't . . .'

'No.'

'That's terrible.'

Ryan shrugged. 'That's the way things are.'

'You talk to her yet?'

'A little, yesterday.'

Charlie nodded, waiting for him to go on.

'She didn't tell me much.' Ryan sighed. 'She didn't seem too happy to see me.'

'She's going through a rough time now, Edward,' Charlie offered.

'Yeah, I know that. I wasn't expecting much from her.'

'You see the kids?'

Ryan smiled. 'Yeah, the boy looks just like him.'

'They're nice children. Maggie's done a good job with them.'

'Hey, I'm not putting Maggie down. I know she's okay. All this other stuff, it's just stuff she got dragged into with Neal. You marry somebody, you marry their past and their problems.'

Charlie nodded and glanced around the bar. 'You're causing quite a stir here.'

'I noticed that.' Ryan lifted his drink. 'You know that couple over by the water there?' Ryan motioned with his beer bottle.

Charlie looked across the room and turned back to Ryan. 'Boland Stutz. He's with the city police. He's fairly new. I think he's only been on the force for six months or so. I don't know who the woman is.'

'Woman doesn't matter.'

'Does Stutz?'

'You tell me.'

'He was the one who found your brother's body.'

Ryan turned to look at him.

'He's okay, Edward. He might be a little on the small-town-cop side, but he's all right.'

'You sure?'

'Yeah. I've had some dealings with him before. He's always been straight with me.'

Ryan went back to his beer.

'What're you planning?'

Ryan ignored him and took his time lighting a cigarette.

'You should stay out of it, Edward. There's nothing you can do.'

'Won't know that until after I've tried.'

'You know what it's like here,' Charlie went on. 'Despite all the tourists it's still a small town. Nothing happens without everyone knowing about it.'

'Maybe that'll make it easier.'

'Make what easier?'

'Easier to find out what happened.'

'What if there's nothing to find out? What if it's just some whacko?'

'Then that'll be all there is to it.'

'That *is* all there is to it. There's nothing else, there's no conspiracy here.'

'C'mon, Charlie. Neal was a CPA, for Christ's sake. Who goes around whacking out accountants?'

'No one sane, that's why you're better off leaving it alone.'

Ryan shook his head. 'Can't do that.'

Charlie sighed, then reached for his drink.

He took him to a restaurant perched on the bank of the Gordon River. They sat at a water table and drank beer and ate steamed shrimp. As the sun set into the Gulf both of them leaned back with cups of coffee.

'You look pretty good. At least what I can see of you behind all that hair does.'

Ryan shrugged.

'How long you been riding around like that?'

'Few years now,' Ryan answered non-committally.

'Maybe about seven?'

Ryan glanced over at him sharply.

'I'm sorry. Forget I said that.'

After a moment Ryan nodded, then looked away. 'How's Gloria doing?'

'Good. She's pregnant again.'

'How many is that now?' asked Ryan, with a trace of awe in his tone.

'Eight.'

'Christ, Charlie, haven't you heard of contraception, or even abstinence?'

31

'Yeah, but I guess I never listened too closely.'

'Obviously,' Ryan commented dryly.

'What about you? Anybody in your life?'

'No, not really.'

'There been anybody since . . .?' Charlie started, then stopped abruptly.

'No, Charlie,' Ryan answered. 'Not since then.' He paused and added softly. 'Just leave it alone, okay?'

Charlie nodded and motioned the waitress over for the check.

'It's a constant battle, but so far we've been holding our own,' Charlie said, as he drove slowly down the main street of town towards the Gulf of Mexico. 'The developers are buying up every piece of land they can, and trying to build their shopping centers and condos. Every time we manage to stop a project all the contractors come down on us, claiming we're putting them, and all their employees, out of work and hurting the economy. It just seems to go on for ever. No one ever seems to stop to take a look around at what's happening. We're tearing the land apart.' Charlie glanced over at Ryan, shaking his head in weary disbelief.

'We've been rationing water for the last three years, but it doesn't stop them from building. I can't wash my car except on Tuesdays, Thursdays and Saturdays. The place where I wash it, which is right outside my garage, used to face an old Florida home. They tore it down last May and now there's a twelve-unit luxury condo there. Makes no sense to me. If I have to watch the amount of water I use, how the hell can they continue to build condos?'

'What about the old part of town?'

'Christ,' Charlie said in disgust. 'That and Royal Port is where they all live, all the contractors and developers. They've got the most stringent zoning laws throughout the whole county. You don't shit where you live,' Charlie added bitterly and turned onto Gulfshore Boulevard. The Boulevard paralleled the waterfront. He drove down and parked at the city parking lot.

Ryan climbed out of the air-conditioned car into the humid night air.

'C'mon, we'll walk out onto the pier.'

Ryan lit a cigarette and followed his friend towards the water. The pier stretched before them a full quarter of a mile out into the Gulf. Lights dotted it, highlighting the faces of fishermen crouched over the railing with their poles.

Half-way out on the pier Ryan felt the first stir of a breeze blowing in from the south-west.

'It always comes out of the west or south-west during the summer,' Charlie explained, stepping over to the railing. He pointed along the south shore. 'All that's the Olde Siena section of town. It meets up, a half mile down or so, with Royal Port. That's where the real money is.' Charlie pointed further south. 'Down that way is Rollins Pass. It used to be owned by the city. About two years ago the city sold it. Two weeks later it was rezoned for residential use. Now there's an eleven-million-dollar home sitting on the property.' He turned to Ryan. 'There's also a fence jutting out into the water, cutting off the beach from public use. It's the first fence that's ever been put up on Siena beach.' Charlie glanced out at the water. 'I hope it's the last, but I don't think it is,' he said sadly.

They walked out to the end of the pier, where it angled into a square with an overhang posted in the center. Sheltered below the small roof, were two benches. A group of fishermen sat there, gathered around a lantern. Charlie and Ryan went past them ignoring their curious glances.

'Feel that breeze?'

Ryan nodded.

'It's one of the reasons, other than the view of course, that makes waterfront property so expensive. It's always cool down here.'

Far off Ryan saw a light bobbing in the dark water. He watched it crawl slowly across the horizon. He turned when he heard the scrape of metal behind him. One of the men had pulled out a bowie knife and was sharpening it. As he ran the blade across the flint, he stared up at Ryan insolently.

Ryan turned back to the water. 'You ever think of leaving here?'

'No,' Charlie said, turning to look at him. 'This is where I live.'

Ryan nodded and started back towards shore. He passed the man with the knife without looking at him. He heard a bark of guttural laughter, but took no notice and continued walking.

'Where you staying?'

'Out on the north Highway,' Ryan answered, climbing into the car.

'I need to pick up my bike,' he reminded Charlie. 'It's back at the bar.'

Charlie pulled out of the lot and took a different route back. He slowed, pointing out new construction sites and recently built condominiums. 'Tore down a house that must have been sixty, seventy years old and put that thing up.' Charlie pointed across the road at a boxy-looking building. 'Place has eight units. Each of them is selling for two hundred and sixty thousand.' Charlie put the car in gear. 'It's been on the market now for over a year and they've only sold one of the units so far.'

Ryan twisted in his seat to look at the building behind him. He tried to imagine paying a quarter of a million dollars for an apartment.

'How involved was Neal in all of this?' Ryan asked, getting out of the car and crouching over to peer inside.

Charlie shook his head. 'Not too much. He didn't like what was happening around here, but he knew that if he became too vocal about it he'd be cutting his own throat.'

'He worked for the developers?'

'Not exclusively, but enough that he didn't want to lose the ones he had as clients,' Charlie said, then paused thoughtfully for a moment. 'I don't think that had anything to do with it, Edward. These people don't have to kill anyone to get what they want. They have enough money they can just but it.' Charlie shook his head and forced a smile. 'I'll give you a call some time tomorrow. We'll have you over for dinner.'

'I'd like that.'

'I'll talk to you then.'

Ryan shut the door and watched him pulled out of the lot. He lit a cigarette and climbed onto his bike. He leaned back but didn't make any move to start up until he'd finished smoking.

He pulled out onto the main highway linking the town with the interstate and drove north, passing gas stations, food franchises and restaurants. He kept riding until he saw a flashing pink neon sign announcing Gatsby's where he wheeled into the lot and parked.

As he walked across the parking lot, he was aware of the measuring looks he received from the two men seated in a patrol car at the edge of the lot.

At the front door, he was stopped by a doorman wearing a skin-tight T-shirt, which displayed every torturously ridged muscle to its best advantage.

'Three dollar cover.'

Ryan paid and started to step around him.

'No trouble, huh,' the man said, eyeing him carefully.

Ryan nodded and continued inside. Despite it being the off season, the bar was nearly full, as was the dance-floor. The air conditioning gave off an almost arctic blast of cold air.

Ryan made his way to the bar and ordered a beer from a young woman wearing a khaki tank-top and tight white shorts. When she bent over to grab the bottle the shorts almost disappeared into the crack of her ass. She presented his beer to him with a flirtatious smile. Ryan paid and watched her serve the other customers. With each sale she attempted the same maneuver. He noticed that her ploy had a definite effect on the amount of money left on the bar top as a tip.

After a while he turned to watch the band and the dance-floor. The band was made up of the standard bass and lead guitar, with a drummer centered between them. The fourth ingredient was the lead singer. She wore a black miniskirt with a red silk top, tucked tightly into the waistband of her skirt. Tied round her wrist was a white sash, which she used to punctuate her performance. The music was top forty and bland.

Ryan took his time with his beer. When he finished he pushed the empty forward and left. He nodded to the bouncer and walked across the lot. The patrol car was still there. He could feel the men inside gauging him, wondering how much he'd drunk.

He pulled out onto the highway and drove further north, stopping at the next night-club he saw.

Three hours later, he drove back towards town. He was about a half mile from the turn-off to his motel when he saw the flashing lights behind him. He pulled over and waited.

'Just stay right where you are.'

Ryan nodded, making no attempt to rise from his bike.

'How much have you had to drink this evening?'

'A couple beers.'

'Step away from the bike.'

Ryan swung his leg over and stood beside it. The cop stepped in front of him. He kept one hand over the butt of his revolver while he examined him. 'Your driver's license.'

Ryan handed it to him.

'You're from California. How long have you been in Florida?'

'Two days.'

The cop looked up at him suspiciously.

Ryan shrugged.

'Just stay right there,' the cop ordered, then walked back to his cruiser. He reached inside and pulled out his hand set. Ryan slouched against his bike, listening to the cop call in his driver's license number and the plate of his bike. 'Everything seems to be in order.'

Ryan took the license back and replaced it in his wallet, wondering if there was going to be more. He glanced over at the cop.

'This is a quiet town. We don't want any trouble here.' Ryan nodded his agreement. 'You keep that in mind while you're here, all right?' the policeman said and waited for Ryan to answer before he turned away.

Ryan drove back to his motel and flopped across his bed. He rolled over onto his back and lit a cigarette. He closed his eyes tightly and drifted until he found a memory that was painless enough to replay. He let it take him until he'd recreated the texture and feel of it.

He was in a canoe on one of the canals leading back into the Everglades. Neal, four years younger than he, was in the bow, excited at the prospect of seeing his first alligator.

'Where are they all?' he complained, glancing back at Ryan in frustration.

'They're here.' Ryan smiled. 'You just have to look for them.'

'Where?'

'Over there,' Ryan said suddenly, spotting the tip of the snout, and the two eyes, just barely breaking the surface of the water.

Neal whirled round in excitement. His momentum upset the precarious balance of the canoe. For one moment Ryan thought that they might still be okay, but then the next Neal screamed, 'I see it,' and started to rise.

The canoe dipped to its side and water rushed over the edge. Neal made one frantic grab for the side before he toppled over into the brackish water. His terrified scream echoed in the torpid air. Ryan quickly went in after him.

'Where is it?' Neal shouted frantically as he twisted in horror, trying to spot the alligator.

'It's okay, Neal. Hang on.' Ryan grabbed his hand and hauled him back into the canoe.

Huddled in the bow, both arms wrapped round his knees and chest, Neal cried hysterically.

Ryan put an arm around his little brother's shoulders and hugged him. 'It's okay,' he promised softly. 'I won't ever let anything happen to you.'

He felt his younger brother's arms reach out and cling to him desperately.

Seven

Every town has one. Usually it's located on one of the strips leading either in or out of the city. It hides between the gas stations, fast food franchises and dry cleaners. It rarely serves anything other than drinks, though sometimes, because of futile zoning attempts, the bar will be forced to serve food. The food served is usually barely palatable and only offered in deference to the zoning requirements.

In Siena the place is called The Buggy. It's a combination package liquor store and bar. The store offers a selection of wine, beer and hard liquor at twice their normal retail prices. Most of its sales take place in the last hour before closing, the majority of the late-night customers being culled from the adjoining bar. Either too drunk or in too much of a hurry to drive the four miles to the next nearest liquor store, The Buggy's patrons grudgingly pay the exorbitant prices.

The bar offers strong, cheap drinks and, for the hungry, something arguably called a burrito. The burrito is something of a joke, though most of the regulars, at one time or another, have been disoriented enough to order and actually eat it. It's a rite of passage for the Buggy regulars.

The bar also offers, independently of its owner, an array of drugs and illicit services that cover just about every possible need and hunger.

It was here that four years ago a winter resident found two men willing to dispose of his wife. In the subsequent trial, The Buggy was named frequently as the initial contact point.

Paging through local court records, The Buggy is a location that often arises in the dispensation of justice. Drugs, property and services are traded, bought and sold with nightly regularity.

* * *

Seated in his usual corner of the bar, the man known only as Surfer plied his trade. His trade was sales, his merchandise was whatever desire his customer wished to fulfill.

He drank a soda water with a squeeze of lime and watched as the bar began to fill. Restaurant people stopped in after work, dragging in friends – and soon to be friends – they had met that evening during their shifts.

Surfer leaned back and waited. He watched the mating rituals of the locals and the summer visitors with cynicism, knowing that eventually they would all come to him. If not tonight, then tomorrow or the next night. His wares were too potent to be ignored.

His first sale was to a young waitress he had dealt with before. She bought a three ball for twenty dollars. Surfer passed it to her beneath the bar top. Watching her look down hungrily at the cellophane baggy, he tried to remember if he'd done this one or not. It was when she glanced back at him and smiled that he remembered taking her to the beach, then swinging up on a sea wall and unzipping his pants. When she had bowed over him that night, the smile she had worn was almost the same as the one she had pasted across her face now. He nodded to her and watched her hurry outside. She returned ten minutes later, her smile deepened, her gait unsteady. Surfer's satisfied nod in her direction was a benevolent benediction worthy of any Vatican dignitary.

Surfer remained in his corner until closing. When he left, he climbed into his Honda Prelude six hundred dollars richer.

He drove back to his condominium. Inside, he checked his answering machine, listening to each message carefully. He ran the tape twice, making notes as he listened the second time.

He opened a bottle of Perrier before he returned to the phone. 'Hi, I need you at The Palms at two forty-five, room 302. It's straight, nothing weird. I'll get together with you tomorrow afternoon some time to settle up,' he said into the receiver, then, after hearing the woman's compliance, hung up.

He made four more calls. Two of them were to women, arranging times and places. The third was to a ship's captain in Everglade City, checking on a shipment of marijuana. After being assured that it would arrive later that morning, Surfer hung up.

He leaned back in his chair thoughtfully, then reached for the phone to make his final call. This time his voice took on a subservience that had been lacking for most of the evening. 'This is me,' he said and waited for the man at the other end to identify his voice.

'Yes?'

'I got your message.'

'I have some questions about last week.'

'What about it?' Surfer asked quickly, feeling a twinge of anxiety.

'Were there any problems that you may have failed to mention?'

'No, nothing. Everything went perfectly.'

'What about the children?'

'No, there's no way they could have seen anything. My guy was far enough away that it would have been impossible for him to have been spotted.'

'How reliable is this person?'

'Completely,' Surfer answered, then growing uncomfortable with the silence attempted to fill it. 'I know him for ever. There's no way he'd fuck around with me.'

'We're still a little concerned about the children. We wouldn't want any unforeseen problems to develop.'

'You want me to take them out?'

'No,' the voice answered thoughtfully, 'but we do want you to watch them. We don't want any surprises. Do you understand?'

'Yes, sir. I'll keep my eye on them, and I can also check in with . . .' Surfer stopped abruptly when he heard the dial tone at the other end.

He carried his Perrier into the bedroom with him and sat down on the edge of his bed. He sipped it, thinking about the voice, wondering who it was. His only contact with the person had been by phone and through the mail. The postal service delivered him fat manila envelopes, stuffed with used twenty-dollar bills. The phone delivered curt assignments that Surfer had quickly realized were much too lucrative to ignore.

What had recently begun to cause him some concern was the gradual escalation of his tasks. What had started out as small drug deals and an occasional woman here and there had somehow become much more serious than that. In his more paranoid moments he almost thought he was being set up.

His transactions with the voice had begun about a year ago. An envelope had arrived at his post office box with fifteen twenty-dollar bills in it. Nothing else, just the money. At first, Surfer had been convinced that it was some lame scam put together by the DEA. He had quickly replaced the envelope in his PO box and left it there. That night he'd received his first phone call.

His instructions were simple. The voice wanted an ounce of Hawaiian. He wanted it left beneath a dumpster behind a local restaurant. Surfer had listened to the voice and readily agreed to whatever it had requested. As soon as he'd hung up, he'd laughed at the idiocy of the local police force. No one else, not even the DEA, would be so stupid to set up such an obvious sting.

The next night he'd received another phone call. The same instructions. Again, Surfer had quickly agreed. This time, though, after he'd hung up he'd begun to worry. He'd quickly cleaned out his condo, then sat back to wait to see what they would do next.

He was called again the next evening. 'Go to your kitchen window,' the voice had ordered.

Surfer walked over to his window and looked out at the street below. Parked across the street was a squad car. Peering down at it he saw someone staring up at his condo.

'I want it delivered this evening, or else my man sitting outside won't be so patient,' the voice had informed him.

Surfer figured he was fucked no matter what he did. If they wanted him that bad they were going to get him. All he might be able to control was the degree of their acquisition.

He went to the dumpster that evening and placed a bag of oregano beneath it, figuring if they wanted him, he would offer them a small piece of himself. A conspiracy charge might be just enough to appease them. Surfer figured at worst, with a decent lawyer, he could probably plead it down to a misdemeanor. Maybe end up with nine months.

The phone was ringing when he got back to his condo that night.

'Last chance, Thomas,' the voice had said softly, and Surfer had frozen. If the person at the other end knew his name, then he knew everything.

'I want the ounce tonight, and I want it right now,' the voice had ordered, and Surfer had to admire the man's technique. He hadn't belabored his knowledge of who Surfer actually was with threats. He had simply let Surfer know that he owned him.

Surfer delivered the Hawaiian and waited for the inevitable bust. What came instead was another envelope. This time there were thirty twenty-dollar bills. The voice called him that night and gave him the room number and the time he wanted a woman to be delivered. 'Someone who doesn't normally do this kind of thing,' the voice had added softly.

Surfer knew a good thing when he saw it. He promised a waitress he knew a quarter gram of blow for a little favor, then took her out and dropped her off at the specified hotel. Everyone was happy.

The calls became more frequent and, slowly, more direct. A woman delivered to such-and-such a room number. A woman who wouldn't mind something a little different, something a little rougher. Each time the calls came, Surfer complied.

During the course of the last year, he'd noticed that the manila folders that appeared in his PO box were unstamped, which meant that whoever the voice was, he had some very serious connections.

Last week had been the first time Surfer had been asked to whack someone, though asked was something of a misnomer. By this time he had become so accustomed to the money that he hadn't even thought about what he was agreeing to until after he'd hung up. Even then it hadn't bothered him particularly. He'd felt that whoever his benefactor was he was a benevolent one and would afford Surfer the same protection that he seemed to enjoy.

Surfer had contacted a friend from out of state, someone he'd done a stretch with an age ago, long before he'd become Surfer.

His friend had supplied a name, a number and an introduction that had cost Surfer two hundred dollars.

Surfer had called the number and explained his predicament. They had quickly agreed on a price. Part of the agreed package was a detailed timetable of the mark's movements. By the time his man had arrived, Surfer had the whole thing scoped. It had gone down without a hitch. His man had come into town on a shuttle flight. Two hours later he had picked up a return flight. His brief visit had made Surfer three thousand dollars richer.

It was only later, when Surfer had time to think about it, that he began to realize how involved he had become with the voice. What had started out as an occasional pot delivery had slowly become much more than that. From small-time drug and pimp deals he had quickly graduated to conspiracy and accessory to first-degree murder. It was a course that he would have thought impossible only a year before.

He had always been on the fringe, but had never been involved in any of the hard-core action. He was mystified at how easily he'd been drawn into the situation in which he now found himself. He'd never before gone for this kind of serious work.

He leaned back thoughtfully across his bed, then rose when he heard the knock.

'I'm Jackie,' the girl said, smiling brightly.

Surfer took in the long legs, the small jutting breasts and teased dark hair, and returned her smile.

'Come on in,' he said, motioning her inside.

He watched the way her ass moved as she stepped around him.

'How about something to sweeten your nose?'

Jackie grinned, tilting her head to the side, and raised her eyebrows in a 'why not?' gesture.

Surfer went into the kitchen, returning a moment later with a mirror and a bowl. He laid each out on the table in front of her, then sat on the rug near her legs and cut up some lines. He waited until she had bowed over the mirror before he cupped his hand over the warm curve of her knee. She giggled, sniffled and leaned over to vacuum up another line.

Surfer shifted his hand to her thigh and kneaded the warm flesh.

'I don't know.'

'Maggie, you must have some idea,' Rachel contended.

Maggie shook her head. 'No, Neal would never talk about it,' she said, avoiding Rachel's glance.

'Then why don't you like him?' her friend asked, aware of her evasion but not willing to pursue it.

'Have you seen him?' Maggie asked incredulously, looking across the kitchen table at her friend.

'No, not yet. Why?'

'He's a biker. And not one of those weekend motorcyclists, but a hard-core Los Angeles biker.'

'You mean like a Hell's Angel?' Rachel asked with an uncertain smile.

'Yes, exactly like that.' Maggie rose to refill their coffee cups. Hearing a thud of footsteps coming from outside the kitchen she yelled, 'Oliver John, don't run. If you want to run, go outside.'

'So what does he want?'

'He said he came back for the funeral.'

'How did he know?'

'What?'

'About the funeral,' Rachel said patiently.

'Oh, I don't know. He still has friends here. I heard he was with Charlie Benning last night.'

'The reporter?'

'Yes.'

'What was he going with him?'

'I don't have any idea. All I know is that I wish he'd go back to wherever it is he came from,' Maggie said and turned away quickly, brushing at her eyes.

'It's okay, Maggie, really it is.' Rachel put a hand on her shoulder.

'No, it isn't Rachel, and it's not going to be okay for a long time.' She paused, shook her head and took a deep breath. 'I will not let this happen to me,' she announced firmly. Rachel watched her closely. 'I'm okay,' Maggie said, lifting her coffee cup and saluting her friend.

'How're the kids taking it?'

'Ollie doesn't even understand what's happened.'

'And Lisa?'

'I don't know.' Maggie shook her head sadly. 'I think she knows but doesn't quite understand what it actually means.'

'Those poor kids.'

'Poor all of us.'

'Have the police said anything?'

'No. They think it was some nut.'

'Do you . . .'

'Oliver, I told you not to run,' Maggie yelled.

'I'm not,' Ollie's voice came through the open doorway.

'I'm not going to tell you again. Next time it's upstairs to your bedroom.'

45

'Mommy,' he groaned.

'No running,' Maggie said and turned back to Rachel. 'What were you saying?'

'Do you have any idea why?'

'Rachel, for God's sake, how would I know something like that? You know Neal. Who would want to do something like that, who would want to kill him?' Maggie said, pushing the words out sharply.

'I'm sorry,' Rachel quickly apologized.

'No, *I'm* sorry. I'm just so confused right now.' Maggie closed her eyes and shook her head.

'It's all right.' Rachel rose and went over to her. She put her hands on her friend's shoulders. 'If you need anything you know I'm right here for you.'

'I know.' Maggie nodded, reaching up to cover Rachel's hands with her own.

Lisa sat outside on the top step of the front porch. She heard Ollie from inside the house making his engine noises and waited for the inevitable. A moment later came her mother's raised voice warning Ollie not to run. Lisa smiled and listened closely.

The noises soon began again and a few moments later she heard the sound of his feet clomping across the living-room floor. Her mother's angry tones carried out to the porch, threatening Ollie once again with his bedroom.

Lisa giggled when a few minutes later she heard Ollie begin to warm up again. She sometimes wondered seriously if her brother wasn't retarded. He seemed unable to remember the simplest things.

She was disappointed when she heard him approach the front door. She didn't want to talk to him.

'What're you doing?'

'Just sitting.'

'How come?'

'Because I want to,' Lisa answered as she heard the screen door open.

'How come you're sitting there?'

'You mean here?' Lisa asked, turning to him.

'Yeah, there?'

'Here?' she asked again, enjoying the confused expression on his face.

'There,' he said loudly, pointing to where she was sitting.

Lisa smiled sweetly, before she said, 'Here?' and watched the way his mouth tightened and his face grew red at her lack of understanding. She barely managed to restrain her laughter as Ollie grew increasingly perturbed.

He scowled at her, turned abruptly and stomped back into the house. She listened as his engine started up and a moment later heard him racing round the living-room.

'All right. That's it, Oliver John, upstairs.'

'Mommy,' he wailed.

'Don't you Mommy me, young man. I told you, now you get up those stairs right this minute.'

Lisa heard his cries fade as he clumped up the stairs.

'You okay, honey?'

She turned to her mother and nodded.

'You sure?'

She nodded again, afraid from the sound of her mother's voice that she might start to cry again. She hated it when her mother did that. She never knew what to do.

'Okay.' Her mother nodded, and started to turn.

'Mom?'

'Yes?'

'Is that man going to come back again?' Seeing her mother's confusion, Lisa added, 'Uncle Eddie.' She felt strange saying it.

Her mother's lips tightened. 'I don't think so, honey. I don't think he'll come back for a while.'

'But he will come back some time?'

'I don't know. I hope not.'

'Why?'

For a moment her mother seemed about to respond, then she shook her head and stepped back into the house.

Lisa waited for the door to close, rose and skipped down the drive. Half-way to the street she paused, then crouched over to examine the black top. Splattered across the tar was a small spot of oil. She touched it with her finger and looked at it. She knew it was from the man's motorcycle. She rubbed it between her thumb and forefinger, feeling the slick texture of it coat the pads of her fingers.

She got up, went down to the street, stood on her toes at the edge of the curb and looked in both directions.

She felt sure she knew something that her mother didn't know. She knew that the man was going to come back, that the man – 'I'm your Uncle Eddie' – wasn't going to leave them all alone.

What she had decided to do was to wait for him. Because this time she wanted to see his tattoo, and maybe also to ask him how come he sounded so much like her father.

Lisa skipped back up to the porch and sat down to wait. From the window above her she heard Ollie starting up his engine. She smiled as she surveyed the street before her.

Eight

Ryan woke early the next morning. He showered quickly, dressed and left his room. The brilliant glare of sunlight waited for him outside his door. The heat, already heavy and moist, swamped around him and beaded his back and shoulders with perspiration.

He walked to the motel restaurant, pausing to pick up a newspaper on the way, and sat at the counter and ordered breakfast. Paging through the local paper, he saw a column by Charlie Benning and read it carefully. Charlie berated the Siena City Council for granting a residential zoning deferment for a beach house being constructed in Royal Port. Ryan could almost hear his voice speaking the words to him. The angry words were similar to the ones he had heard from his friend last night.

When he was finished with the paper, he ordered a refill of coffee and lit a cigarette. He smoked, trying to decide where to begin.

Ten minutes later he went outside and made his way to his motorcycle. He pulled out of the lot and turned towards town. A newer model Mercedes pulled in front of him. The car maintained a steady speed of fifteen miles an hour. Ryan peered in through the rear window and saw only a gray head and two hands on the steering-wheel. The rest of the driver was hidden behind the back of the seat. He snorted ruefully and kicked down into second gear.

He followed the car in front of him along the main street of town leading towards the beach. Boutiques, with colorfully displayed windows, lined the sidewalk.

At the intersection to the beach he waited patiently while the driver of the Mercedes laboriously attempted to parallel park. After the fourth attempt, the car finally managed to glide crookedly into the slot. Ryan glanced over at it as he passed. He saw a tiny wrinkled

49

face turned towards the door, struggling with the door handle.

Ryan turned into the old section of town. He drove slowly along the narrow roads, examining the houses and yards around him. Palm and banyan trees graciously lined the street. Avocado, lime, and mango trees sprouted from the meticulously manicured lawns to each side of him.

He passed a sign announcing his arrival into Royal Port. There was an almost immediate change in the size of the houses and yards. Everything here seemed constructed on a much larger scale. The houses were all two or three storeys and sat on acreage seemingly denied the rest of the community. As he drove, Ryan became aware of the ubiquitous small rectangular blue signs planted at the foot of each of the estates. Each announced that the premises were protected by Point Blank Security.

The houses all seemed to be named. Across their mailboxes, in bright splashes of color, Ryan read, Rogue's Rest, Palm Haven, Skipper's Reef. The blatant opulence of the area astounded him. The lush colors and fastidious maintenance of the grounds and homes seemed almost preternatural. Everything was so neat and clean that it appeared very nearly surreal.

He pulled off onto a dead-end street and parked beneath the overhanging roots of a banyan tree. He lit a cigarette and leaned back, examining the mansion in front of him. It sat on a small rise and backed onto a canal leading to the Gulf of Mexico. Bobbing gently along the wharf, was a forty-foot yacht. Ryan tried to imagine the kind of money it would take to maintain the boat and the house. He gave up when he realized that the home before him was only the owner's winter retreat; his main home was somewhere up north.

Ryan shook his head in disbelief, then stubbed out his cigarette and started his bike. He was about to pull onto the road when a newer model Ford Bronco pulled up and stopped beside him. Printed across the passenger's door was the blue logo of Point Blank Security.

'How you doing,' the man greeted him, after leaning over to roll down the passenger window. His smile did not reach his eyes. 'Can I help you with anything?'

'No, just looking around.'

'Nice up around here.' The man nodded agreeably. He wore a

long-sleeved blue shirt, ribbed with black stripes. Placed beside him on the car seat was a black cap and a walkie-talkie.

The man continued to smile as he eyed Ryan closely. Then, with a final nod, he rolled up his window and pulled off the road in front of Ryan's motorcycle.

Ryan circled the bike to the main street and drove back towards town. In his rear-view mirror he watched the Bronco follow him. It remained behind him until he passed into the old section of town.

Ryan tugged his T-shirt away from his body, feeling perspiration beading beneath his arms and along the small of his back. It fell damply back into place. He stepped through the doors, welcoming the sudden rush of cool air, paused at the directory beside the elevator and took the stairs up to the second floor. He walked down the hallway to a glazed glass door with the words 'Burdick and Ryan: Certified Public Accountants' painted across the center.

'May I help you?' the woman behind the desk asked, eyeing him suspiciously.

'Yes, I'd like to see Mr Burdick.'

'He isn't in right now, would you like to leave a message?' she answered without hesitation.

Ryan smiled and shook his head. 'Maybe I'll just wait until he returns.'

'I don't expect him back until late this afternoon.'

'That's okay, I don't have any plans.'

Ryan took a seat and pulled a magazine from the table. He slouched back, negligently stretching his legs across the table top. He felt the woman's eyes boring into him but refused to acknowledge her. A moment later she pushed back her chair and disappeared through one of the two doors behind her desk.

'Yes, is there something I can do for you?' a voice inquired coldly.

Ryan glanced up at the man standing in the doorway. A little behind him stood the secretary.

'I'm Edward Ryan. Neal's brother.' He stood, examining the man before him. He was dressed conservatively in a gray cotton suit with a dark tie. In his right hand he held a folder. He tapped it nervously against his leg.

'I'm sorry about your brother. He was a good friend.' The words came out smoothly, without imparting any meaning.

'If you don't mind, I'd like to ask you a few questions.'

'About what?'

'About my brother.'

'What exactly did you want to know?'

'How long did you know him?'

'Why?'

'Just wondering.'

'I really don't have time for this.'

'Things pretty busy right now?'

'Yes, they are,' Burdick answered curtly.

'Maybe I should come back some other time.'

'I don't think it will matter. With your brother's absence all his work has fallen to me. So, unless there was something specific you wanted to ask, I don't think I can be of too much help to you.'

'Who killed him?' Ryan asked abruptly. The grin he wore contradicted his words.

His question startled Burdick. His eyes shifted, then came back to Ryan's face. 'I have no idea.'

'What was he working on?'

'I honestly don't have the time for this. If you're interested in speculations about his death I suggest you talk to the police,' Burdick said and with a brisk nod turned into his office. His secretary stepped into the room and closed the door behind her. She turned to face Ryan.

'Nice guy to work for, I bet.' Ryan smiled.

The woman stared back at him impassively.

'Have a nice day,' Ryan said a moment later, then turned and left.

When he walked through the main door the man behind the desk immediately stiffened. Ryan smiled and went over to the desk. 'I'm Edward Ryan. I wanted to talk to someone about my brother, Neal.'

The policeman eyed him closely. His lips twisted with distaste as he took in Ryan's appearance. 'I don't know if there's too much I can do for you,' he drawled insolently.

'Well, why don't you just call someone who can, then?'

The policeman casually reached for his coffee and raised it to his lips. He never took his eyes off of Ryan.

'There's no hurry. Take your time, I got all day,' Ryan told him.

'That's good, because it might take me some time to figure out just who it is you should talk to.'

'I'll just sit down over there.' Ryan motioned towards a vinyl chair by the door.

He lit a cigarette, leaned back and closed his eyes. He saw Zella smiling at him from across the restaurant. He moved quickly towards the smile and all the promises it held.

He opened his eyes when someone kicked his leg. Two policemen stood over him. One of them was the man he had seen the night before in the restaurant. Stutz. The other, the one who had kicked him, stood in front of him casually resting one hand on his gun belt while he examined him.

'What do you think this piece of trash's doing here, Bo?'

Stutz shrugged and glanced towards the desk.

'He's looking to talk to someone about his brother,' the man behind it called over.

'And who might that be, or maybe what might that be would be a better question?' The man grinned.

Ryan smiled back at him easily. 'Neal Ryan,' he said and added, 'He was shot to death in your park in front of his two kids. I was just wondering if you'd had some time to think about that at all, or if you were too busy checking beach permits to get around to it.'

'Why you mother . . .'

Stutz grabbed the other man's arm and pulled him back. 'C'mon, Hal, let it alone,' he cautioned his partner, pushing him towards the front door.

Ryan glanced up at Stutz, then looked over at the desk. The policeman was watching the three of them intently. He seemed disappointed when Stutz pulled his partner out through the door.

Ryan leaned back and glanced out of the window. He saw Stutz shaking his head and talking to his partner. As they reached their squad car, the other man turned to glare at Ryan.

'Captain says he'll talk to you now,' the cop behind the desk called and nodded towards a hallway leading off to his left.

The man stepping around the desk to greet him was Florida bred and born. Ryan could easily read the imprint of the sun and the land in the man's face and bearing.

'I'm Captain Rainey.' He held out his hand.

Ryan took it, surprised by the man's easy acceptance of him.

'Sit down.' He motioned to a chair. 'Can I get you some coffee or something?'

'No thanks.'

'All right; tell me what I can do for you.'

'You mind?' Ryan asked, pulling out a cigarette.

'Not if you don't.' Rainey smiled, reaching into his breast pocket and coming out with a cigar.

'I was wondering what was going on about my brother.'

'Neal.' Rainey nodded, tapping a file on his desk. 'There's not much I can tell you. He was shot once in the back of the head.' Rainey paused, throwing a measured glance at Ryan before he went on. 'Bullet ended up lodged beneath the sternum. We were able to recover it. A .22 long. Ballistics guess it was fired with a Colt Woodsman. We found an area, approximately twenty feet from where he was shot, where we think the shooter waited.' Rainey glanced over at Ryan expectantly. He answered his own question before it was asked. 'The area was trampled and littered with cigarette butts. I know that doesn't sound like much, but it's all we've got at this point. It was relatively early in the morning, so the possibilities of someone else being there for that length of time are pretty slim,' Rainey finished and leaned back in his chair, blowing a stream of smoke above his head.

'You think the guy was waiting specifically for Neal?'

'Looks that way right now, but as I said, we don't have too much. Could've been someone else hanging around there, but the time of day would make that improbable.'

'So it was a hit?'

'Maybe.'

'You have any idea why?'

'No.'

'You talk to Burdick?'

'Yes.'

'Anything there?'

'Nothing so far. Your brother's share of the business passes on to

his wife and everything he was working on seems pretty straight-
forward. Nothing we could find that might embarrass anyone.'

Ryan leaned forward to stub out his cigarette. 'Why are you telling
me all this?'

'He was your brother. Man should know what's going on when
something like that happens.'

Ryan examined him closely.

Rainey, aware of his scrutiny, smiled back at him and nodded.
'Yep, we knew each other. Maybe there's a few years' difference
between us, but we were both born within twenty miles of each
other. Probably ran some of the same canals when we were kids.'

'A lot's changed since then.'

'Sure has,' Rainey agreed. 'This town's one of them. Fifteen years
ago I bought a house in the old section. Paid sixty thousand dollars
and thought it was more than the place was worth. It was just valued
last year at two hundred and sixty. Lot of new money coming into
this area.'

'That affect Neal's business?'

'I'm sure it did. He wasn't a fool. He knew where his bread
was buttered.'

'You think he could have gotten involved with the wrong kind
of money?'

'You're talking drugs now.' Rainey nodded thoughtfully. 'Lot of
that around. No question about that. It comes in up and down the
coastline. Everglade City used to be one of the main drops, but a
couple of years back the county police, along with the DEA, went in
there and bagged almost half the town. Things have quieted down
some since then. Most of the action has moved further north, up
around Bonita and Fort Meyers.' Rainey paused, puffing thoughtfully on his cigar. 'I don't think drugs had anything to do with your
brother's death.'

'Then what did?'

'We'll find out.'

Ryan nodded.

'I had a call earlier from Mr Burdick. He said you were harassing
him.'

'I just asked him a few questions.'

Rainey met his gaze and nodded. 'There are some questions that people don't like to be asked. It makes them uncomfortable, reminds them of things they'd rather forget.'

'Maybe those are the questions to ask.'

'Yeah, as long as they're being asked by the right person.'

'Meaning leave it alone?'

Rainey shrugged. 'This is my town. I don't want any trouble.'

'Seems to me I've been hearing that quite a bit lately.'

'Well I know you heard it at least once last night, when you were pulled over by one of my men. And I'd guess you probably heard it again from that security guard up in Royal Port.' Rainey caught Ryan's surprised glance. 'It's my business to know what's going on, and also to know what's happened in the past,' he said, pushing away a file to reveal another one beneath it.

Ryan glanced at it then up at Rainey.

'I knew your father. I ran into him when I'd just started on the force. He was one mean old son-of-a-bitch, no offense intended.'

'None taken.' Ryan smiled.

Rainey leaned back and squinted across his desk at the other man. 'You usually wear colors?'

'Used to, but I ride alone now.'

'They weren't too sure about that out west.'

'Well you can clear that up for them now.'

'I'll probably do just that.'

They locked eyes for a moment. Ryan was the first to look away. He pushed out of his chair and offered his hand.

'You have any questions you feel free to stop by and ask them,' Rainey told him, taking it.

'I'll do that.'

'You have a nice day now.'

Ryan nodded and left the room.

He drove out on the highway and slowed as he turned onto a residential street. He glanced over at the house and saw the little girl sitting on the front porch. For a moment they stared at each other before she hesitantly raised her hand and waved. Ryan waved back and drove on. He stopped at a drugstore on his way back to the motel.

He carried his purchases into the bathroom and set them out on top of the sink. He eyed his reflection in the mirror, grinned and filled the basin with water. When he was done, he pulled on a pair of swimming trunks and walked down to the pool.

A woman smiled lazily up at him from the heat of her *chaise longue* as he stepped out onto the diving board. The cool blue water rippled enticingly below. He bounced once on the board, then dived awkwardly. He climbed out, dived again and continued diving until he entered the water smoothly. He rubbed some sun-block on his face and body and positioned one of the lounge chairs so it faced the sun. He lay back, feeling the heat press against him, and closed his eyes. He drifted back, recreating the house in his mind.

It stood unevenly on its stilts. A huge banyan tree grew unchecked in the back yard. Its root system spread voraciously beneath the stilts supporting the house. At the edge of the back yard the ground grew marshy where it eased into the mangroves that banked the canal. There was a narrow clearing leading down to it. At the foot of the clearing was a small plywood wharf with a canoe and a mullet boat tied to it. Ryan remembered sitting on the wharf in the early evening, pulling in snapper and grouper; rebaiting his hook with shrimp and casting out at the foot of the mangroves; watching the way the shadows crawled across the brackish water, bringing with them the first cool breath of air felt throughout the day.

Sound of Neal racing down to the wharf. Excited peal of his voice, as he pulled up the shaved willow fork to examine his brother's catch.

Neal sitting beside him, eagerly staring out at the water, both hands wrapped tightly round the pole. Wildly jerking it at the first hit; pulling it so hard that the hook flew up and almost hit him in the face. Sound of his laughter. Ryan reaching over and putting an arm round his shoulder.

Backfire of a truck pulling up to the front of the house; both boys turning and glancing behind them. When they turn back to each other, their smiles are gone. Ryan's face is impassive and, as he looks at his brother's, all he sees is the fear.

Ryan opened his eyes and quickly pushed himself out of his chair. He stepped onto the diving board. Perspiration dripped along his shoulders and chest. He sprang into the air and knifed cleanly into the water, feeling it close around him, drawing him into its cool silence.

'Who is this guy?'

'He's Neal's brother.'

'I don't understand what he wants,' John said, nervously shredding his cocktail napkin.

Richard took a leisurely sip of his martini before he answered. 'It's understandable that he would want to know what happened. It was his brother after all.'

'I don't like him asking questions, and I don't like the way he looks.'

'He does look a bit rough, I'll grant you that. But that should be a point in our favor.'

'Why?'

'Who's going to take him seriously?'

John glanced away and motioned to the bartender. He waited until they were both served before he said, 'I don't want any more calls at the office.' Richard smiled. 'I'm serious, Richard.'

'Didn't you enjoy yourself?'

'That's not what I'm talking about.'

'From what I heard, you had quite a good time,' Richard said pointedly and waited until John glanced away before adding, 'You really should try to temper yourself just a little. The girl was in hysterics.'

John refused to meet his eye. His fingers tapped against the bar top.

'Don't worry about the brother. He's being taken care of,' Richard offered.

'How?'

'That's not your concern.'

'I thought we talked about this before. I'm a part of the whole operation. I think I should be told what's going on.'

Richard turned to look at him. This time John refused to be intimidated.

'Okay.' The other man nodded, then, smiling slightly, lifted his martini. He held it before him, examining it thoughtfully. 'The brother is being watched. He's not doing anything that we don't know about.'

'What if he finds out something?'

'Then something will have to be done.' Richard sipped his drink.

Satisfied with this response, John nodded. 'What about the children?'

'Nothing new has developed. I don't think we have anything to worry about from that quarter.'

John's sigh of relief was audible.

With a bemused smile, Richard said, 'You really do worry too much. You know that, don't you?'

'Someone has to,' John answered, his foot shifting nervously against the rung of his stool.

'Well everything is under control. The funeral's in two days and I would assume the brother will disappear a day or two after that. And then', Richard said with a satisfied tilt of his head, 'everything will return to normal.'

'God, I sure hope so. This whole thing is getting out of control.'

Richard's speculative glance went unnoticed as John reached for his drink.

Nine

At seven-thirty the man stepped up to Charlie Benning's door. He wore a pair of cotton khaki pants and a white short-sleeved shirt. His hair was neatly trimmed and cleanly ridged along the collar of his shirt. There was no attempt at facial hair to hide the two scars adorning his face. One of them drifted down a quarter inch from his lower lip. The other bisected his right eyebrow.

The man straightened his shirt and knocked at the door.

Charlie answered. He glanced at the man, then over at the Chevy Caprice parked in the drive. 'Can I help you?'

Suddenly the man smiled. 'Charlie, for Christ's sake.'

'Edward. That you?' Charlie crouched forward and squinted into the freshly shaven face.

'What do you think?' Ryan lifted his chin in profile.

'I think I better lock up Gloria.'

'As fertile as she is, that might not be a bad idea.'

Charlie quickly ushered him into the house and introduced him to all seven of the children. The youngest was only two. Taking the boy's small hand in his own, Ryan couldn't help being reminded of his nephew. Each of the kids solemnly shook his hand, then quietly disappeared upstairs.

Seated over dinner, with Gloria at one end of the table and Charlie at the other, Ryan felt himself relaxing for the first time in days. They talked about old times, carefully, yet not uncomfortably, avoiding the more painful memories.

'. . . Sure she was.' Charlie grinned.

Both he and Ryan turned to look at Gloria.

The bright rush of color to her face only added to their amusement. 'Charlie, don't.'

'Well you were,' he maintained.

'I didn't know you were valedictorian,' Ryan said.

'Probably because you were too busy with Nancy Belke,' Gloria retorted.

'Nancy, that's right. I haven't thought about her in years.'

'You two were pretty hot stuff back then.'

'I'll say, that's all any of us ever talked about in the locker room. We always wondered if she was actually doing "it" with you.'

Ryan glanced over at Gloria.

'Were you, Edward?' she asked coyly, raising one eyebrow.

'Whatever happened to her?' he asked.

'Married and living up in Michigan, and don't avoid the question.'

'I'm not. I'm just not going to answer it.'

Gloria glanced down the table at her husband.

'Don't ask me.' Charlie shrugged. 'He never told me one way or the other.'

'She was a nice girl.'

'That's why we all wondered what on earth she was doing with you,' Gloria commented wryly.

'Jeez, Glo, give him a break.'

Stifling a laugh, Gloria added, 'Well, it's true. You remember how he was. He had that Sean Penn look about him, as if he was just waiting for someone to say one wrong word to him, and then pow.' Gloria glanced over at Ryan. 'You did have a terrible chip on your shoulder, Edward.'

Ryan nodded and leaned back in his chair. 'I agree. I was looking to prove something.'

'I suppose that's understandable,' she said softly.

Charlie quickly rose and began to gather plates. 'No, go ahead, you sit. I'll do it,' he admonished his wife, as she started to rise.

'I won't argue.' Gloria settled back in her chair.

Ryan lit a cigarette and toyed with his coffee cup.

'It's nice seeing you again, Edward. I just wish it could have been under happier circumstances.'

'It's good seeing both of you. It's been a long time.'

'Almost ten years.'

'Yeah, just about that,' Ryan said, nodding thoughtfully and glancing away.

A moment later he brought his gaze back to her. 'What was he like, Gloria?' he asked hoarsely.

'What . . .' Gloria started to ask, startled by the intensity of his question.

'Neal. What was he like?'

'Oh, Edward.' She reached over to touch his hand.

'Was he okay?'

'He was fine, Edward. We didn't see him very much, but when we did, he seemed . . .' she paused, searching for the word, '. . . happy.'

She caught Ryan's glance, shrugged and added, 'He did change. He became more focused. It was like the only things that mattered to him any more were his job and his family. He didn't do much else.'

Ryan nodded and reached for a cigarette.

'Have you seen Maggie and the kids?' Gloria asked quietly.

'Yeah.'

'How're they doing?'

'Okay, I guess. I haven't spent much time with them.'

'You should try, if you can.' Gloria paused, looking over at him closely. 'It's time to let go of the past, Edward.'

'I'm willing to do that, Gloria. I just don't know if she is.' Ryan met her gaze.

'Give her a chance, Edward. She got caught right in the middle of the two of you. She never had a choice.'

'No, she didn't.'

'Didn't what? Charlie asked suspiciously, as he came back into the room. 'Are we still talking about Nancy Belke? Has that question finally been answered?'

'You're never going to know.' Gloria grinned up at him.

'Yeah, I will. You'll tell me as soon as he leaves.'

'Not a chance.'

'I have ways of making you talk.' Charlie stepped behind her and planted a kiss on the side of her neck.

'You guys keep this up and you'll be looking at number nine in no time at all.'

'Eight is it,' Gloria said definitely.

Ryan caught Charlie's shrug.

'It is, Charlie. This is the last.'

'We'll see.' Charlie grinned.

They carried their coffee and brandy out to the porch. Gloria and Charlie took the two chairs while Ryan sat on the top step and leaned back against the railing.

'Always nice this time of night. We get a little bit of that west wind off the Gulf.'

Ryan felt the barest hint of cool air ruffle along his jaw. 'I'd forgotten what the heat was like.'

'You'll get used to it again.'

Ryan nodded and sipped his brandy. 'I saw Captain Rainey today.'

'He's okay.'

'Seemed to be. He was more helpful than I'd expected.'

'He's home grown, which I think makes it pretty tough for him to do his job sometimes.'

Catching Ryan's inquisitive glance, Charlie elaborated. 'The town is controlled by the tourist season, and by the Royal Port crowd. It's not often that the two of them agree.'

'I don't know if that's quite true, Charlie. Some of the people up in Royal Port own shops in town.'

'Yeah, but for them it's more of a hobby than anything else. They come down here to retire, get bored and open a business.'

'I was talking to Linda the other day,' Gloria said and explained to Ryan, 'she owns a women's clothing store over on Third Street. She was telling me that she's spent almost ten years building up her clientele and stock, and then Julia's opened up right down the block from her. The proprietor spent almost a million dollars remodeling and stocking it. Linda says she doesn't know what she's going to do. She just can't compete with that kind of money. She has one bad season and she's in serious trouble. The woman who owns Julia's has a bad season and all she's looking at is a tax write-off.'

'How bad was this last season?'

'Not too bad, but not great. We have another like it and a lot of people are going to start hurting.'

'You know, I always hated that,' Ryan said. 'That total dependency on the tourists.'

Charlie shrugged. 'What else can you do? It's either that or industry. And the way industry treats the environment, I'll stick with the tourists,' he said, offering a toast with his glass.

Gloria kissed Ryan on the cheek. 'I expect to see you more often,' she said solemnly, pulling back and locking her eyes on his.

Ryan promised that she would and wished her good-night.

Charlie returned and filled their glasses. He put the brandy bottle beside his feet. 'You learn anything from Rainey?'

'He thinks it was a hit.'

'I hadn't heard that before.'

'Yeah, that's what he said. He thinks the guy was waiting specifically for Neal.'

'He have any idea why?'

'No. He said they went over the company's books and there wasn't anything they could find. You know Burdick?'

'Slightly.'

'What's he like?'

'Professionally or personally?'

'Both.'

'Professionally, he's very good. From what I've heard he and Neal counterbalanced one another well. Each compensated for the other's weaknesses.'

'What were Neal's weaknesses?'

'He was a little wild.'

Ryan grinned.

'He had a tendency to want to move too quickly. Burdick is much more cautious. At least that's what I've heard. It's all hearsay.' Charlie shrugged.

'And what about personally?'

'Guy's an asshole. He lives alone in the old section of town. No wife, no kids and no real friends that I've ever heard about. His only interest seems to be work.'

'Why's that make him an asshole?'

'I don't know how to answer that. You've met him, what'd you think?'

'I thought he was an asshole.'

'Why?'

'He's too tight. He's one of those guys you expect to go off at any time.'

Charlie nodded his agreement. 'There's something about him that's cold. I can't quite put my finger on it, but I just don't like him. What did Rainey say about him?'

'Said he'd checked out.'

'What're you going to do now?'

'I don't know, just keep asking questions, see if anything happens.'

'And if it does?'

Ryan shrugged.

'Is that what the new look's all about?'

'Yeah, I figure I'm undercover now.' Ryan grinned.

Charlie shook his head. 'If it was a hit, Edward, whoever these people are, they're playing for keeps.'

Ryan glanced at the palm-trees lining the street. 'So am I, Charlie,' he said softly.

There was no doubt in Stutz's mind about the guy's condition. He didn't even need the balloon, but he knew that the videotape alone wouldn't be enough.

Earlier he had pulled his squad car off the road, sheltering it between two jacaranda trees. He had then slouched back in his seat and begun to wait. A little over fifteen minutes ago, about two thirty in the morning, he'd spotted the headlights weaving down the street.

Stutz had hunched forward over the steering-wheel and watched the car's reckless approach. As soon as it had passed in front of him he had pulled out and hit the lights. He'd had to hit the siren as well before the driver became aware that he was there.

The late-model Jaguar XKE had wobbled over to the curb. A moment later the driver's door had opened and its occupant had sprawled out onto the street. Stutz had immediately flipped on the camcorder. It had filmed the driver's fall for posterity.

He had the driver propped up against the side of his car and was just about to hand him the balloon, when the headlights pulled up in front of him. Stutz took a protective step back. His hand rose and released the safety harness of his service revolver.

'How you doing there, officer?'

The headlights abruptly flashed off. Stutz blinked in the sudden darkness. When he refocused his eyes, he saw one of the Point Blank Security people coming towards him.

'Who you got here?' the man asked, moving up beside him. The security guard crouched forward, peering into the face of the driver. 'Mr Dressler, don't you know better than this?'

The man awkwardly raised his head and squinted at the security man. He muttered incoherently and waved his arm in Stutz's direction.

'Don't you worry about a thing, sir.' The security man turned to Stutz. 'It's okay, officer. I'll see that he gets home safely.'

Stutz's sudden smile was one of surprise.

The security guard took it differently. He reached over to grip the drunken man's shoulder.

'Wait just a minute there,' Stutz said, astonished at the audacity of the guard. 'What do you think you're doing?'

'Taking him home.'

'Well that's a nice offer, but we've got a little DUI problem here.'

'I know that. That's why I'm taking Mr Dressler home. He really shouldn't be driving.'

'No, I don't think you understand what's going on here,' Stutz said, attempting to control his anger. 'And if you don't take your hand off that man, right now, I'm going to make damn sure that you understand real fast what's happening.' The security man turned to face the younger policeman. 'Now why don't you just get back into your truck and get the hell out of here.'

The guard locked eyes with Stutz. A moment later he dropped his gaze and turned round. Stutz watched him climb into his truck and went back to the drunk Mr Dressler. He was just attempting to get a reading off the balloon when he heard his call sign come over the radio. He propped the drunken man against the side of the squad and reached in for the hand set. He called in, throwing a disgusted glance at the truck still parked in front of him. Identifying himself, he waited for the return call.

'Twenty-eight, code 64. I repeat code 64.'

'Wait a minute,' Stutz shouted into the receiver.

'That's a 64, 28, over.'

Stutz stared in astonishment at the dead receiver and hung up. He pulled his head back out of the squad and watched as the security guard walked over and collected the drunken man. He led him back to his truck and gently helped him into the passenger seat.

Stutz waited for the man to look his way. He figured if he did, screw code 64 and everything else. He was going to run the son-of-a-bitch in. The guard, as if sensing his mood, never once glanced in his direction. Stutz watched the truck start up and drive into Royal Port. He turned back and climbed into his squad.

Code 64 was an immediate recall to the station. Officers were required to respond at once.

Stutz quickly drove back to the station house. He stormed into the watch commander's office and demanded to know just what the hell was going on.

Surfer took delivery of fifty-two keys of marijuana off a side street in Sabal Bay. He climbed into the back of the Ryder van and checked the count. Satisfied that everything was in order, he locked up and started the truck.

He drove along the highway leading into Siena and turned into the downtown area. Carefully he kept within the posted speed limits and turned south once he hit the waterfront. He drove down the empty streets of the old section of town, passing a squad car along the way. He kept his eyes locked on the road before him, fearing any type of contact might somehow subliminally alert the policeman.

He drove into Royal Port. The houses were all criss-crossed with security spotlights.

Surfer cut his headlights and pulled up in front of a construction site. He parked at the curb, quickly climbed out and locked up the truck. He walked two blocks until he found the Volkswagen bug parked by the side of the road. The keys were in the glove compartment. He started the car and drove back to his condominium. Once there, he replaced the keys in the glove compartment and walked away. He knew the car would disappear some time during the night. It always had before.

He carried a bottle of mineral water over to his phone and waited. Within fifteen minutes the call came. He assured the man that everything had gone as planned.

The voice at the other end congratulated him, then asked about the children.

'Nothing,' Surfer told him. 'There hasn't been a cop near them since I've been watching.'

'What about the brother?'

Surfer cleared his throat.

'Well?' the voice demanded impatiently.

'I lost him,' Surfer said quickly.

'Explain?'

'I followed him back to his motel and waited to see what he would do. He never came back out. I sat there for almost four hours before I started to wonder what was going on. His bike was still parked in front, so I just assumed he was still in there.' He paused.

'And?' the voice prompted.

'So what I did was I went over to take a look. He wasn't there.'

'But his bike was still in place.'

'Yeah, it was parked right out in front. It hasn't moved.' Surfer listened to the thoughtful silence at the other end.

'Do you have someone watching the place now?'

'Yes.'

'Did you go into his room?'

'Yeah, there wasn't anything there.'

'What do you mean?'

'I mean there was just clothes and stuff, nothing else, nothing that meant anything.' Surfer paused for a moment, then hesitantly asked. 'What do you want me to do?'

'For the time being, keep someone on the motel room. If his bike's there, he's bound to return.'

'And if he doesn't?'

'You'd better hope that he does.'

Surfer listened to the sound of the receiver being replaced at the other end. 'Asshole,' he muttered, picked up his mineral water and carried it into the bedroom.

'What's wrong?' the girl sprawled across the sheets asked.

'Nothing.'

She shrugged happily and rolled over to the bedside table. She pulled a mirror onto her lap and crouched over it. Surfer listened to the congested sound of her nostrils snorting up the fine white powder.

'Roll over,' he ordered curtly.

When she had spread herself face down across the bed, Surfer knelt between her legs and began to undo his pants.

Ten

Ryan registered at a motel on the outskirts of town. He quickly checked into his room, then drove out along the highway. He pulled in to Gatsby's lot and parked.

The same bouncer was at the door. 'How you doing this evening, sir?'

Ryan nodded amiably.

'There's a three dollar cover, sir.'

Ryan paid the man and stepped into the night-club. He took a seat at the edge of the bar and ordered a Heineken. He drank slowly, surveying the crowd. When he was sure that his presence had gone unnoticed, he went back out to his car. He drove past his previous motel and glanced over towards his unit. He saw his motorcycle still parked in front of his old room and continued on to town.

He turned south and drove up into the Royal Port area, passing a Point Blank Security vehicle along the way. The man inside waved to him. Ryan waved back and continued his drive. He circled and drove back to his motel room.

He paused in front of the mirror. His new appearance still startled him. He ran a hand along the line of his jaw, surprised by the smooth feel of his flesh.

He sat at the table overlooking the street, lit a cigarette and leaned back closing his eyes. He drifted along within the always present memories, then, with a conscious effort, forced them away. He turned his concentration to Neal, focusing his thoughts on the questions he wanted answered.

He began to plan.

The phone's shrill squeal pulled Charlie from sleep. He untangled himself from his wife's body and groped for the receiver. 'Yeah,' he grunted.

'Who is it?' Gloria asked sleepily.

'The paper,' Charlie whispered, putting a hand on her hip to quiet her questions.

'Get down to the pier.'

'Why, what's going on?'

'Couple of fishermen just pulled in a body.'

'Okay.' He yawned and hung up.

'What did they want?'

'Nothing,' Charlie answered, pushing himself out of bed.

'What is it, Charlie?'

He felt her hand on his side and covered it with his own. 'A story,' he said and rose to his feet. 'Go back to sleep.'

He dressed fast and walked down the hallway, pausing at each of the doors to listen to the sleeping sounds of his children.

Charlie pulled up to the foot of the pier and climbed out of his car, balancing an econo cup of 7–11 coffee in one hand. The pier was cordoned off by two squad cars.

'Hold it,' one of the officers yelled, then recognizing him motioned him forward.

The sun was just shooting highlights of color up into the eastern sky as Charlie joined the small huddle of men standing at the end of the pier. 'What've you got?'

Captain Rainey turned to him. Charlie was surprised to see him at the scene. 'Two guys hooked in to him,' Rainey said, motioning to a blanket-clad body sprawled across the wooden slats of the pier.

'Who is it?'

'No identification yet.'

'Local?'

'Probably.'

'Why?' Charlie asked, glancing up from his notebook.

'Guy's got a tan, a real one, not one of those touristy fake ones.' Rainey turned to look at the body. 'And his shoes.'

Charlie glanced over at the figure. Two feet jutted out from one end of the blanket. 'What about them?'

'They're dress shoes. No tourist comes down here and wears dress shoes. Maybe deck or casuals, but not dress.' Rainey shook his head and glanced expectantly at Charlie.

Charlie nodded his approval, unwilling to voice any other possibilities. 'How long's he been dead?'

'Day or so.'

'What happened to him?'

Rainey turned away.

'What?' Charlie called to him.

Rainey ignored him and stepped over to two fishermen leaning against the railing. Each of them had a cigarette going. Warily they watched the Captain approach.

Charlie tried to join them, but was halted by another detective. 'How'd he die, Al?'

Al glanced over towards Rainey, then back at Charlie. 'Took one in the head,' he whispered.

'Burton, get the hell over here,' Rainey shouted, glaring over at the detective. Al shrugged sheepishly and walked over to Rainey.

Charlie turned back to the body, hearing Rainey's angry voice berate the detective.

The sun had just started to peek over the trees by the time Rainey stepped back to the reporter. 'You want to take a look, since there's not much left to hide?' he said, throwing a disgusted glance at Al Burton.

Charlie followed him over to the body. Rainey pulled back the top of the blanket, revealing the corpse's head. The face was leached of all color, which made the red-rimmed hole in the center of his forehead that much more startling. Charlie took a step back, then forced himself to move forward. He leaned over to examine the face. 'I don't know. He looks kinds of familiar.'

'Yeah.' Rainey sighed, dropping the blanket back in place.

Three of the corpse's fingers jutted out from one side of the blanket.

'I feel the same way about it. Maybe he's just got one of those faces.' Rainey stretched and yawned hugely. 'We'll know soon enough.'

'Anything about the weapon?'

Rainey glanced at him sharply.

Charlie pretended not to notice.

'Nothing yet.'

'ME been out?'

'Came and gone. We're waiting on the goddamn EMS,' Rainey said. Before he'd finished they both turned to see the flashing red lights pull up at the foot of the pier. 'Now that's timing.' Rainey grinned.

Charlie took notes, then talked to the two fishermen. Neither had much more to offer. One of them had snagged the body and dragged it to the surface. Interspersed with various big-fish jokes they explained how they had tied off the line to one of the pilings, then called the police.

Charlie took their names and turned to watch the two EMS men load the body onto a gurney and wheel him off the pier. He followed. A small group composed off predominantly elderly people gathered at the foot of the pier.

'Look at them,' Rainey said in disgust. 'Give them something to talk about at their bridge game this afternoon.'

Charlie watched him climb wearily into his unmarked car and pull away. He turned and caught up to Al as he was opening the door of his car.

'Get away from me, Charlie. You already got me in trouble once this morning.'

'Hey, Al, I just wanted to ask you a few questions.'

'No way, buddy. Rainey was pissed off as hell that I said that thing about the gun.'

'I would have found out anyway,' Charlie said reasonably.

'Yeah, well, at least it wouldn't have been from me.'

'They know what caliber it was?'

'Charlie,' Al warned.

'C'mon, what's the difference if you tell me or I get it from the ME in a couple of hours.'

'My ass is the difference,' Al said, climbed into his vehicle and pulled away.

Charlie made his way back to his car, ignoring the curious questions directed at him from the group surrounding the pier.

He drove to the newspaper and went into Phil Luard's office.

The night editor was seated at his desk with a cup of coffee and a sheaf of contact sheets in his hand. 'Which one?' he asked, handing Charlie two of the sheets.

Charlie glanced at the two circled prints. Each of them showed a pretty young woman standing in front of a pig. The only difference between the two photographs was the angle of the camera.

'This one?'

'Why?'

'Shows a little of the woman's thigh. Who wants to look at a pig?'

'You'd be surprised.' Phil sighed wearily and straightened his shoulders. 'What you got?'

'Male, caucasian, between sixty and sixty-five, shot once in the head, been dead at least five hours and no longer than twelve. Two fishermen hooked into him about five forty this morning. Rainey thinks the victim might be a local. He arrived at that brilliant deduction by the man's shoes.'

'His shoes?' Phil asked incredulously.

Charlie grinned. 'They're dress shoes. Rainey doesn't think tourists come down here and wear dress-up clothes.'

'Christ, I guess it makes sense.'

'With Rainey, things usually do,' Charlie agreed. 'You want me to write it up now, or wait for the ME's report?'

'When're they expecting it?'

'Later this afternoon.'

'Can we make the afternoon edition?'

'I don't know. It'd be close.'

Phil raised his coffee thoughtfully and nodded. 'Write up what you have. Whatever we miss we'll follow up tomorrow.'

Charlie nodded and started towards the door.

'Oh, by the way, I heard Neal Ryan's brother is in town.'

Charlie turned.

'There anything in that?'

'No.'

'There's a lot of background in that family,' Phil said cautiously.

'Leave it alone, Phil. All of that was a long time ago.'

'It's news.'

'It's just dirt. Nothing was ever proven.'

Phil leaned back. 'Okay.' He nodded. 'I know he's a friend of yours, so we'll let it go. But don't let your friendship interfere with the paper.'

Charlie shrugged, turned and went out to his desk to write the article. He finished it in time to get to the city council meeting scheduled for ten o'clock that morning. Up for discussion that day was a condominium project planned for the north end of town. The project pitted the developers and store owners against the growing number of environmentalists. One side contended that the project would increase employment and offer tax relief. The other argued that the area should be protected under the federal wetland policies.

The final outcome held little surprise for anyone cognizant with the practises of the local government. The final vote was five to one in approval of the project. They would break ground within the next thirty days unless the environmentalists could convince the state legislature to issue a temporary injunction, a possibility that had very little chance of occurring within the allotted time. Charlie's objectivity was sorely tested as he wrote the article.

He stopped at home for a quick shower and a change of clothes, and was at the county hospital in time for the release of the ME's report.

The victim was estimated to have been killed no less than eleven hours earlier and no more than eighteen. His age was approximated at sixty-five. He had been dead before he had entered the water. Ballistics had ascertained that the bullet was a .22 long. The consensus was that it had been fired from a Colt Woodsman. There was still no response on his prints.

Charlie added the material to what he had already discovered and went back to the newspaper to write up the additional information.

He left his office late that afternoon and drove out to a small restaurant lounge on Rattlesnake Drive. He entered the dimly lit bar and paused for a moment in the doorway to allow his eyes to adjust to the sudden contrast of light. He made his way along the bar, nodding to a few of the officers he knew. Spotting Al Burton seated at the end he stepped down to join him.

'Hotter than shit,' Al greeted him.

Charlie agreed and ordered them both a beer.

'What's going on?'

Charlie smiled and reached for a handful of popcorn. 'Just got the Examiner's report,' he said round a mouthful of popcorn.

'So?'

'It was a .22 long.'

'Like I said, so?'

'Kind of odd, don't you think?' Charlie said casually, looking at the other man's reflection in the mirror.

Al turned to him. 'What do you mean, odd?'

'That's the second person, in less than a month, that's seen the wrong end of a .22.'

'Charlie, don't make anything out of this that isn't there,' Al said tiredly.

'I don't think I am. I just think it's a little on the coincidental side. This isn't Miami. This is a small, quiet little town.'

'We've got our share of problems.'

Charlie agreed. 'Domestics, drugs and the occasional robbery. Nothing like this.'

'And what exactly do you think this is?'

'I think it's a hit,' Charlie said, watching the other man closely.

Al snorted in derision. 'Maybe you should talk to Rainey.'

'Tried to, but he didn't have time to see me.'

'So you came to me.'

'Who else?' Charlie shrugged, smiling at the impatient scowl on Al's face.

'Charlie, I can't tell you anything. you know as much about this as I do.'

'So tell me what you think.'

'I don't think anything.'

'C'mon, Al. Two guys, both hit with the same caliber bullet. Don't you think that's a little strange for Siena?'

'It's not even my case, Charlie. Talk to Wetherford or Arnold. They're the ones handling it. Leave me alone.'

'Did they run a comparison on the bullets?'

'Charlie!'

'Did they?'

Shaking his head in disgust, Al sighed. 'You want a lot for one beer.'

'Let me get you another.'

'You want a lot for two beers.'

'Gloria's talking about making some ravioli.'

Al glanced over at him thoughtfully.

'Probably next week some time.'

'Jesus Christ, Charlie, you're ruthless.'

'Did they run a comparison?'

'They were talking about it. Take a day or so. The other slug's up in Tallahassee. They're still running some tests on it.'

Charlie ordered them each another beer.

Al took a long sip and turned. 'What time's dinner?' He grinned.

Surfer opened the afternoon paper. He examined the headline story carefully. Satisfied that everything had gone according to plan he quickly discarded that section of the paper.

He was just starting on the sports page when the phone interrupted him.

'Yes?'

'Surf, ain't nothing going on here. How long I got to sit here looking at this guy's fucking cycle?'

'Hang on another hour. Someone'll be out to relieve you.'

'That'd be nice. This is getting pretty fucking old.'

'Anyone notice you?'

'Shit, it's too hot for anyone to notice much of anything. I been sitting in this fucking car for almost six hours now.'

'No one's been around?'

'No, nothing, just the maid came by is all.'

'Hang on another hour,' Surfer promised.

Surfer slowed as he passed the motel. He glanced over and saw his man slumped behind the wheel of his car, glumly staring across the street at the motel. Surfer kept driving and headed out to the east end of town.

He pulled up in front of a small one-storey cottage and honked. A moment later the front door opened and a man stepped out onto the porch. He squinted at the car, waved and disappeared back inside the house. When he returned he carried a small plastic shopping bag with him.

'What's that?'

'Lunch.' The man grinned, settling himself into the passenger seat.

Surfer started up the car. He opened his windows as the smell of fish began to permeate the small space.

He parked a block away, then motioned the man out and over to the car parked across the street from the motel.

'All I do is sit there and wait?'

'That's it.'

'What am I supposed to do if I see someone?'

'Just call me. Nothing else, all right?'

The man nodded and trudged across the road.

Surfer watched as the two men exchanged places. The one who'd taken the first watch climbed out and raced over to Surfer's car.

'Jesus, hit the air, man. I'm fucking dying,' he said, fiddling with the controls on the dashboard.

Surfer drove him home. He handed him a fifty dollar bill as he pulled in front of a run-down apartment complex. Three children stood at one end of the building, watching as a fourth urinated against the wall. They all turned to stare at Surfer's car.

'You going to need me again?'

'I don't know. I'll give you a call some time tonight if I do.'

The man nodded, closed the door and started up the sidewalk.

A woman, hugely pregnant, stepped awkwardly out onto the porch to greet him. Shading her eyes, she glared at Surfer's car, turned and directed a scowl at the man walking up to her. Surfer pulled away, hearing her angry voice rise behind him.

He pulled into the lot off St Christopher's Road, one of the more exclusive mainstays in the restaurant world of Siena, and parked.

He took a seat at the corner of the dark bar and waited.

'How you doing?' the barmaid greeted him warmly.

'Pretty good. How about yourself?'

'Better now.' She grinned coyly, turning away to make his drink.

'Johnny Black and water.' She beamed at him, placing the drink on a coaster near his hand.

Surfer took the drink. The small package of aluminum foil he had left on the bar quickly disappeared into the woman's hand. She winked and stepped out from behind the bar. Surfer watched as she made a beeline to the women's room.

When she returned her eyes glittered excitedly. 'Really good shit, Surfer.'

Surfer nodded. 'How much you want?'

'An ounce.'

'You think you can handle that kind of weight?'

She leaned over the bar towards him.

Surfer admired the tops of her breasts.

'These guys don't give a shit about money.' She grimaced, motioning to the room around her.

'All right, anything else?'

'Not yet.' She grinned. 'But it's still early.'

Surfer finished his drink and walked out to his car. He opened the trunk, pulled out a beige Coach purse, and carried it self-consciously back in. 'This it?' he called out awkwardly, walking into the lounge.

'Yeah,' she answered. Her laughter at his obvious embarrassment was joined by some of her other customers at the bar.

Surfer handed her the purse and quickly exited the restaurant. He drove through town and out along the highway, making his rounds. He dropped off whatever was needed with his contact people in the restaurants and hotels, and took orders and collected for previous services. On his way home, he stopped at a Limpy's burger franchise and picked up an order to go.

He returned to his condo before sunset, went into the kitchen, trashed his burger and fries and pulled out a Perrier from the refrigerator. He carried it with him into the living-room and spread out the day's take on the table before him. The phone interrupted his count. He put down the wad of bills to pick it up.

'Anything?' the voice asked without preamble.

'Nothing so far.'

'Are you sure?'

'Yeah. I've had people on the room right around the clock.'

'He's moved.'

'You want I should look for him?'

'Yes, but I don't want him to know about it.'

Surfer grinned. 'He shouldn't be too difficult to find, looking the way he does.'

The voice hesitated for a moment. 'Yes, he wouldn't be, would he?' came the distracted response.

'Anything else?'

'Yes, I want a boy out at The Regency at eight thirty this evening, room 301.'

'Anything special?'

'No older than eleven and no younger than eight.'

'Okay, you got it,' Surfer answered.

The man hung up and turned to his companion. 'I think the brother's becoming a problem.'

'Why?'

'He hasn't returned to the motel.'

'Maybe he met someone.'

'No, I don't think that's what happened.'

'It would be logical. There is, from what I understand, a certain type of woman who finds that kind of man appealing.'

'If that were the case he would have returned for his motorcycle.'

The other man nodded thoughtfully.

'I think he's out there planning something.'

'What could he possibly plan? He doesn't know anything.'

'Maybe that's something we need to consider. What does he know?'

'You're over-reacting. There isn't any way he could have learned anything. Everything Neal was involved with has been destroyed. There are no links to our group.'

'Are you sure about that?'

'Yes.'

'Are you willing to gamble everything on that assumption?'

The other man grew uncomfortable beneath his gaze. 'What do you suggest?'

'I think our primary directive should be to locate the brother.'

'I agree.'

'Then I think we should neutralize him.'

'We tried that. We couldn't interest the paper in the story.'

'Then maybe it's time to think of something a little more drastic.'

'Don't you think we should wait to see what happens, before we make that kind of move?'

'I don't think we should wait,' the man answered, with a note of finality in his tone.

He stepped over to a picture window, offering a panoramic view of the Gulf of Mexico. The sun was just touching the horizon, beginning its rapid burn into the sea. The man stood watching the sun's descent. When all that was left was a trail of blooded clouds, he turned back to his companion. 'I think it's time we called the group together. This is something that should be decided among us all.'

'Do you have something specific in mind?'

The man smiled. 'I was just thinking that if we were to stop all our activities there would be nothing to discover. The brother won't stay for ever.' The man's smile deepened. 'And what do we care about time.'

His companion's answering smile gave way to laughter.

The man turned to the window and watched the last trail of color fade from the horizon. 'Beautiful, isn't it.' He commented softly, listening to the slow ease of laughter behind him.

Eleven

Ryan bought a cheap cardboard briefcase and threw it into the front seat of his car. He drove out and parked two blocks from the house. Feeling slightly ridiculous, but not ridiculous enough to change his plan, he slowly began to work his way towards it.

He stopped at each of the homes on the block. He would knock at the front door and if anyone answered he would immediately go into a sales pitch for vacuum cleaners.

At one of the places where he stopped the woman started to display a certain interest in his fictional merchandise. Ryan quoted an outrageous price and was abruptly shown the door.

He saw the little girl, Lisa, when he was half a block away. She sat on the front steps with a book spread across her lap. He became aware of her curious glance as he walked up to the front door of the lot adjoining hers. Her gaze seemed too intent to be mere curiosity.

'How come you're like that?' She nodded to his clothes.

Ryan pushed at the foot of her porch, surprised that she'd been able to recognize him. It made him wonder if he'd made a mistake. 'It's a surprise.'

She nodded solemnly. Her eyes never left his face.

'What is it?'

She glanced away, then brought her gaze back to him. 'How come . . .' She hesitated.

'What?' he asked softly.

'How come you sound like my daddy?'

Ryan sighed. He put his briefcase down on the top step and sat beside her. 'Do you know who I am?'

She nodded. Her eyes flicked across his face, seemingly unable to find a point of focus.

'I'm your uncle, right?' He waited for her nod. 'So that means I'm your father's brother. Just like Ollie's your brother.'

'How come I don't know who you are?'

Ryan glanced out at the street. 'Well, your daddy and I got into an argument a long time ago and he was still angry.'

'What about?'

'Something dumb.' Ryan smiled at her.

'I get in arguments with Ollie.'

'I'll bet you do.'

'Sometimes he's real retarded.'

'He didn't seem that bad.'

'He is,' she said and held up a finger. 'Listen.' Ryan cocked his head. He kept his eyes on his niece's face. 'Hear that? That's Ollie making his engine noises. He makes them all the time now, no matter how many times you tell him not to.' Ryan heard the noises coming from inside the house. 'Even when he's eating he makes that noise. The only time he stops is when he goes to bed. That's the only way I can tell when he's sleeping.'

'When your father was small he used to make noises too.'

'What kind of noises?'

'He used to make boat noises,' Ryan said and closed his eyes for a moment. He opened them abruptly, threatened by the vividness of the memory. 'He used to drive us all nuts.' Lisa smiled. 'Is your mother home?' Ryan asked, pushing to his feet and reaching for his briefcase.

Lisa nodded. 'But I don't think she wants to see you.'

'Well why don't we find out if that's true.' He held his hand out. A moment later Lisa took it, stood up and led him into the house.

Surfer took the call late in the afternoon.

'Anything?'

'Nah, mailman, woman from next door and a salesman. That's it. How long I gotta do this, Surf?'

'Little while longer. No cops show up?'

'Nope.'

'I'll get back to you later. Keep watching.' Surfer hung up and went back to the dining-room table. On top of it were two piles of bills. The bills were ragged from use and made up of denominations no larger than twenty. One pile was considerably bigger than the other. Surfer examined the larger pile in dismay, then, with an abrupt shake of his head, put it in a brown manila envelope. Across the front he wrote, Acme Construction. The smaller pile he put in a coffee can and returned to his top kitchen cabinet.

He carried the manila envelope out to his car and drove out to an abandoned construction site in Royal Port. Parking off the main street, he quickly went over to any empty office trailer standing on the site. He taped the manila folder to the side of the door and walked back to his car.

He drove back through town and stopped at a little bar set back from the street. The small, dimly lit Budweiser sign in the window was the only indication of the business inside.

The abrupt transition from the bright day to the dark interior of the bar left Surfer momentarily blinded as he stepped through the doorway. The inside was illuminated by two heavily shaded lamps at each end of the bar and there were candles placed in the center of each of the six tables that formed a half circle around it, which did little more than highlight the faces of the people seated there. Their bodies tapered off into the darkness.

'Leon here?'

The young man behind the bar wore a white string T-shirt and a pair of black leather shorts. Both garments seemed more painted onto his body than worn.

'He's at the back table.' He gestured. His voice was softly pitched, and he had trouble enunciating his esses.

'Surfer, my good friend.' The man leaned forward, his face suddenly appearing above the light of the candle. His eyes were heavily caked with make-up.

Surfer pulled out a chair and sat across from him.

'You have some very rough friends.' The man tittered.

'Hey, that's how it goes.' Surfer shrugged dismissively. 'How much I owe you?'

'One fifty?'

'Higher than usual.'

'It was much rougher than usual.'

Surfer counted out the money and pushed it across the table.

The nails on the hand that reached out to gather the bills were polished a deep red. 'Will I be hearing from you again?'

'Probably.'

'Soon, I hope.' The man grinned, his fingers gently caressing the money.

'We'll see.' Surfer pushed himself out of his chair and headed for the door.

He drove back to his condo and carried a Perrier and his phone onto his deck. He leaned back in a *chaise longue* and drank his mineral water as he looked out at the gentle swell of the Gulf and waited for his phone to ring.

The boy walked awkwardly across the pavement. With his feet pointing out, he shuffled along the entrance way of the motel to his room.

'Tony?' He turned. 'What're you doing? You want go down to the beach for a while? Me and a couple of the other guys are going. Jim's got a car.'

'Nah, I don't think so. I'm just going to hang out here.'

His friend looked at him closely. 'You okay?'

'Yeah.' Tony shrugged, turned and painfully made his way into his room.

The other boy watched his progress. He waited until Tony had disappeared through his door before he raced back along the hallway of the motel to the parking lot.

'Tony coming?' someone called from the car.

The boy laughed as he opened the door and climbed inside. 'Nah, I think he's going to soak his asshole.'

'Again,' someone shouted gleefully from the back seat, and amidst the sound of childish laughter the car headed for the beach.

Inside his room Tony removed the bloody menstrual pad he had placed in the bottom of his underwear. He examined it closely and, seemingly satisfied, discarded it in the waste basket. He poured Epsom Salts into the tub and filled it with hot water. The box of Epsom Salts, along with a tube of KY jelly and a Bible, were among the hospitalities provided by the management.

Tony undressed and slowly eased himself in. He leaned back and laid his head on the edge of the tub. With his eyes closed he didn't have to see the pinkish tinge that began to color the water.

* * *

'How you doing?' Judy greeted him cheerfully. Stutz grunted and took his customary seat at the chickee bar. 'Something wrong?'

'Nothing's wrong, just got me a beer, would you, please.'

'Sure.' Judy nodded.

Stutz watched her stoop into one of the coolers and retrieve a Budweiser. She unscrewed the top and set the bottle in front of him.

'You okay?'

'Yeah, I'm just dandy.' Stutz picked up his beer and drank. He didn't put the bottle back onto the bar until it was half empty. He felt Judy's eyes on him. 'Just a bad day,' he explained and raised his beer again. He killed it and shoved the empty forward. Judy replaced it with a fresh one.

Stutz lit a cigarette and watched as she served another customer. Even the sight of her shorts riding up the back of her thighs didn't do anything to improve his mood.

He looked across the bar towards the pool. The pool-side tables were strictly reserved for occupants of the hotel. There were four couples seated on *chaise longues*. Beside each of the chairs were small circular plastic tables. On top of these were multicolored drinks, sporting fruit and shaded by miniature umbrellas. Stutz examined the couples closely. None of them was younger than sixty.

'Jesus, you're in a mood.' Stutz scowled at her. 'What's wrong? One of the bad guys get away?' Judy smiled. Stutz glanced at her sharply. 'Hey, I'm sorry. I was just trying to lighten things up a little.'

Stutz picked up his beer and swallowed thoughtfully. 'You know something. This town sucks.'

'Tell me something I don't know.'

Stutz shook his head. 'It does. I don't know what the fuck I'm doing here. It's all old people and old money. They're the ones running the fucking place,' he said bitterly, aware of Judy watching him closely, waiting for an explanation.

For a moment he was tempted to tell her about last night, about his little meeting with the watch commander.

'What the hell were you doing in Royal Port?' the man had demanded angrily.

'My job.'

'Don't be a wiseass. You want to do your job, do it where it counts. There's nothing happening in that area.'

'I've got a videotape that might prove you wrong, sir,' Stutz had answered politely, tacking on the sir as an afterthought.

'You keep fucking with me, I'm going to show you right from wrong so fast you're not going to know what the hell hit you,' the man had responded, leaning across his desk to glare at Stutz. 'I want that videotape on my desk in ten minutes, and then I want you out in The Gate for the rest of your shift. And if I ever hear of you in that area again, you can kiss your ass goodbye, Mr Stutz. You understand me?'

Stutz hadn't answered. He'd gone out to get the video, which he'd brought back into the office and thrown on the commander's desk. He'd turned away when the man had picked up the tape and dropped it into the waste basket.

Stutz sighed heavily and toyed with his beer bottle.

Judy leaned across the bar towards him, her breasts coming to rest just inches from his hands. 'I get off in half an hour.'

Stutz raised his eyes to hers and attempted a smile. It felt stiff and insincere to him, but seemed genuine enough to please her.

'Half an hour.' She winked and stepped to the end of the bar to serve a waiter.

Stutz glanced over at the pool as one of the elderly couples impatiently signaled for service. A moment later a waiter appeared beside them. Stutz looked away when the elderly woman began to loudly berate him.

'Fucking town,' he muttered disgustedly under his breath.

'Here, this'll make you feel better.'

He looked at the shot glass Judy held out to him.

'Tequila. It'll pick you right up.'

Stutz smiled his first genuine smile of the day as he reached for the glass and with a toast in her direction, threw it back. He felt it burn all the way down his throat.

An hour later the two of them sat downing shots of tequila at a bar up in Bonita Beach.

'You know who runs this town?' Stutz asked, attempting unsuccessfully to enunciate each word.

'Money.' Judy shrugged indifferently. Stutz examined her. 'Hey.' She smiled 'Are you just finding that out?' Stutz picked up his glass. 'Jeez, Bo, where you been hiding?'

He drank, then replaced the glass on the bar and turned to her.
'Tell me about that.'

'About what?'

'About money running the town.'

Judy shrugged. 'Nothing to tell.'

'Then how come you said that?'

'Because it's true.'

'How do you know that?'

Judy glanced away.

Stutz gently touched her chin and turned her gaze back to his.
'C'mon, tell me about it.'

'There's nothing to tell, Bo.'

Stutz examined her closely, then, with a shrug, grinned at her and
turned to the bartender. He motioned to their glasses. He sipped his,
watching over the rim as Judy knocked her drink back in a well-
practiced move.

Three hours later, Judy was stretched across the front seat of his
car, resting her head on his lap.

Stutz said carefully, 'God, there's a lot of money in this town.'

'Tons of it.'

'You must see a lot of it, working where you do.'

'They all come in there,' Judy said bitterly.

'You don't like them?'

'They're assholes. Cheap assholes who think they can do whatever
they want to do.'

'Do they?'

'Do they what?' Judy glanced up at him, blinking her eyes in an
attempt to focus.

'Do whatever they want to do?'

Judy laughed, then nodded knowingly. 'Anything they want, they
get.'

Stutz looked down at her. He touched her hair and asked softly,
'Like what?'

'Like girls, boys, anything they want to try, they just buy it,' Judy
answered. She paused for a moment, as if considering what she was
saying, then, with a shrug, went on talking.

Stutz listened carefully to everything she said.

*   *   *

'Shhh,' Lisa warned Ollie, holding a finger to her lips.

Ollie smiled and nodded eagerly. They both sat outside the closed door of the kitchen.

'Is that Daddy?' Ollie whispered.

Lisa shook her head. 'It's Uncle Eddie.'

'He has a motorcycle.'

Lisa nodded and leaned forward, trying to hear what they were saying in the other room. Ollie, seeing her do this, did the same, until his head leaned against her cheek.

'Let it go,' he heard Uncle Eddie say.

'Why should I. Neal didn't. You think just because he's dead everything's forgotten.'

'Why are you doing this? None of this had anything to do with you. It all happened long before you ever met him.'

'He was my husband. Just because he's gone doesn't change anything.'

There was a long silence. Lisa became aware of Ollie looking at her curiously. She motioned for him to remain quiet, then heard her Uncle say, 'It should, Maggie. It should change everything.'

'Well, it doesn't.'

'That's Mommy,' Ollie said.

Lisa glared at him, quickly grabbed his arm and pulled him away from the door as she heard her mother's footsteps.

'What're you two doing?' she demanded, leaning through the open door.

'Nothing,' Lisa said, sitting on the floor in front of the couch.

'Well then do it outside, and take your brother with you.'

'Mommy, can't we . . .' Ollie started to say, when Lisa pinched him. He squealed. His bottom lip began to protrude.

'Outside, both of you, right now.' Her mother motioned towards the porch.

Lisa rose and started for the front door.

'Lisa, take your brother with you.'

Lisa turned back for Ollie. When she tried to take his hand he jerked it away. 'You pinched me,' he accused.

'Did not.'

'Did too.'

'Did too,' Lisa quickly answered, smiling at his sudden confusion.

'You're both going to end up in your rooms if you keep this up,' her mother threatened.

Lisa moved towards the door. She heard Ollie trailing behind her. She could tell he was there by the sound of his engine starting up.

'And stay in the front yard. I don't want you in the street,' Maggie told them and waited until the front door had closed before she turned back to the kitchen. She took a deep breath and, with a sigh, stepped back into the room. She felt Eddie watching her closely as she went over to the sink and leaned against it. Both her hands tightly clenched the counter. 'What do you want, Eddie?'

'I want to know what happened to Neal.'

'It's a little late for that kind of interest, isn't it?'

'No,' Ryan answered curtly, meeting her eye until she glanced away.

'I don't want you here.'

'I don't care. I'm here. You can either help me or ignore me, but it's not going to matter. I'm staying.'

Maggie turned to the window. 'The funeral's tomorrow,' she said softly.

'I know.'

'Sometimes, it's so hard to . . .' she shook her head, stopping her flow of words.

Ryan rose and went over beside her. 'Maggie.'

'No, Eddie. It doesn't feel right talking to you now. Maybe later it will, but right now, everything's just too strange, too . . .' She stopped again and turned her head to meet his gaze.

Ryan searched her eyes and took a step back. He nodded, then reached down to pick up his briefcase.

'Do you really think you need to do that?' She smiled thinly.

'Someone killed him, Maggie. Someone was out there hunting him. Hunting Neal.' Ryan turned to the door. 'I'll see you at the funeral,' he said and walked out.

He found Ollie and Lisa sitting on the front steps. 'Where's the motorcycle?'

'I left it at home.' He smiled.

'Can I have a ride?'

Lisa elbowed her brother. He gave her an injured look and turned back to Ryan expectantly.

'Sure.' Ryan nodded. 'We'll do that as soon as I can.'

Ollie smiled happily, then made a screeching sound as he reached across the porch.

'See,' Lisa said, shaking her head impatiently. 'He always does that.' Her voice came out so weary that Ryan smiled. He started towards his car.

'You promised,' Ollie reminded him.

'I promise,' Ryan assured him and glanced over at Lisa. 'Maybe all three of us can take a ride.'

Lisa smiled and glanced away shyly.

Ryan drove back to his motel room changed into a pair of ragged jeans and sprawled out across his bed. Even with the air conditioning going full blast he could feel perspiration dotting his arms and chest.

He pulled the phone over and dialed Charlie's house. He reached Gloria, who told him that Charlie was still at the office. She gave him the number, after eliciting a promise that Ryan would stop by before the funeral tomorrow.

'There's been another one,' Charlie told him. 'They fished a guy out of the Gulf this morning. He'd been shot once in the head. It looks like a professional hit.'

'That's the second in three weeks. That must be making people a little nervous.'

'If it is, no one's saying anything,' Charlie said. 'I was down at the station when they identified the guy's prints. I overheard two of the detectives talking about it.'

'Who was he?'

'No one's talking about it downtown. I think they were pissed off that I was there. Rainey called me in and grilled me about what I'd heard. I told him I hadn't heard a thing. I don't know if he believed me or not.'

'Is there a connection with Neal?'

'Could be. They were both shot with the same caliber gun.'

'Can they match the bullets?'

'I don't know. They sent them up to Tallahassee, but the comparison won't come back for a couple of days.'

'What do you think?'

'I think this is a small town, and I think it's a little too coincidental that two men are both shot with the same caliber gun, in what looks like an obvious assassination, to think that there isn't a connection.'

'Who was the guy?'

'Why?'

'C'mon, what do you think I'm going to do?'

'I don't have the faintest idea, which is why I'm a little reluctant to tell you.'

'Charlie, just talk to me, okay?' Ryan asked.

'Don't fuck around, Edward. This is getting a little weird.' Charlie paused. 'Guy's name was John Caldwell, he's a retired banker from Pennsylvania. He came down here about seven years ago and dabbled fairly successfully in real estate.'

'Did Neal do any work for him?'

'Not that I could find out. I talked to Burdick.'

'What did he say?'

'He said he'd never heard of the man, which I don't believe.'

'Why?'

'Caldwell was fairly well known, maybe not by sight but certainly by reputation. Even you've probably seen his signs around town. I don't see how Burdick could have missed them. I don't think Caldwell was actively working in the office any longer, but he was definitely overseeing things.'

'Why would Burdick lie?'

'I don't know. He wouldn't tell me,' Charlie said dryly.

'Maybe I should ask him.'

'I don't think that's such a good idea.'

'Then what is?'

'Give me some time with Burdick. Maybe I can dig something up in the back files.'

'What're the police doing?' Ryan asked. His question earned him a thoughtful silence from the other end.

'Caldwell represents some pretty big money,' Charlie answered cautiously.

'What does that mean?'

'He lived out in Royal Port. I got the impression that Rainey wants to be very careful about what he does.'

'Is he doing anything?' Ryan asked impatiently.

'I don't know, Edward. No one's talking. I would assume that

Rainey's moving very slowly. I'm sure he doesn't want to step on anyone's toes over this thing.'

'Who the hell's toes could he be stepping on?'

'I think that's the question that's bothering him.'

'Well maybe he should get his ass in gear and find out,' Ryan retorted heatedly.

'Take it easy. This isn't LA. You can't just kick in a door out here without having a pretty damn good reason.'

'Especially if the door just happens to be in Royal Port,' Ryan retorted bitterly.

'Hey, don't take it out on me.'

'Sorry.' Ryan paused. He reached over to the end table for his cigarettes. 'You'll let me know what's going on?' he asked, as he lit one.

'You know I will.'

'Thanks, Charlie.'

'That's okay. Just take it easy, all right?'

'Yeah, I will.' Ryan answered and repeated his promise to Gloria to stop by the house before the funeral tomorrow.

He hung up and went over to the side table, opened the phone book and traced the column of names until he found a listing for John Caldwell on Galleon Drive. He wrote the address down and walked over to the window. He looked out at the pool. An elderly couple shuffled along the far side of it. Ryan watched as they cautiously lowered themselves into two pool-side chairs.

The harsh glare of the sun splashed down across the water and deck. The two people sat and stared. They each wore long-sleeved shirts and long pants.

Ryan shook his head incredulously and ran a hand across his chest. It came away moist with perspiration. He pulled the complimentary map over to the bed and traced the roads leading out of the downtown section. The map ended abruptly at the edge of the Royal Port area.

He stubbed out his cigarette and lay back on his bed to wait for sunset, closing his eyes and letting himself drift.

He saw Neal standing before his father. The small figure of his brother stood unyielding beneath his parent's drunken gaze. He watched as the old man's hand rose and flashed across Neal's face. The blow spun him to the ground. Ryan raced over to his brother's side.

'You keep the fuck away from him, or you're going to get some of this too,' his father bellowed at him.

Ryan glared back at him. The old man seemed momentarily disconcerted by the directness of his gaze. It lasted only an instant. His father's foot lashed out and caught Ryan in the ribs. The kick toppled him to his side. The next kick thudded into the same spot. Ryan moaned and curled up, trying to protect himself from the other's boots. When the next kick came, he tried to roll away but his father followed, kicking and screaming inchoherently at him. He heard something crack inside his chest, then felt a sharp lancing pain flash up into his lungs.

He remained curled tightly on his side until he felt Neal touching his shoulder. He tried to straighten his legs but the pain stabbed deep into his chest. He groaned and wrapped his arms round his body.

'I'm going to kill him,' he heard Neal sob.

He forced himself to reach out to his younger brother. 'It's okay,' he said painfully. Each word dug sharply into his lungs.

'I'm going to,' Neal threatened.

Ryan nodded. They both waited until the sounds of their father's angry voice quieted inside the stilt house.

The silence was finally broken by the sound of the side door opening. They turned to see their mother creeping silently down the stairs.

She helped Ryan to his feet. Between the two of them they half carried him to the bed of the truck. They laid him gently on top of some burlap bags and drove him to the county hospital.

Neal sat with him, holding his head on his lap.

At the county hospital, Ryan listened as his mother explained to the doctor how he had fallen down the stairs. Neal sat silently beside him.

On the ride home Ryan, awkwardly trying to find a position that didn't put any pressure on his two fractured ribs, caught his brother's eye as they pulled into their drive.

'I'm going to kill him,' Neal promised.

Ryan shook his head sadly, feeling a sharp stab of pain lance through his chest that had nothing to do with his ribs.

Twelve

Ryan left his motel room at three o'clock in the morning. He drove along the nearly deserted streets to the pier and parked in the city lot across the block. Few other vehicles were there at that hour of the morning.

Walking towards the Gulf, Ryan could see the shadowed figures of fishermen patiently leaning against the decking of the pier. At its foot he turned to the stairs leading down to the beach. Moving quickly out of the circular splash of light surrounding the pier, he headed southwards along the edge of the water. The waves washed up behind him, wiping away his footprints.

He walked quickly along the shore, avoiding the harsh glare of the security spotlights illuminating the houses and grounds fronting the Gulf. About a mile further south he came to the Royal Port Country Club. Once he had passed it, he stepped away from the water and up to the sea wall running parallel to the Gulf. He followed the concrete wall until he came to a wooden stairway. He went up the stairs and paused at the top. Before him was a narrow half lot, leading out to the main street that bisected Royal Port.

Ryan moved quietly to the edge of the street. He kept beneath the overhang of a banyan tree as he checked the road before him. Satisfied that it was empty of travelers, he crossed quickly and made his way along a hedge bordering the side of the road. Two blocks later he came to Galleon Drive.

All the houses on the block had mailboxes jutting out into the street. Caldwell's was carved in the shape of a pelican. Its beak was the receptacle for his mail.

Ryan saw the small Point Blank Security sign as he moved towards the cast-iron fence surrounding the property. He was just pulling himself over the top when he heard a vehicle coming up on the road behind him. He threw himself over the fence and rolled behind a jacaranda tree. He watched as a Point Blank Security truck slowly approached the house. The driver flashed a spotlight towards the building behind Ryan. The light flashed by the bush, then moved on, passing across the yard and on to the next home on the block.

Ryan waited until the vehicle returned. It drove slowly along the opposite side of the street, shining its light on the homes across from Ryan. He waited until he heard it turn onto the main road before he moved.

Wiping at the perspiration dotting his forehead he stepped swiftly across the grounds to the rear of the house. It backed up to a canal. A covered speedboat bobbed gently against a small dock, built out from the center of the property. A granite pathway led from the dock up to the pool behind the house. In the shallow section of the pool Ryan could see three bar stools bolted to the bottom. Along the edge, above the stools, was a stainless steel service bar, off to the left of the service bar a hot tub.

The back of the house was all windows. The glass ran from the ground right up to the second floor. The main floor was dimly lit by a lamp near the front entrance way.

Ryan stooped down to examine the window. At the bottom he found a small metal lead embedded in the glass. He traced it all round the edge of the rectangular piece of glass. The adjoining sheet held the same type of metal lead.

He moved round to the side of the building until he came to a small opaque window and again found the alarm system. He circled, checking each window, but in all of them the alarm system was clearly evident.

He returned to the back and walked out to the dock. After carefully checking the boat for an alarm system he unclasped the canvas tarp and slipped beneath it. He pulled a flashlight from his pocket and moved it over the interior of the boat. The deck work was meticulously maintained. The highly polished wood and chrome glittered brightly beneath his beam of light.

Ryan moved down the stairs into the cabin and began to search. He started with the neatly made-up bunk and then methodically went through the rest of the stateroom.

When he finished he leaned against the bulkhead and surveyed the cabin. It no longer resembled the impeccably maintained room he had entered only fifteen minutes before. He turned and climbed up to the deck and started his search again.

He crawled from beneath the tarp and moved quietly across the lawn to the back of the house. He paused to check the time. It was four thirty. Sunrise wasn't until six fifty.

Ryan moved to the side of the patio doors. He traced the window until he found where the wire leads joined and entered the lintel of the doorway. He pulled a chisel from his pocket and wrapped it with a torn section of towel he had taken from his motel room. He spread out another section of the towel on the ground below the window. He placed the chisel a little above the area where the wire leads disappeared into the doorway, then, using the heel of his hand, hammered it into the stucco exterior. The chisel made little noise as it chipped into the surface. He worked at the stucco, pausing often to listen, until he created a jagged hole about two inches in diameter.

He cleaned the hole, carefully capturing the dust in his hand and putting it in the towel on the ground. Then, using his flashlight, he peered into the opening he had made.

A little below the hole he could see the two wire leads going into the side of the wall. Each of them was insulated with different colored rubber tubing. Ryan pulled a strand of wire from his back pocket. Using his pocket-knife, he cautiously scraped away the insulated tubing until he had revealed the wire beneath. He connected each of the bared wires with the wire he had brought with him until he had created a circuit.

He picked up the towel and carried it with him to the edge of the pool. He separated a small pile of the dust to the side, then, knotting the towel, dipped it quickly into the water. Massaging the towel, he stepped back to the doorway. He paused for a moment and, after taking a deep breath, reached in and quickly cut the wires leading out of the doorway. He opened the towel and slapped the wet muddy dust into the hole. When it was almost level with the rest of the surface of the house he took the dry chips and brushed them gently along the face of the hole. He froze when he heard the sound of a vehicle pulling up in front of the house. He stepped back, flashed his light at the wall, then quickly raced out to the dock and onto the boat. He dived beneath the canvas tarp as he heard the sound of a car door opening and closing.

He clipped the tarp back into place and peered out at the house through the narrow opening. A man came towards him. Ryan could see the sweep of his flashlight moving across the grounds and up towards the back of the house. He heard another man approaching from the opposite side and watched as the two men met.

'Anything?'

'Nah, nothing, what about you?'

The man shrugged, training his light on the ground before him. The other man began to move along the back of the house, checking the windows and doors. As he came to the patio door, the first man walked over to the pool. 'Jesus, would you look at this. They got a fucking bar in their pool, for Christ's sake.'

'Money,' the other man snorted disgustedly, turning away from the patio to join his companion by the pool-side.

'What about the boat?'

'What about it?'

'Shouldn't we check it?'

'You can if you want. I'm going back to the truck,' he said, turning and starting back.

His companion hesitated for a moment, shrugged and followed him.

Ryan didn't move until he heard the sound of the vehicle turn on to the main street. He glanced at his watch and raced across the yard to the patio door. Quickly he pulled a strip of duct tape from his pocket and taped the window and, using his elbow, cracked the pane of glass.

He paused and listened for a full five minutes, before he removed the broken glass from the frame, reached inside and opened the door.

He started on the top floor and methodically moved through each of the rooms. The upstairs rooms yielded nothing of interest.

Downstairs, in a small alcove set off from a guest bedroom, he found a series of drawers built into the wall. He quickly went through them, discovering nothing of interest. As he closed the last drawer it made a curious hollow sound. Ryan crouched over and examined the structure carefully. He tried to remove the drawer, but it automatically locked in place at the end of its roller system. He started at the top of the bureau and again began to work his way through it. This time he concentrated on the drawers themselves, rather than what they contained. In the second-to-bottom drawer he found a beveled strip of aluminum on the side of the shelving. He pressed it as he pulled on the drawer and the drawer came out smoothly.

Ryan flashed his light into the opening, then quickly reached for the next drawer. It came out just as easily. He removed all of them and peered into the small compartment built behind the bureau.

He checked his watch, then raced upstairs and into one of the bedrooms. He grabbed a pillowcase and swiftly returned downstairs. Quickly he gathered the material.

Without taking time to examine it Ryan shoved it into his makeshift bag. He replaced the drawers and let himself out through the patio door, moving silently along the side of the house to the road and retracing his steps to the beach. By the time he reached the pier, light had started to shred the eastern sky.

He drove back to his motel room, dumped the contents of the pillowcase across his bed and lit a cigarette.

A few moments later he sat down and carefully began to go through the material.

'How will he take the funeral, Charlie?'

'I don't know.' Charlie shrugged. 'He's had a lot of practice with funerals.'

'Is he seeing anyone?' Gloria asked quietly a moment later.

Charlie paused, catching sight of her reflection in the corner of the mirror. 'No, not really,' he answered and resumed straightening his tie.

'Is that because he hasn't met anyone or because . . .' Gloria finished her question with a shrug.

Charlie turned, patting his tie into place. 'I don't know. I didn't really ask.' He stepped over and sat beside her on the bed. 'You know how he is about that stuff.'

'Yeah, but I thought maybe he'd changed.'

'You should have seen him when he first hit town.'

'Was he really that bad?'

'Christ.' Charlie smiled, shaking his head. 'You wouldn't have known him. He looked like something out of one of those old Peter Fonda biker movies.'

'It just seems like such a shame.'

'Well there's nothing we can do about it.'

'Isn't there?' Gloria asked quickly.

'No, there isn't, Glo. You should just leave it alone.'

She glanced away.

'Edward deals with things his own way. He always has.' Charlie stood and pulled his suit coat into place. 'What do you think?'

After an appraising glance, Gloria, pronounced, 'You look weird.'

'What's that supposed to mean?'

'Well I never see you in a suit. All you ever wear are those old blue pants and that short-sleeved white shirt. Wait'll the children get a look at you. They won't even know you.' Gloria pushed herself to her feet and turned to the door.

'I don't always wear those blue pants,' Charlie called to her retreating back.

The children, as Gloria had predicted, each had a comment about Charlie's attire. From giggles from the two oldest, to a solemn 'You look pretty, Daddy' from the youngest.

Of all of them, Charlie decided, the youngest was the closest to the truth. He swooped him up in his arms and carried him into the kitchen, where he found Gloria at the sink.

'What time's the sitter coming?'

'About ten.'

'Edward call?' Charlie asked, putting down his son and turning to watch him race into the living-room.

'No, he said he'd just come by about the same time as the sitter.'

Charlie poured a cup of coffee and sat at the kitchen table. He watched his wife at the sink, admiring the line of her back, the way it flowered gently around her hips, then tapered to her thighs. The thin cotton dress she wore fitted snugly round her hips and chest. He rose and stepped behind her, pressing his body against hers, crossing his hands across her chest and cupping her breasts. She leaned into him for a moment, then pushed him away.

'The kids,' she whispered.

'You look wonderful.'

'So, what else is new?' was her blasé response.

Charlie smiled and went back to his coffee.

'I think he still blames himself,' Gloria said abruptly a moment later.

'I don't think he does,' Charlie answered, knowing immediately to what she was referring.

'Then you don't know him.'

'C'mon, Glo, I've known Edward since he was thirteen years old. How can you say something like that?'

'Because you're a man.'

'This is a gender thing, is it?'

'Yes.' Gloria nodded, refusing to rise to the bait.

Charlie sighed and shook his head. 'What happened, happened almost seven years ago. I can't believe Edward's still carrying it around with him.'

'Charlie, look at him. For god's sake, take a look at what he's done with himself in those seven years. Nothing. All he does is drift. You've seen his letters. They're postmarked from all over the country.'

'He likes to travel.'

Gloria glared at him and turned back to the sink. 'You're being purposely obtuse. It's a typical male reaction. I don't know what it is about men that makes them think admitting pain is somehow effeminate.'

'Gloria?' She turned. 'Don't say anything to him, okay?' She glanced away without answering. 'The woman's dead, let's just leave it alone,' Charlie said and after a moment headed for the living-room.

Gloria abruptly turned off the faucet and glanced out of the window above the sink. The bright sunshine splashed across the back yard. Its harsh glare had burnt the grass to a smudged yellow color.

'Men,' she muttered, and with a disgusted shake of her head went in to join the rest of her family.

In the drift, Ryan was seated in a bar across the street from the San Francisco Greyhound bus station. He had a shot of Daniels accompanied by a beer chaser in front of him. The window before him looked out at the wet street. Ryan leaned on the bar and stared out at the inclement weather, feeling a certain measure of warmth and security at being inside.

A bus pulled up and parked in front of the station across the street. Suddenly Ryan's end of the bar became crowded. Five or six men moved quickly up to the window and stared over at the bus station.

Ryan glanced around curiously, then, seeing the direction of their gaze, watched with them as the passengers began to disembark. The first few people to step onto the sidewalk caused little reaction in the group of men around him.

Suddenly a young girl appeared; framed in the doorway of the bus. The men around him craned forward as she stepped down to the street. She clutched a worn duffle bag in both hands as she moved tentatively into the station. Examining her, along with the rest of the men, Ryan was sure she wasn't much older than fifteen.

Two of the men in the bar quickly moved out of the door and across the road. Through the windows of the bus station Ryan watched the two men walk up and begin talking to the girl. He was distracted when another man left the bar. This one approached a young boy who had just come down off the bus. He said a few words to him and with a smile pointed down the street. The two of them walked away together.

The bus closed its doors and pulled away. The remainder of the men slowly returned to their bar stools. Ryan glanced over at the bus station as the two men who had left earlier went out onto the sidewalk. Walking between them, smiling happily, was the young girl.

'Next one's at four fifty-eight.'

Ryan looked over at the smiling face of the bartender.

'That's the one you want to catch. It's the meat run.' The bartender winked and asked if he'd like another drink.

Ryan quickly left the bar. He tightened his collar round his neck, trying to hide from the cold spattering of rain, and climbed onto his bike.

He hooked up with the interstate and headed north. He kept seeing the girl, the fearful way she had exited the bus, her bag clutched tightly in front of her body as if it might offer her some protection. The two men's smiles as they escorted her onto the street. The girl's young grin as she followed them.

He kept the speedometer at an even seventy-five, letting the wind wash away the image, until it was replaced with only the sound of the engine and the feel of the bike becoming a part of his body.

Thirteen

There were nine men seated round the conference table. Richard sat at the head. There were pastries from the French Bakery Shop, decoratively displayed on a sterling-silver service tray. Beside the glittering, polished tray was an accompanying coffee pot. Each man had a bone-china cup and saucer in front of him, along with a spread sheet of their organization's financial activities.

'I apologize for the inconvenience of this meeting, but I felt it might be advantageous to bring you all up to date about the current status of our group.' Richard paused to lift his cup delicately. 'I think all of you have been made aware of some of the problems we have recently encountered.'

'What the hell happened with John?' the man to Richard's immediate right demanded.

Richard turned to face him. 'If you'll wait just a moment, Leonard, I'll be more than happy to explain. But first I think a brief elucidation of recent events might make the subsequent course of action concerning John a little more understandable.'

Leonard nodded impatiently for Richard to continue.

'As you all know, Neal Ryan was a rather serious mistake.' Before Richard could continue, he was interrupted again.

'Exactly whose mistake was that?' Richard glanced down to the other end of the table. 'Was it ours or was it Neal's?'

'A moot point at best. We took what we thought was the correct course of action at the time.'

'In retrospect, it would seem we were wrong,' the man responded truculently.

Richard shrugged. 'It's academic. It's done. To question it now is futile. We have to concentrate on our current situation.'

'Yes, but our current situation is a direct result of that initial directive.'

'Are you attempting to make a point with these observations, Roland, or are you merely being provocative?'

'I'm simply calling attention to a very obvious mistake we,' the man paused to look round the table, including each of the men in his glance, 'made. And I think it would behove us to remember this the next time a question of this nature is brought to the floor.'

Richard nodded his agreement.

'So what the hell was the deal with John?'

'Yeah, forget all this other bullshit. We all know what's going on. Just tell us about John.'

Richard waited for silence before he went on. 'John was vacillating. It would have been only a matter of time before he did something foolish.'

'Who decided this?'

Richard met Roland's glance. The two men locked eyes; neither of them looked away.

'I did,' Richard said quietly.

Roland nodded thoughtfully. A barely perceptible smile tugged at his lips. 'You acted on your own, Richard? When the ultimate responsibility for your action falls on all of us?'

The men turned their glances from Roland to Richard, awaiting his response.

'We've all taken similar action in the past.'

'But this was slightly different, this was something that directly affected the group.'

'It would also have directly affected the group if John had decided to talk to someone.'

'That may be, but it was something that should have been a group decision. When we started this, we decided that we were all equal and that nothing that affected the group could be instigated without the group's prior approval.'

'And since that time, Roland, we've realized that there are circumstances that sometimes circumvent that directive.'

'Minor circumstances, Richard. Nothing like this.'

'I felt it was a situation that demanded immediate attention.'

'You also felt that the situation with Neal demanded immediate attention, and look what happened there.'

The men turned to Richard, who sensed he was losing them. He glanced down to the other end of the table. Roland looked back at him impassively, with the barest trace of a smile twisting his lips.

'Our decision concerning Neal was arrived at by the group. The right or wrong of it is incidental at this point. Our major concern now should be the ramifications of that action. We can discuss what we should or shouldn't have done for the next twenty-four hours and still not reach a conclusion. Even if we had paid the additional money Neal demanded, would he have talked eventually? I for one thought he might, and enough of you agreed with me, so we decided to take the appropriate action. I think we should simply accept that fact and move on to what has developed since then. If you have a better idea, Roland, why don't you share it with us,' Richard concluded.

Roland's smile disappeared. It was now being worn by Richard.

'All right.' Roland nodded curtly. 'Let's get on with it.'

'Thank you.' Richard said magnanimously, without showing a trace of the victory he felt he had just won. 'Neal's funeral is this morning. As far as we have been able to ascertain the children are no longer a consideration. Neither of them appears to be a problem. Neal's brother is still an unknown factor. We lost sight of him but expect to locate him this morning at the funeral. The consensus is that he will leave within the next day or two.'

'What if he doesn't?' Leonard asked.

'At this point I think it would be premature of us to speculate otherwise.'

'Who's covering the funeral?'

'Someone we can trust. I also took the added precaution of advising our man to photograph the proceedings.' Richard hurried on before the expected questions were raised. 'I think pictures of those in attendance would be advisable. I would like to be able to recognize the brother, as well as anyone else who might have been close to Neal.'

'Do you think he talked to someone?'

'No, I don't. I think if he had, we would have been made aware of that fact already.'

'Then why the photographer?'

'We all need to know the brother, and I think it's vital for all of us to be aware of just exactly who Neal's friends were.'

'What about John, Richard? What happened there?' asked Roland.

'As I said earlier, we were losing John. I think we all knew this. At our last meeting we had even talked about the possibility of this happening.'

'But we also agreed that no action would be taken.'

'I realize that, Roland. But I also realized that if our group was in jeopardy our primary concern should be for its protection.'

'Was John that close to talking?'

'I think he was,' Richard said unequivocally.

It was Roland who broke the momentary silence in the room. 'It's unfortunate, isn't it, Richard, that you were the only one to realize this.'

Richard met his gaze. 'No, Roland, I think it was quite fortunate that I was there to stop him.'

'Enough of this. Let's get to our immediate concern. What are we going to do now?'

Richard pulled his gaze away from Roland.

'What about my end of things?' a man seated at the center of the table asked. 'Does this mean I have to close down the motel? If I do, what am I going to do about the boys?'

'Does everything have to stop?' another asked.

'Everything stops,' Richard said, bringing immediate silence to the group. When he had their full attention, 'We've come this far by being cautious. Some of us have thought too cautious,' he commented, throwing a quick glance in Roland's direction. 'But no one can argue that our caution has been ill advised. It has proven to be tremendously lucrative, as you can all verify by the balance sheets before you. I move that in view of recent events we take a two-week sabbatical. This would include all facets of our activities.'

'But what about what we've already set up? We can't just walk away from that?'

'No, we can't. All our prior commitments, up until this moment, will still be honored. But any new order of business should be postponed. I think we all need to take a temporary leave of absence.'

Richard paused for a moment to glance round the table. 'After all, gentlemen, time is ultimately our most formidable resource.'

Amidst the answering smiles and laughter Richard caught sight of Roland's implacable gaze. It was enough to freeze his smile.

'You okay?' Gloria asked, after giving him an appraising glance.

'Yeah.' Ryan nodded, stepping into the house.

'Charlie'll be out in a minute. He's in the living-room threatening the kids.'

Ryan glanced towards the other room. He could just make out his friend's voice, explaining to his children the drastic changes that would take place in their lives if they didn't follow their babysitter's orders. He turned when he felt Gloria's hand on his shoulder.

'Edward,' she said, meeting his eye, 'I'm really sorry.'

'I know,' Ryan responded softly and opened his arms.

'Jeez, what's this?'

Without releasing him, Gloria glanced over Ryan's shoulder at her husband. 'This is sympathy,' she said, turning out of the circle of Edward's arms, but keeping one arm round his waist.

Eyeing the two of them closely Charlie asked, 'What about me? I could use a little sympathy.'

Ryan held out his arms. He heard Gloria's laugh and watched as Charlie quickly stepped round him.

'That wasn't quite what I had in mind.'

Ryan shrugged.

'Let me get my purse and we can leave.'

Ryan went over to Charlie. 'After the funeral I have some things I want to show you.'

'Like what?'

'Just some things I picked up.'

Charlie's next question was interrupted by the return of his wife.

The surface quality of the water table, along with the transient population, made the cemetery business relatively unprofitable in south-western Florida. Most of the departed in this section of the state either opted for cremation or were transported for burial back to their home towns.

Meadow Gardens was situated in the far north corner of the city. It encompassed a scant three acres of land. The cemetery was sparsely dotted with modestly sized crosses. In the center was a mausoleum which housed as many of the dead as the land itself.

The cemetery grounds, despite that constant sprinkler system, had leached to a yellowish hue beneath the humid weight of the July sun. Banyan, palm and scrub pine-trees offered a minimum amount of shade. The land immediately around the cemetery tapered off into sandy scrub, twisted with sand spurs and scree. At the entrance way of the cemetery was a small chapel.

Charlie pulled up and parked in the front lot. He turned off the engine and glanced at Ryan in the back seat. 'Okay?'

'Yeah.' Ryan nodded, staring out at the cemetery.

'Looks like there's quite a few people,' Gloria said, glancing round the crowded parking lot.

Ryan pulled his gaze away and saw Gloria and Charlie looking at him intently.

He smiled softly in response to their unstated question. 'It's all right. I'm fine.'

He pushed his way out of the car into the oppressive heat, feeling sweat begin to form beneath the collar of his shirt and under his arms.

'I can't even remember the last time I wore a suit,' Charlie said, his head rising over the roof of the car.

'Neither can I,' Gloria said tartly.

Charlie grimaced at her and started walking towards the chapel.

Gloria stepped up beside him and took his hand. She paused at the front door to wait for Ryan. She reached out for his hand and linked her arm through his. The three of them went inside.

Ryan sat at the back of the chapel with his friends. He saw Maggie in the front pew. Beside her, holding her hand, was another woman. Neither of the children appeared to be there. The room held about twenty-five people. Ryan saw Captain Rainey seated towards the middle of the room. It was the only other face he recognized. In keeping with the ambience of Siena most of the people appeared to be much older than Neal had been.

The service ended quietly and people rose and moved towards Maggie, offering their condolences.

'Who are these people?'

'Mostly clients.'

Ryan turned to look at them filing towards the door. He spotted Rainey in the middle of the crowd. The policeman threw a curious glance his way. A moment later Rainey looked back, examining him much more closely this time.

Ryan waited until the people surrounding Maggie had thinned before moving into the aisle and walking up to her. He stopped a few feet away and waited. She glanced up at him, then, with a decisive shake of her head, opened her arms. Ryan hugged her tightly. He felt the small bones of her back quiver beneath his hands. 'It's okay,' he whispered.

She held his hand as they walked outside to join the small group of mourners surrounding the burial plot. As they reached them, Ryan overheard someone ask why Neal hadn't wanted to be cremated. Maggie's sharp intake of breath let him know that she had overheard as well.

Ryan stood beside her while the minister offered a benediction, then stepped back as the casket was slowly lowered into the grave. He caught sight of Rainey, looking pointedly in his direction. Ryan lit a cigarette.

'It was a nice service.'

He glanced at the woman before him, immediately identifying her as the person he had seen seated beside Maggie in the chapel.

'I'm Rachel Thomas. I'm a friend of Maggie's.' She glanced over at Maggie who now stood before the grave site with Charlie and Gloria by her side.

Ryan nodded to the young woman. 'I'm . . .'

'Eddie,' she interrupted. 'The older brother.'

'Do I know you?' Ryan asked, looking at her closely.

'No, we've never met, but I've heard a little bit about you from both Neal and Maggie.'

'I didn't know they even talked about me.' Ryan paused. 'Neal and I had a disagreement a long time ago,' he said, looking at her inquisitively.

'No.' She smiled softly. 'I don't know anything about that. I only know that you were the wild one, the black sheep,' she said, still hanging on to her smile.

Ryan was about to respond when Rainey came over to him. 'Ryan.' He nodded curtly to Rachel, then motioned Ryan off to the side. 'I'm surprised to see you here.'

'Why? He was my brother.'

'That's true.' Rainey nodded judiciously. 'But I heard there was more than a little bit of bad blood between the two of you.'

Ryan locked eyes with him. 'Can't always believe what you hear.'

'Is that supposed to mean something?' Rainey asked quietly.

Ryan shrugged and looked away.

'Hey, I asked you a question.' Rainey grabbed his shoulder, as Ryan attempted to step round him.

'And I didn't answer it,' he told him, shrugging away from the hand and moving towards Charlie and Gloria.

'What was that all about?'

'Nothing.'

Rachel kept pace with him. 'Are you coming by the house?'

'I don't know,' Ryan answered, glancing at Maggie.

'You should.' He turned to her. 'She needs all the support she can get. It may not seem like it, but she would like you to be there.'

Before Ryan could respond, she walked away.

'. . . come by the house,' Ryan overheard Maggie saying to Gloria and Charlie.

As he reached the group all three turned to him. Without looking at Ryan, Maggie said softly, 'You're welcome as well, Eddie,' and moved off.

Ryan watched as Rachel joined her and the two of them walked towards the lot and climbed into her car.

'What do you want to do? Gloria and I thought we'd go by the house for a while. If you'd rather, I could just drop Gloria off, and we could . . .' Charlie paused as Ryan turned to him.

'No, that'll be fine,' he said and walked over to the grave site. He looked down at the casket. Sand had begun to pool slowly along the sides and top of it. He scooped up a handful of dirt and slowly let it trickle through his fingers onto the casket.

He closed his eyes tightly and felt himself abruptly shift in time. He felt his brother's small body quivering in his embrace, and heard a younger version of his own voice promising Neal that he would never let anything happen to him. He opened his eyes to the harsh glare of the sun and the casket before him, and quickly turned away.

Gloria and Charlie caught up with him. Silently they walked back to the car.

The group had adjourned to a smaller room set off from the main conference room. The nine men sat facing the front of the unlit room. Set on a table was a large-screen TV set. A videotape played across the face of the screen. The men watched it silently. The only sound was the sometimes excited inhalations of their breath.

On the screen was a young girl, no older than thirteen, possibly as young as eleven. She stood self-consciously beside a bed. The camera panned the room, displaying the rest of the interior. The room was decorated in typical motel style. The queen-size bed dominated the carpeted floor. On the wall over the bed was an innocuous print of a river scene. Opposite was an ersatz wooden bureau, with a full mirror hanging over the top of it. In a corner off to the side was a TV set fixed on a free-standing shelf. As the camera traveled towards the door, past the closed shades and the small table situated in front of them, the girl suddenly stepped into the picture and approached the door.

She opened it.

The man coming in made the girl seem even younger. He wore a herring-bone gray suit, with a white shirt and a paisley tie.

He smiled warmly at the girl, turned and locked the door behind him. He bolted and chained it before he turned back to her. This time his smile seemed hungry.

The girl stepped back, her arms involuntarily rising to cross over her chest.

The man spoke, and although the video was without sound each man in the small room knew what he was saying. He was simply telling her not to be frightened. The men in the room knew this, because most of them had said those same words, in a room not that dissimilar from the one on the screen before them.

The man sat on the edge of the bed. He smiled at the girl and patted his knee. For a moment the camera caught her darting sideways glance as she looked towards the door. It lasted only an instant and then her shoulders sagged as she came over to the bed and sat on the man's lap. His hand immediately rose to her neck, then traveled along her shoulder, moving beneath the white blouse. The fabric shifted revealing the pale, thin strap of her brassiere.

The nine men watched as the man gently began to disrobe the girl. He did it slowly, often pausing to speak to her. When, finally, he had completely undressed her, he rose and stepped back to examine her.

The camera did the same. Her breasts were barely formed, imparting only the slightest indication of how she might look once she matured. Her ribs were clearly outlined beneath her pale flesh and tapered almost straight down to her legs with only the leanest curve at her hips. She had a sparse dotting of wispy brown hair between her legs and the lips of her sex were clearly visible.

The man standing before her, still fully dressed, only accentuated her nudity. He reached up and loosened his tie. A moment later, beneath the girl's unwavering gaze, he pulled off his shirt and slowly began to unbuckle his belt.

The nine men in the room became even more quiet. The only sound was the quickening of their breath as they watched the now naked man manipulate the girl across the top of the bed.

When he'd finished with her, he stood and moved into the bathroom. The camera remained focused on the crumpled form of the girl spread across the bed. It zoomed in for a close-up and picked up the tears at the corners of her eyes. A moment later it also caught the twist of nausea crossing her face and then the sudden retching as she leaned over the side of the bed and vomited.

As she crouched over it traveled lovingly along her thin back, down across the barely rounded globes of her buttocks and then lowered to the slightly dirty soles of her feet.

The screen suddenly went black. For a second there was utter silence in the room, broken when one of the men began to applaud.

A moment later the other eight joined him.

'Where's Daddy?' Ollie asked and looked up expectantly.

Ryan glanced over at Lisa and caught her quick grimace.

'He couldn't make it.'

'How come?'

'Ollie,' Lisa cautioned.

Both Ryan and Ollie looked at her.

116

'He just does that so you'll give him something,' Lisa explained.
'Do not.'
'Do too.'
'Do not.'
'Enough,' Ryan said, holding his hand up to halt them. They both looked up at him solemnly.

Ryan stood in a corner of the kitchen with the two of them. The sounds of the rest of the group, huddled in the living-room, filtered in through the open doorway.

'Is it your birfday?'
'No.'
'Is it Mommy's?'
'Not that I know of.' Ryan stooped down in front of him. He reached out to straighten Ollie's collar.

'Then how come we're having a party?' Ollie shrugged.
'Just because,' Ryan answered.

This seemed to satisfy Ollie. He grinned at Ryan, started up his engine and disappeared through the kitchen doorway.

Lisa rolled her eyes at him.

'Tough having a little brother?' She nodded, looking up at him closely. 'What is it?'

'How come you shaved it all off?'
'Don't you like it?'
Lisa looked away. 'It's okay.'
'I think it makes me look younger.'

She looked at him quickly and went back to examining the floor. 'Do you still have . . .' She paused. One hand reached up and began nervously twisting a strand of her hair.

'Do I still have what?'
'That tattoo?'
'Yes.'

Lisa raised her eyes to his. Ryan smiled at her and rolled up his sleeve.

'It's a snake,' she said, tentatively reaching out to trace the design on his arm. 'What's that say?'

'It says "*enfants perdus*". It's French. It means lost children.'

She looked up at him curiously.

Ryan avoided her question. He stood up and reached for her

117

hand. 'C'mon, let's go see what your mother's doing.'

He led her into the living-room where small groups of people stood around. Many of them glanced at Ryan curiously as he led Lisa towards the front porch. Standing outside the doorway on the porch were Rachel, Maggie, Charlie and Gloria.

'Where's Ollie?'

'He's inside,' Lisa answered, pointing into the house.

'Are you watching him?'

Lisa nodded.

Maggie abruptly reached over and hugged her tightly.

Ryan glanced up and caught Rachel's eye.

'We should go,' Charlie said quietly.

Ryan nodded, breaking away from Rachel's glance.

'You'll call if you need anything,' Gloria said, wrapping her arms round Maggie.

'I will.'

'You promise?'

Maggie nodded, turned and embraced Charlie.

Ryan stood awkwardly beside them. He glanced down when he felt Lisa's hands close round his own. She tugged on it. He stooped in front of her.

'You promised to give Ollie a ride,' she whispered.

'Yes I did,' he whispered back.

'Are you going to?'

'A promise is a promise,' he said seriously and was rewarded by her answering smile.

He rose to face Maggie.

'Thanks for coming,' she said stiffly.

Ryan nodded and reached out tentatively to touch her shoulder. 'I'll talk to you,' he said softly, turned away and started down the stairs. Half-way down the steps he heard Ollie buzz through the front door onto the porch.

'Uncle Eddie?'

Ryan turned.

'You promised,' he called.

Ryan smiled. 'You're right, I promised.'

Ollie grinned widely, turned and screeched back into the house.

Ryan carried the smile with him to the car.

'So what's this big mystery you have to show me?' Charlie asked, after closing Gloria's door.

Ryan's smile disappeared. 'Let's drop Gloria off first and then we'll take a ride out to my place.'

Charlie seemed about to ask something more, but shrugged instead and climbed behind the wheel.

Ryan glanced back at the house. Maggie and Rachel still stood on the porch. He felt them watching him as he climbed into the car. As they pulled out of the drive Rachel waved. Maggie stood stiffly beside her, staring impassively at the departing vehicle.

'Give her time, Edward,' Gloria said, turning to look back at him from the front seat. Ryan nodded, looking out of the window at his brother's house until it disappeared from sight.

Fourteen

Stutz had a studio apartment four blocks from the beach. The entrance hall opened into a small kitchen area, then passed into a large rectangular room which served as a combination living and sleeping space. A full porch stretched across the end of the apartment. It looked out onto an expanse of lawn that ended abruptly at a residential street. Stutz spent most of his time on the porch. It was the only place that managed to catch the elusive west breeze coming off the Gulf.

Seated there, with a cup of coffee beside him, Stutz reviewed his notes. Since his early-morning meeting with the Watch Commander after the incident with the Point Blank Security people, and his subsequent conversation with Judy, Stutz had decided to look around cautiously at some of the more covert workings of the city. His original motivation had been anger at what had happened in Royal Port. This had quickly given way to curiosity, after hearing what Judy had said. But now, two days later, having compiled four pages of notes, he realized that what he was unraveling went far beyond an explanation of mere curiosity.

Stutz leaned back, resting his coffee cup on his chest. Prior to Siena he had worked for two years as a patrolman in a small industrial mid-west town. The job had consisted predominantly of traffic violations and drunks, with the occasional breaking and entering thrown in for variety. It had quickly grown monotonous.

He had heard about the opening in Siena through a friend he had made at the Academy. In a burst of enthusiasm but without much hope, he had submitted a resumé. Realistically, Stutz had realized, he'd only been out of the Academy for two and a half years, and his experience in law enforcement was limited to barely two years. He had been surprised when he'd been invited for an interview. He'd flown down the following week, trying unsuccessfully to rein in his excitement.

His meeting with Captain Rainey had gone better than he had expected. Rainey had been quick to inform him that he was looking for someone with only a limited amount of experience. He wanted a man he could groom for the job, rather than someone with preconceived ideas of how it should be done.

'This is a very sensitive area, Mr Stutz,' Rainey had told him. 'There's a great deal of money around, and the people who live here expect to be treated accordingly.'

Quickly Stutz had agreed with him, claiming he understood the discretionary rules of enforcing the law. Even where he had been, as small as it was, there was still a strict social system, demarcated by finances.

Three weeks later he had been offered the job. The rate of pay was five thousand dollars higher than he had been receiving. But even without that, the thought of never seeing another mid-west winter was more than enough incentive for him to jump at the offer.

Stutz glanced down at the notebook on his lap. On the front page, covering three columns, was a list of DUIs issued over the last two months. He had correlated them according to the addresses of the drivers. The first column covered The Gate. The second and third were relegated to North and East Siena. There wasn't one issuance of a DUI to anyone living in either Olde Siena or Royal Port. These were the two sections of the city where the moneyed lived.

The second page of notes chronicled the arrest reports for prostitution. There were only two columns on this page. The first column listed thirty-five names of prostitutes and the men who had suborned them. The men were later charged with conspiracy to commit, and for the most part were quickly found guilty and fined. All the men listed lived outside the two areas Stutz had begun to examine.

The other column on the page, consisting of forty-two names, was a list of the women charged with prostitution. There were no accompanying charges for conspiracy to commit. There were no men involved in the arrest reports at all. Stutz was fairly sure he knew why.

The third page showed the ratio of crimes committed to crimes solved. Most of the crimes were relatively minor in nature. Loitering, criminal intent, vagrancy and the occasional breaking and entering. Of the twenty-nine charges leveled in the Royal Port and Olde Siena area, twenty-eight had been cleared. Of the one hundred and thirty-seven crimes committed in the rest of the city, fifty-one had been closed.

The fourth and final page of his notes was a breakdown of man-hours in relation to the layout of the city. The patrols were sparsely scattered throughout the east, north, and the The Gate area. Royal Port and Olde Naples were heavily patrolled, in an almost four-to-one ratio, despite the fact that arrest reports did not justify this concentrated effort.

If the arrest reports could be believed, the percentage of crimes was almost three to one in favor of the rest of the city, as opposed to the Olde Naples and Royal Port area. Active enforcement did not even come close to this hypothesis.

Stutz slouched back in his chair and looked out at the street in front of him. His porch was largely shaded by an Australian pine. Outside the circle of shade, the glare of the sun beat relentlessly down on the street and grass, which had yellowed and thinned.

Stutz rose and stepped into his small kitchenette. He poured himself another cup of coffee and returned to his seat. He watched as a wild parrot took perch in the tree outside his screen and began to screech. When he glanced away, his eyes fell on the pad on the floor beside him. He hesitated for a moment, picked it up and put it on his lap. Sighing wearily he opened it and once again began to review his notes.

Surfer stood at the railing of his condo, looking out at the Gulf. A boat slid gracefully across the surface of the water, its white sails blossoming as they managed to catch the wind.

Surfer snorted in disgust and abruptly turned away from the railing. On his way into the kitchen he paused to glare at the phone. Fifteen minutes before, the voice had called to inform him that everything was going to be closed down temporarily. Surfer had been so surprised that at first he had been unable to respond.

'Everything's going so well. Why are we shutting down?' he'd asked, when he managed to compose himself.

'That means everything, Thomas,' the voice had responded coldly, ignoring Surfer's question.

'I have commitments. I can't walk away from them. It's taken me almost a year to set up some of these things. No one's going to hang around waiting for me for two weeks. These people don't care who they buy from, all they want is . . .'

'Everything, Thomas,' the voice had repeated emphatically and hung up.

Surfer's occupation was not one which engendered loyalty. His customers' buying habits were regulated strictly by what was available and who was offering it at the cheapest possible price. A two-week break, in any other business, would prove negligible over the course of a year. In Surfer's business it could spell doom. Once his people realized that he was no longer reliable they would simply find somebody else who was. It wouldn't matter that the quality might not be the same. Something was better than nothing and, if the voice was to be believed, nothing was all Surfer was going to have to offer for the next two weeks.

He carried his Perrier into the living-room and sat by the phone. He retrieved his own personal phone book from the desk and began to thumb through it. Pausing at a page that listed numbers with a Miami prefix, he picked up the phone and began to dial.

'Yeah,' a voice answered.

Surfer hesitated.

'Hello?'

Taking a deep breath, Surfer responded, 'My man, Jerry, how you doing?'

'That's Caldwell, isn't it? Ryan asked, standing alongside Charlie.

Charlie nodded, staring at the photograph in his hand.

The photograph was of a barely pubescent girl. She was tied face down across a bed. Her buttocks were criss-crossed with welts. The man standing over her was naked from the waist down. He grasped his erection in his hand as he bowed over the supine body of the girl. The incongruity of the white shirt and tie he wore with the naked lower half of his body only made his nudity the more obscene.

'Jesus Christ.' Charlie shook his head in disbelief, then flipped the photograph onto the bed to join the others. Altogether there were twenty-six pictures. All of them featured John Caldwell in various stages of sexual conclusion. Each of the pictures also featured a young girl. They were usually tied, though in one exposure the girl was encased in a black leather constriction suit. The only visible openings in the body suit were at her genital area, her breasts and her mouth. In this photograph Caldwell was fully undressed and stood behind the slight figure. The painful tilt of the girl's head left little to conjecture about where the fifth opening in the suit might be.

'Where the hell did you get this stuff?'

'Do you really want to know?'

Charlie glanced sharply at his friend and shrugged. 'No, but I think I should.'

Ryan nodded as he pulled and lit a cigarette. 'I got them from Caldwell's house.'

'How?'

'I stopped in there last night. I found them stashed away in a secret compartment behind a bureau. They weren't hidden very well. I have a feeling Caldwell never expected anyone to be looking for them.'

'How the hell did you get into the house?'

'That you don't need to know.' Ryan shook his head and walked over to the bed. He picked up a magazine and handed it to Charlie. 'Take a look at this.'

Charlie took the magazine. On the front cover were three young girls tied together at the waist and neck. They were tied in such a way that they formed a triangle, the fronts of their bodies making the outside of the angle. Surrounding them were three men. All the men were naked and obviously excited.

Charlie snorted in disgust threw the magazine onto the bed. He stepped over to the window.

'Nice guy this Caldwell,' Ryan said softly, sitting on the edge of the bed and reaching for the catalogue. 'Did you know there's a mail-order house up in Orlando that specializes in S&M and Bondage devices?' He glanced over at Charlie and went on, 'It says here you can get a mouth retractor for $29.95. There's also something called an anal intruder. And here's another catchy little device; this one's capable of giving off minor electrical charges at that "penultimate moment of supreme pleasure",' Ryan quoted.

Charlie turned. 'What's this got to do with anything? Caldwell was a pervert. Big deal. There's a lot of them out there. What the hell do you want me to do about it?' he said angrily.

'Do what you do best, Charlie,' Ryan said softly. He gestured towards the pile of material spread across the bed. 'Find out all you can about this stuff. Where it comes from, who gets it. Anything and everything you hear.'

'Why?'

Ryan examined his friend closely. 'What are you doing, Charlie?' he asked quietly. Charlie looked back at him quizzically. 'Look at this crap. This is your town and this shit's going on, man. Doesn't that bother you at all?'

'You don't give a shit about this stuff,' Charlie said, stepping over to the edge of the bed. 'All you care about is what happened to Neal.'

'So what?'

'So don't come on to me like some self-righteous protector of public morality.'

Ryan stared into the angry face of his friend. He shook his head and leaned back against the headboard. 'What's the problem here, Charlie?'

'There's no problem.'

Ryan watched as Charlie went over to the window and looked out. 'Only thing you're interested in is land deals, is that it?'

'What's that supposed to mean?'

'You knew about this, didn't you?' Ryan said quietly. Charlie's hands clenched into fists. 'You've known all along about these little games Caldwell was playing up there in his Royal Port home.'

'That's not true.' Charlie turned back to the window. 'I never knew anything about this stuff.'

'Then what did you know?'

'There was talk, but it was only gossip.' He shrugged without turning. 'I never had any idea that . . .'

'You never looked into it? You never followed up on it?'

'Edward,' Charlie pleaded, 'it's not that I didn't follow up on it, it's that there was nothing to follow up on. It was just talk.'

'Who are you trying to convince, me or yourself?'

Charlie turned away.

Ryan rose and moved over beside him. Without looking at him, he said, 'Something you might want to think about, Charlie. Those pictures, Caldwell didn't take them.' Ryan paused. 'There had to be someone else in the room, someone who was either just watching, or maybe waiting his turn.' He shook his head. 'Some of those girls aren't much older than yours.'

'Fuck you, Edward.' Charlie turned towards the door.

Ryan grabbed him by the shoulder and swung him round. 'You take this.' He shoved one of the photographs into Charlie's breast pocket. 'And you find out everything you can about it. Where it was developed, where it was shot and anything else you can come up with.' Charlie jerked away from Ryan's grip and stalked across the room. 'And Charlie,' Ryan's voice stopped him at the door, 'if you're not interested in doing that you can just keep the picture, maybe take it out and look at it the next time your daughter doesn't show up when she's supposed to.'

Ryan watched him climb into his car and pull out of the lot. He lit a cigarette and walked over to the bed. Carefully he sorted through the pictures until he had chosen three of them. He used his pocket-knife to cut off the bottom half of each picture, leaving only the face on display.

Gathering up the remaining material he replaced it in the pillow-case. He checked out of the motel and returned the car to the rental agency, then walked the three blocks back to his original motel room. After his appearance at the funeral, whatever he had hoped to accomplish by hiding had been negated.

Ryan put the pillowcase in the bottom of his duffle-bag, then changed into a pair of worn jeans and his Harley T-shirt. He sat at the table in front of the window and lit a cigarette. His bike was parked directly in front of his room. The sun glinted brightly off the chrome. He closed his eyes and leaned back in his chair.

'You ever think you're going to do anything?' Zella asked, the smile taking the sting out of her question.

'Like what?'

'Something.' She shrugged. 'All you do is drift. Doesn't that get boring after a while?'

'Did until I met you.' He smiled.

'I don't know if that's enough.' She sat up, wrapping her arms round her knees.

Ryan ran a hand along her spine, all the way down to where it disappeared into the folds of the mattress. He felt her shiver beneath his touch.

'It's not enough for me, Eddie.' She turned to look at him, shrugging away from his hand. 'I want more than this.'

Ryan glanced round the motel room. It was no different from all the others he had occupied over the years.

'How much more?'

She smiled down at him. 'Maybe more than you're willing to give.'

'Try me.'

She leaned over him, grazing the tips of her breasts across his chest. 'I might just do that,' she threatened and slowly lowered herself into his arms.

Drifting with it, letting it lull him, Ryan could almost feel her in his arms again, the soft warm weight of her, the sense of her life inextricably becoming a part of his own.

The scream crashed into him. It was a shriek shredded by agony so intense that the sound bore little resemblance to anything human.

The vivid memory of sound abruptly jerked Ryan out of his chair and to his feet. He stepped to the window and looked out. The perspiration dotting his forehead had little to do with the heat of the room.

He climbed onto his motorcycle and started it. The steady roar of the engine soothed him. He pulled the clutch, popped it into gear and whirled it towards the street.

He raced out to the highway and ran it quickly up into fifth, letting the speed cleanse away the memory, until the scream was forced to return to where it was so carefully hidden.

When it was buried deep enough, Ryan turned and headed for the beach.

Fifteen

In an inlet off the south-western tip of Florida, approximately thirty miles south of Siena, is a cluster of islands referred to as Ten Thousand Islands. The largest of these is Camora Island. It boasts a population of fifteen thousand in the off season, and four times that during the season. Unlike Siena, its beaches are cluttered with condominiums and motels. Public access to these beaches is strictly limited to the owners and occupants of these structures. There are those in Siena who look at this arrangement with envy. The envious are usually those distinguished by considerably more than healthy financial resources.

Access to Camora Island is restricted to a single bridge, traversing a quarter mile of the Gulf. That and a small local airport at the furthest eastern point of the island are the only two entry points. There are numerous docking and boating facilities that also access the island, but local use is predominantly attained by the bridge.

At the Radisson Hotel, in room 709, Joe Ball sat at the window overlooking the Gulf. He found the sight of all that water infinitely soothing. It was nothing like home. Home was Leslie, Georgia. A small town about ninety miles south of Atlanta and a little over ten miles from Lake Blackshear. The lake was a poor substitute for what Joe was able to see so clearly from the window of his room.

Far out on the horizon he was able momentarily to make out the blurred mast of a boat before it slipped out of sight. He leaned back in his chair and cradled his Dixie beer against his chest. Condensation ran down the sides of the can and pebbled coolly on his pale skin. He rubbed a hand along his flesh, spreading the cool moisture through the thick mat of dark hair covering his chest.

When he'd finished his beer he rose and walked over to the small refrigerator, set beneath the counter that separated the kitchenette from the rest of the room. He pulled out another can of Dixie. He'd had to bring a case down with him, having learned from prior experience that it was almost impossible to obtain in this part of the country.

As he pulled the beer out he did a quick count of the remaining cans. He was down to eight. Joe Ball figured it would be enough to get him through the rest of the night. Early tomorrow morning he was booked on a shuttle flight up to Tampa. From there he would pick up a connecting flight into Atlanta. By late tomorrow afternoon he expected to be sitting on his front porch, assured of an inexhaustible supply of Dixie beer.

Joe Ball had arrived in Camora four days ago. It was a trip that he had not anticipated, coming so quickly after his last visit. It had caused him more than a little anxiety.

Joe was a very careful man. In his business, success was measured by the amount of care taken in the completion of each assignment. He was not allowed to make any minor mistakes. All it would take would be one rash moment to obliterate his fifteen-year record of success.

Failure, in Joe Ball's occupation, would mean much more than the simple loss of an account, or a few dollars less on his bank statement at the end of the month. It would mean prison, or worse. Florida still resolved some of its problems with capital punishment. He had no interest in becoming part of that resolution.

He'd flown into Camora, rented a car and driven up to Siena. He'd taken a room at one of the numerous mid-dollar-range motels on the main highway. He'd connected with his man the following morning and picked up the brief. It had been collated exactly as he had requested. It made everything so much easier when he dealt with someone who knew what he was supposed to do and did it. Initially this had surprised him. Thomas was not a guy that Joe Ball would have expected to be this meticulous in his work.

After their first job together, Joe had become quite sure that Thomas was being run by someone else, which was just fine with him. He'd figured there was no way Thomas would have told his superiors who he was. It would have opened the possibility for his superiors to cut Thomas out. And if nothing else, Joe Ball was quite sure of the depths of Thomas's greed.

On the evening of his third day in Florida, he had driven to the beach and parked in one of the public lots overlooking the shore. He'd been tempted to walk down to the water, but knew that his pale complexion would make him conspicuous. He'd leaned back comfortably in his seat to watch the sun begin its descent into the water.

By the time it had touched the far horizon Joe Ball had spotted his man coming down the street behind him. The man wore a pair of white shorts and a short-sleeved green shirt with a little alligator above the breast pocket. He was riding a bicycle.

Joe Ball had followed his approach carefully in his rear-view mirror. After a quick check around, assuring himself that the other sunset revelers' concentration was firmly focused on the western horizon, Joe had quietly unlatched the driver's door. He'd watched the man in his mirror and waited.

As the man came up to the car, Joe Ball had suddenly thrown open his door. The man had made a feeble attempt to get out of the way. He might have made it, if not for Joe's help.

Joe Ball had grabbed the handlebars of the man's bike and yanked him towards the door.

'What the . . .' were the only words the man had managed to get out, before Joe Ball's right fist crashed into his jaw. Within seconds, he had thrown him across the front seat. He'd wheeled the bike over to the side and unhurriedly returned to his car. The whole incident had taken less than three minutes.

Joe Ball had pulled out of the lot, glancing in his rear-view mirror to see the multicolored sky slowly begin to darken. He'd been forced to hit the man once more when he threatened to regain consciousness. He had been careful not to draw blood. Blood would only complicate the situation.

He'd driven away from the richer section of town, moving north, but keeping within sight of the Gulf. According to the tide tables, he had forty-five minutes. More than enough time.

He'd driven northwards until he was forced to cut east by a large inlet. He'd followed it round as far as a stop sign, where the road redirected him back to the Gulf, then as instructed had turned left.

This way had taken him to a dead end. At the end of the road was an abandoned construction sight. The nearest condominium complex was a quarter of a mile away and the sparsely lit building was a clear indication that most of the residents were seasonal.

Joe Ball had pulled his man out of the car and dragged him across the site to the foot of the Gulf. The water was rapidly pulling away from the sand. Joe had welcomed the sound of the waves. He'd crouched beside the man and pulled out a .22 caliber Woodsman. He'd placed the barrel of the gun in the center of the guy's head and pulled the trigger. The sound of the surf had made the silencer he carried with him superfluous. He had then rolled the body into the surf and watched as the water quickly drew it out. He had been back in his motel room forty-five minutes later with a cold Dixie in his hand. It was the kind of work that Joe Ball liked. Easy and uncomplicated. No trying to make it look like an accident, or worrying about hiding the body. Just a simple whack-out. That's how it used to be. Now, it seemed to him as if everyone was trying to get tricky about things. It was something he didn't understand. The shortest distance between two points was a straight line, why fuck around with all this round-about shit.

Joe Ball opened the room service menu and began to study it. He had it narrowed down between the Prime Rib and the Seafood Platter when the phone rang. He glanced at it curiously. There was only one person who knew he was there, and there was no reason for this person to call unless there were problems.

Cautiously he picked up the phone.

Before he had a chance to speak, the voice at the other end stated, 'Joe Ball.' It was an unfamiliar voice. 'I have work for you.'

'You must have the wrong number.'

'No. I don't think so,' the voice responded, and Joe Ball could hear the other man's amusement. It irritated him. He was about to pass his irritation on to his caller when the man said, 'You're Joe Ball from Leslie, Georgia. You're the man who kills people. Is that correct?'

'Who the fuck . . .'

'Someone who has work for you,' the voice interrupted. 'If you're not interested, I'm sure I can find someone who might be.'

'Listen, my friend, I don't know who you are, or what you're talking about.'

'If that's true, then it probably wouldn't disturb you if I were to pass on some of my misconceptions to the local police force.' The voice paused to give him an opportunity to respond.

Joe Ball felt perspiration begin to bead along his shoulders. There was only one person who knew of his existence in town. Joe planned to remedy that problem as soon as he found out what the hell this guy wanted.

'I assume your silence means you're interested in my proposition?'

'Go on,' Joe Ball grunted.

'I would like to purchase your services. If you go down to the front desk, you'll find a package waiting for you. Inside is your standard fee for this type of assignment. Ten thousand dollars, along with a brief. I think that's the proper terminology you use of the intended recipient.' The voice paused. 'Do you have any questions?'

'Yeah. There's ten thousand dollars sitting downstairs waiting for me. Is that right?'

'Correct.'

Joe Ball smiled.

'You're not that stupid,' the voice said, as if sensing his smile. 'If I know who you are and where you live, then it would be extremely foolish of you to underestimate what else I might know. Don't you think so, Mr Ball?' the voice asked conversationally.

Joe Ball reluctantly agreed and asked, 'What if I need more information?'

'You won't. The brief has been prepared in strict accordance with your operating procedures. Do this well, Mr Ball, and I think we may be able to offer you future assignments that might prove equally lucrative.'

Joe Ball took the elevator to the lobby. A large manila folder was waiting for him. He tucked it under his arm and returned to his room. Unlocking his door, he again thought about the person who must have turned him. He planned on having a talk with him as soon as possible. It would be strictly a one-sided conversation.

He retrieved his can of Dixie and carried his beer and the manila envelope over to the chair by the window. He took a long sip, then opened the envelope and pulled out the photograph inside.

* * *

'Roland.' Richard rose to greet his guest as the other man was shown into his living-room.

The room fronted the Gulf. The western wall was one solid piece of glass. Opposite the window was a huge stone fireplace that tapered up to a cathedral roof and disappeared through the ceiling. The air conditioning silently chilled the house to such an extent that the blazing fire became a necessity rather than an affectation.

'A cognac?' Richard asked, going to a mahogany bar built into the wall.

Roland surveyed the room around him. The black-leather cherry-wood couch and accompanying chairs, along with the sleek Italian brass-and-crystal table, impressed him. He stepped over to the wall to examine a photograph. It was a Joel-Peter Witkin original. He turned as Richard offered him a crystal balloon glass of cognac.

'You do yourself well, Richard.'

The other man shrugged disparagingly.

Roland sipped his drink and moved over to the window.

'It's quite spectacular at sunset,' Richard commented, coming up beside him.

'Yes, I imagine it would be.' Roland turned to face the other man. 'This is all very nice, Richard, but to be perfectly frank, we really don't like each other very much. So what's this all about?' Roland walked away from the window and sat down.

'I think,' Richard began thoughtfully, 'that we need to understand each other. Both of us are aware of the potential of the group; more so, I think, than any of the others.'

'So?'

'So, I think rather than being at odds with each other, it would prove much more beneficial for us to work together. We agree on the end results, it's only the means that seem to cause us conflict.'

Roland nodded. 'So what are you suggesting?'

'A truce. No more of this bickering in front of the others for control. It only causes dissension. It serves no purpose other than to salve our own egos and neither of us is really that deprived in that regard.' Richard smiled wryly.

'You know what I think?'

'What?'

'I think this is just an attempt on your part to take total control of the group. You've been manipulating everything in that direction since the beginning. I think you're just trying to appease me, and once you think you've accomplished that you'll make your move. God knows, you've almost got it now. There's only myself and Leonard who ever seem to disagree with you.'

'I've noticed that as well.'

'Well it's not going to work, Richard. I'm not going to put up with it.'

'What can you possibly do about it?' Richard asked casually.

Roland leaned forward. 'I can begin by forming the rest of us into a solid block of votes, which would negate whatever plans you have.' Roland smiled.

Richard shook his head sadly. 'That would be quite unwise.'

'And why is that?' Roland challenged.

'Because I'd have you killed.'

The ease with which Richard said these words startled the other man into silence.

'I'm quite serious about this, Roland. Oppose me and I'll see to it that you are quietly, and most finally, removed. I will not stand for any opposition.'

'Just who the hell do . . .' Roland began, rising angrily to his feet.

'The man who can do it,' Richard interrupted and glanced toward the door. 'Good night, Roland.'

Roland suddenly became aware of Richard's servant, standing patiently in the doorway awaiting his departure.

He looked back at Richard.

'Try to be reasonable about this. I would hate to lose you, Roland. You're quite good at what you do. It would be very difficult to replace you, but I'm sure I could if the situation arose.'

Roland followed the servant to the front door. He pulled round the circular drive to the main street and drove the six blocks to his own home.

Eleanor raised her eyes as he stepped into the living-room.

'How's Richard?'

'Just fine,' he answered curtly and stalked into the den.

Eleanor glanced over at the closed door, then returned her attention to *Most Wanted*. Pictured on the television screen was the brutal face of a man wanted for rape and murder in Lubbock, Texas.

Eleanor shivered. She thought he looked quite a bit like the bag boy at Publix. She poured herself another scotch and leaned forward intently to hear the rest of the gory details.

In the dream, everything's been leached of color by the sun. It blazes overhead, turning the land into a blur of heat. The trees are misshapen and bare of all foliage. The ground is patterned with sand and scraggly tufts of grass that barely manage to push themselves from the earth. In this inferno of heat and glaring light is the rhythmic squeal of a rusty chain swinging back and forth. The persistent sound inundates itself into the brain, until its shriek becomes heavy with portent, signaling the arrival of some creature who thrives within this habitat.

Suddenly, in the center of this desolate landscape, a pond appears. The sunlight glints coolly along the rippling water. For a moment a breeze rises and passes over her. Its cold feathery touch washes along her face and body.

Lisa smiles and begins to move across the arid ground towards the pool. She hears laughter behind her and turns to see her father swinging Ollie up onto his shoulders. She points towards the water and watches as her father's gaze darts to the pond, then back to her. His smile is one she knows and loves. She laughs, then pauses, waiting for them to catch up.

Her father swings Ollie to the ground and crouches before him.

Lisa's too far away to hear what he's saying, but somehow she knows he's telling Ollie that they will have a race to the water. Ollie's excited squeal carries over to her.

Before her father rises completely, Ollie is off, running along the sand, his laughter carrying to her.

'Faster,' she screams at Ollie, peering behind him to see her father suddenly slowed to a standstill by the heat. His hand gradually rises to his forehead. Lisa looks at Ollie racing towards her, an awkward jumble of bouncing arms and legs, then she glances back at her father. His movements are still locked in a slow drift of heat and time.

'I did it,' Ollie squeals, standing before her proudly.

Lisa looks down at him, then watches as he starts to turn to look back at their father. Suddenly his motion is slowed as well. Of the three of them she's the only one who seems able to move at normal speed.

She hears a firecracker explode. She glances off to the right and sees a blur of movement by the swing set. She turns back to her father. His hands are now tightly clenched to the back of his head. His eyes roll upwards and close. She hears Ollie's delighted laugh and watches as her father slowly begins to topple to the ground.

She screams.

'Honey, what's wrong?'

'Daddy,' Lisa whimpered as she felt her mother's arms move round her.

'It's okay. It was just a bad dream.'

'Where'd Daddy go?'

'Daddy went away for a while,' her mother said softly. Lisa buried her head in her shoulder. 'It's all right, honey. It was just a nightmare.'

Lisa closed her eyes tightly but it didn't help. When she opened them she sobbed.

'Oh, honey, don't,' she heard her mother say and felt her arms tighten and begin to rock her.

The movement soothed her, and the sound of her mother's voice, even if it was that sad sound that Lisa had come to know so well over the last two weeks, slowly eased her back to sleep.

Maggie pulled the sheet up to her daughter's waist and turned to glance over at Ollie. He was sprawled diagonally across his bed with the sheet twisted between his legs. She straightened the bedclothes and kissed him gently on the forehead.

She stopped in the doorway of her bedroom and stared across the room at the double bed. Quickly she turned and walked into the kitchen. She turned on the night light and sat at the kitchen table with a cup of coffee. The dim light softened the corners and the edges of the room. She sipped her drink and stared at the envelope on the table. It was a rectangular business envelope, yellowed by time. It was still sealed. Across the face of it, in her husband's recognizable scrawl, was printed the name Edward Ryan.

She'd found it three days ago, stuck between the pages of his dictionary. She had no idea it was there, or even how long it had been there.

She'd been all set to open it when Ollie had suddenly appeared in the doorway. The sight of him had startled her. It had made her reconsider what she was about to do.

Before Ollie's sudden appearance she hadn't even thought about it. She would have just opened it and read what was inside. The sudden sight of her son abruptly made her realize that what she was about to do was wrong.

Over the last three days she had agonized over the letter. She couldn't bring herself to open it, yet at the same time she was reluctant to give it to Eddie. Somehow, in a way that she didn't quite understand, it seemed as if she would be giving away all that remained of her husband.

She rose and rinsed her cup out at the sink, then turned and picked up the letter. She carried it with her into the living-room and lay down on the couch. She held the letter against her chest and listened to the silence of the house. In an indefinable way the house seemed much larger and more quiet now.

Maggie drew up her knees and crossed her arms over her chest. She felt the corners of the envelope crumple against her robe. She fell asleep cradling the letter to her chest.

Sixteen

Ryan had just pulled into Olde Siena when he caught sight of the squad car in his rear-view mirror. A block later, its light flashed him over to the side of the road. He cut his engine and swiveled round on the seat, watching as the policeman he had seen twice now stepped out of the car and approached him. It took him a moment to remember the man's name.

'Stutz,' he said thoughtfully, when the patrolman stepped over to him.

'That's right, and you're Edward Ryan. Took me a moment to recognize you without all that hair.'

'Well now that you have, what can I do for you?' Ryan paused to pull out a cigarette. 'I think I was within the speed limit,' he said, glancing at the other man, a slight smile on his lips.

Stutz ignored the smile. 'The captain wants to talk to you.'

Ryan nodded, then reached for his handlebars.

'Why don't you just park that on the side and I'll give you a ride in,' Stutz told him.

'Both ways?'

'Sure.' Stutz nodded, turned and walked back to his squad without looking back.

Ryan climbed into the squad car. He leaned against the seat, feeling a rush of cool air from the air-conditioning unit. 'Haven't ridden too often in the front,' he commented.

'Somehow that doesn't surprise me.'

'You have any idea what the captain wants to talk to me about?'

'Nope.'

A moment later, Ryan offered, 'By the way, I appreciate your pulling your friend off me the other day.'

139

'It's my job,' Stutz shrugged.

'Right,' Ryan replied sarcastically.

Stutz glanced over at him. 'You trying to say something?'

'Charlie Benning said you were all right.'

'That sure makes me feel warm all over.'

'I trust Charlie's judgment.'

Stutz nodded without commenting.

'He said you were the one who found my brother's body.'

'Yeah,' Stutz admitted wearily. 'I was the one.'

'It must've been tough,' Ryan said, then added, 'with the kids.'

The patrolman sighed. 'They didn't even know what was going on. The little boy kept asking me when his daddy was going to wake up.'

'They're good kids.'

Stutz hit a red light and looked closely over at Ryan. 'What is it you want to know?'

'Nothing, I was just making conversation.'

'Well we're about three blocks from the station now, so if you've got a question I suggest you ask it before we get there.'

Ryan examined the younger man carefully and, nodding thoughtfully, said, 'There was another man killed a few days ago. Same caliber gun, same professional feel to it. You think that's coincidental?'

Stutz glanced away without answering. He drove through the intersection towards the station.

As they pulled up in front of it Ryan said, 'Something's wrong with this town. Charlie told me you've only been around here for half a year or so.' Ryan waited for the other man to cut the engine before he asked, 'Haven't you noticed anything that bothers you?'

'We're here,' Stutz said curtly. 'I think you know the way.'

Ryan climbed out of the car and walked into the station. The desk sergeant nodded him towards the hall without a word.

'Mr Ryan, I'm glad you came by.'

'I didn't know I had a choice.'

'This is America.' Rainey smiled. 'Everyone has a choice. Why don't you sit down.'

Ryan sat and lit a cigarette.

'Do you know a man named John Caldwell?' Rainey asked abruptly.

'No, I don't think so.'

Rainey kept his gaze locked on Ryan's face. 'He was killed a few days ago.'

'Sorry to hear that.'

'Happened in much the same way as your brother.'

'That's interesting,' Ryan said casually.

'Yes, it is, isn't it.' Rainey leaned back in his chair. He interlocked his fingers and braced them against the back of his head. 'Same caliber gun as the one that killed your brother, but according to this,' he said, nodding towards a folder on his desk, 'bullet wasn't fired from the same gun.'

'Would have been stupid if it had been.'

'Yeah, it would have been. But then I've noticed over the years that people are capable of doing some pretty stupid things from time to time.' Rainey paused, bringing his eyes up to Ryan's face. 'Sent a couple men out to Caldwell's place to look around.'

When the other man didn't go on, Ryan asked, 'They find anything interesting?'

Rainey smiled. 'That's the funny thing about it, when they got out there they noticed that someone else had already gone through the house.'

'Sounds like you have some kind of conspiracy going on here.'

'That what you think?'

Ryan shrugged.

'Conspiracy theories seem to be pretty popular right now. I see where they're talking about reopening the whole Kennedy thing again.' Rainey shook his head sadly. 'Some people just can't seem to accept the truth, even when it's right there before their eyes. You one of those people, Mr Ryan?'

'No, I have no problem with the truth. When I see it.'

'That's good,' said Rainey, bringing his hands down to grip the edge of his desk. 'Because I don't want anyone thinking they know something I don't. We're all after the same thing here. You just keep that in mind, Mr Ryan,' Rainey said, picked up a folder from his desk and leaned back to examine it. He glanced up at Ryan a moment later. Feigning surprise, he said, 'You still here?'

'No, I'm not here at all.' Ryan smiled, rose and walked out.

Stutz was still parked in front, waiting for him.

'Captain's a real nice guy,' Ryan said dryly, as he slid into the passenger seat.

Stutz dropped him off beside his cycle and watched as Ryan started it up and drove towards Olde Siena. He turned the squad around and headed back to the station. He checked in at the desk and walked down to the computer room where he pulled up Ryan's file. He was surprised by its size, and even more so when he began to read it.

Ryan had first come to the attention of the Park County police when he was only thirteen years old. He'd been arrested for assault. The case had been dismissed before it went to trial.

His second arrest had come two years later. This time he'd been arrested and charged with first-degree murder. The case had gone to trial and Ryan had been acquitted.

Stutz scrolled back to the indictment. The victim's name had been Elsa Ryan.

Stutz glanced quickly through the rest of Ryan's record which consisted of numerous trash charges: disorderly conduct, loitering and not much else of any import. The most severe charge Stutz could find was a DUI about seven years ago.

Stutz copied down the file number of the murder charge, turned off the computer and pulled a hard copy of the court transcripts.

Elsa Ryan was Edward and Neal Ryan's mother. Her husband, Abner, made up the rest of the immediate family. Their house had caught fire and Elsa had been trapped inside. She had been the only person in the house at the time. Both boys had claimed to have been elsewhere. Their corroborating testimony, along with their ages, had been the deciding factor in Ryan's eventual acquittal. Fire inspectors had determined that the fire had been deliberately set. The case remained opened.

Stutz read the transcript carefully. He found a section where Abner Ryan had been called to take the stand. It had been the father's testimony that had originally implicated Edward. On the stand he had claimed to have seen the boy deliberately douse the base of the house with gasoline.

The defense attorney for the boy had shredded the father's testimony. By the time he had finished his cross-examination, it was clear to Stutz, as it must have been to the jury, that Abner had been drunk and had been so for at least a week leading up to the day of the fire.

Stutz replaced the file and retrieved the statements concerning Ryan's prior assault charge. He glanced at the report quickly. The victim had been a teacher at the local school. Edward Ryan had approached the man during school hours and attacked him. The teacher had suffered a broken jaw and sprained wrist.

Stutz glanced curiously at the top of the file, which gave a brief description of the defendant. Ryan had been only thirteen years old at the time.

He went back to the statement. The day before the beating the teacher had called Neal Ryan to the front of the class, where he had proceeded to berate him before his classmates. He had then testified to administering a paddling. Neal had responded by calling the teacher an 'asshole'. The teacher had suspended him from school for three weeks. The next afternoon Edward had visited the teacher.

Stutz returned the file to the cabinet and went back through the station to his squad car. He climbed in and drove out towards the northern sector of town. He found a secluded spot and parked, ostensibly setting up a speed trap. What he did instead was lean back in his seat and think about the notes he had so carefully recorded over the last few days, and try to decide what he could possibly do with this discovery.

Ryan parked in the city lot opposite the beach. He swung off his bike and walked out to the pier. To either side of it, the sand was almost hidden beneath a colorful array of towels and blankets.

Ryan lit a cigarette and surveyed the people below. Most of them were young, running in age from mid-teens to early twenties. A volley-ball net was set up near the foot of the pier. Two men and four women, split into equal teams, darted across the sand in pursuit of the ball. The women, he noticed, barely managed to keep the tops of their suits in place. With each strike at the ball they would slip, revealing a startling expanse of white flesh. He noticed his interest was shared by a number of men on the pier, as well as some of those seated below on the sand.

He glanced towards the water as two young women raced into the surf and watched as they swam out towards a speedboat anchored fifty yards off shore.

The two men in the boat put down their beer cans and greeted the women with wide smiles. After a couple of minutes' conversation they lowered a ladder and helped the women aboard. A few moments later the engine roared to life and the boat pulled out to sea.

Ryan turned his attention back to the men around him. He glanced at them curiously, feeling the weight of the sun starting to settle on him. Perspiration began to run along his sides and back. He pulled off his T-shirt and wadded it into a ball.

A fisherman passed behind him. Ryan watched as the man's eyes darted towards the volley-ball game. He followed the direction of the man's gaze, and looked on as one of the women leaped into the air to spike the ball. For a moment the top of her suit slipped, revealing the dark aureole of her nipple. He heard two men to the side of him laugh and glanced over at them. They were both in their early twenties. Each of them had a carefully cultivated three-day growth of beard that shadowed his face. One had a pony-tail, pulled back and tied with a brightly colored elastic band. The other's hair was cut short with unruly spikes jutting out from the top. They both wore shorts and T-shirts, the latter luridly colored with advertisements for rock bands. Each of them was deeply tanned.

Ryan lit another cigarette and observed them. He edged closer until he was able to hear their comments. Their conversation was liberally punctuated with names.

Ryan could feel perspiration dripping along his ribs and down to the waistband of his pants. He ran a hand across his chest and it moved smoothly through the beaded moisture.

The two men beside him finally began to move towards the foot of the pier. Ryan let them get slightly ahead of him before he followed. They walked off the pier towards the parking lot. Ryan stepped along the shaded sidewalk behind them, welcoming the temporary relief.

In the parking lot, pony-tail moved away from his friend and climbed into a newer model pick-up truck. The other man continued along the sidewalk.

Ryan caught up to him at the end of the block. 'Hey, I talk to you a minute?'

The man turned, watching without interest as Ryan approached him.

'How you doing?'

'All right,' the young man answered cautiously.

'I was wondering if you could help me.'

The other man stared back at him silently.

'I was looking for this girl,' Ryan said, reaching into his back pocket for one of the pictures.

The man smiled. 'Don't know her.' He shrugged without glancing at the photograph and started to turn away.

'You didn't get a good look at her.'

'Fuck you.'

Ryan grabbed him by the shoulder and jerked him round. 'Take another look.' He smiled politely.

'Hey, man, I don't know who you think . . .'

Ryan punched him once in the solar plexus. It was a short jab, blocked from anyone else's view by his body. The blow doubled the man over. Ryan's grip was the only thing keeping him on his feet. 'What's your name?'

'Tommy.'

'Well, Tommy, why don't you take another look at this picture for me,' Ryan said conversationally.

'I don't know her.'

'I don't think you looked close enough.'

'What'd you want her for?'

Ryan smiled widely. 'I'm asking the questions, Tommy. You're answering them. Okay?'

Tommy tried to meet Ryan's eye, but quickly glanced away. He muttered a name.

'What? I didn't quite catch that?'

'Lailya. All right. That's her name.'

'Where can I find her?'

'Man, I don't understand . . .' Ryan raised his fist. 'She works out at the Limpy's on the north highway.'

Ryan released him. Tommy quickly moved out of reach.

'Thanks,' Ryan said and started towards his bike.

'You looking for some of that you're going to have to pay.'

Ryan turned to see the cruel smile on the other man's face.

145

'Lailya, man, she'll fuck anyone as long as he's got some coin.' Tommy laughed, and after a glance at Ryan's face quickly turned and ran.

Ryan climbed onto his bike and headed for the north highway. He found the fast-food franchise bracketed by a fan store and a second-hand boutique.

At the counter he stood patiently behind an elderly woman who meticulously counted out eighteen pennies, then slowly smoothed out three one-dollar bills, before she reluctantly pushed the money over to the girl behind the register.

Ryan ordered a Limpy cheeseburger and fries as he surveyed the girls behind the counter.

He carried his burger over to a table that offered him a view of the counter. He pulled out the picture, examined it and again studied the waitresses. He wouldn't have recognized her if she hadn't suddenly yelped and jerked her hand back from the grill. It was the momentary look of pain shifting across her face that allowed him to identify her.

Ryan finished off his burger and walked out to his bike. He spotted a combination restaurant and lounge across the highway and, leaving his bike in the Limpy's lot, walked over to it.

He went into the lounge and ordered a beer. There were three men seated at the bar and another six at the tables, all of them well into their sixties. They drank their drinks quickly, as if afraid they wouldn't be around long enough to finish them.

Ryan carried his beer over to a window table that looked out at the restaurant across the street. He drank slowly, glancing often at the clock.

At three thirty he was half-way through his third beer when he saw her step out from behind the building. She had removed the Limpy's hat and was dragging a garbage bag towards the dumpster at the side.

Ryan quickly downed the rest of his beer and walked across the street. He lit a cigarette and started up his bike. The girl appeared a few moments later. She had changed into a pair of ragged cut-off denim shorts and a man's large white shirt. She eyed him appraisingly as she passed and walked out to the sidewalk.

Ryan wheeled his bike up to the entrance way and stopped. He waited for her to walk up to him.

'How far are you going?' He smiled, looking over at her. She glanced up at him shyly. 'Hop on, I'll give you a ride.'

She looked back at the restaurant, then returned her gaze to him. 'I'm just going a little ways up.' She shrugged, eyeing the bike excitedly.

Ryan shifted forward on the seat and motioned for her to climb on the back.

She grinned, stepped up to the bike, swung her leg over the seat and slipped in behind him. Her arms locked round his waist. He pulled out onto the street.

'I live the other way,' she said without a trace of concern.

'We'll just take a little ride. It's a nice day,' Ryan called back to her and felt her hands twist and press tightly against his stomach. He drove into his motel lot and parked.

'What're we doing here?'

Ryan smiled and helped her off the bike. He held her hand and led her towards his room.

'What d'you think you're doing?' She giggled.

Ryan opened the door of his room, released her hand and motioned her inside.

She smiled at him coyly and darted in.

Ryan followed her, then turned and locked the door behind him.

Seventeen

Joe Ball stood impatiently outside the door – he was not happy about the way things were going. He'd had to postpone his flight home until tomorrow morning. There hadn't been another flight, outside of Miami, leaving before then. Normally this wouldn't have bothered him. There really wasn't anything that important waiting for him at home. The problem was that he was down to his last can of Dixie.

He turned his attention back to the door as he heard footsteps approaching. It swung open and he took a certain vindictive pleasure in the look of astonishment on the other man's face.

'What the hell are you doing here?'

'We got some problems,' Joe Ball said curtly and pushed his way past.

Surfer quickly closed the door and turned to see Joe Ball stepping over to the couch.

'What's going on? You shouldn't be here.'

Joe snorted in disgust. 'You think I'd be here if I could help it. We got a problem.'

'What problem?' Surfer went into the living-room. He picked up a bottle of Perrier off a side table.

'Get me something to drink, would you?'

Surfer nodded and moved into the kitchen, returning a moment later with a bottle of Heineken for his guest. Joe Ball grimaced.

'What the hell's going on, Joe?' Surfer sat across from him.

'This.' He threw a manila folder on the table between them, watching as Surfer picked it up and opened it.

The first thing Surfer saw was a three-by-six color photograph of himself. He glanced over at Joe Ball and back at the photograph. The picture was stapled to a sheet of notebook paper. Printed at the top of the page was Surfer's given name and address.

'What the fuck,' Surfer muttered softly and quickly examined the other two pages in the folder. Each page outlined his daily schedule, listing restaurants and bars he frequented, along with the probable times he could be found there.

'This is . . .'

'A brief,' Joe Ball finished for him. 'Your brief.'

'Where did this come from?'

'I don't know. Someone left it for me at the hotel.'

'This is all they left?'

'That and ten thousand dollars.'

Surfer glanced over sharply at the other man.

Joe Ball smiled and shook his head. 'No, don't worry about it. If I was going to do you, you would have already been done by now.' Surfer carefully examined the man sitting across from him. 'Hey, c'mon, Thomas, cool it, would you. We got other stuff to worry about.'

'Like what?' Surfer asked suspiciously.

'Like just who the hell is this guy and how does he know who I am.'

'I don't know.'

'Who's the man you're working for?'

'What makes you think I'm working for someone?' Surfer asked slyly.

Joe Ball gave him a disgusted glance. 'This set-up you've been running is just a little too clean for you, no offense.'

Surfer glared across the table.

'You tell him about me?' asked Joe Ball, ignoring the other man's look.

'Never your name,' Surfer answered churlishly.

'You ever talk times with him?'

'No.' Surfer shook his head. 'How do you know it's the same guy?'

'Who the hell else could it be? Who would even know I'm in town?' Joe Ball paused. 'If it isn't the same guy, we're both fucked, because whoever this is, he knows everything that's going on.'

Surfer abruptly rose and walked over to the window looking out at the Gulf. 'I don't get it, man. It doesn't make any sense that he'd do something like this. Why would he want to blow me away?' he asked, then suddenly stopped. He remembered his call to Miami and the talk he'd had with Jerry.

'What is it?'

'Nothing.' Surfer shook his head. There wasn't any way the voice could have known about that.

'What're we going to do?'

Joe Ball picked up his beer. 'We got to find out who this guy is and how come he knows so much about us.'

'I don't know, Joe. I've been trying to figure that out ever since the first time I heard from him.'

'How long ago was that?'

'First time was about a year and a half ago.'

'And you haven't found out anything?'

'Nothing. I haven't been able to find out one goddamn thing about this guy. I don't know how he knows the stuff he does. Seems like he's never around, but he knows exactly what I'm doing, and how much I'm making when I do it.'

'What's he taking?'

'Almost eighty percent.'

Joe Ball looked around the condo. 'Doesn't seem like it's hurting you too much.'

'Shit, man, the money's amazing. Even twenty percent is more than I was doing on my own. Whoever this guy is, he's got some weight.' Surfer grinned, but the smile disappeared as he spotted his photograph on the table. 'Christ, what the fuck are we going to do?'

'I don't know.' Joe Ball shook his head. He carefully set the Heineken bottle on the table. 'You got some aspirin or something. This shit's giving me a headache.'

'Yeah, hang on a minute.' Surfer turned and walked towards the bathroom. 'We're just going to have to play it out, maybe pretend you did me, and then see what the guy does,' he called over his shoulder.

He stepped into the bathroom and opened the medicine cabinet. He shook out two Bufferin into his palm, closed the cabinet door and turned.

Joe Ball was standing in the doorway. 'I took the guy's money, Thomas,' he explained sadly.

'Joe. C'mon, man. Don't?'

Joe shrugged. 'I got a reputation here, and I think,' he said regretfully, 'you got a big mouth.'

He lashed out with the side of his hand. The blow caught Surfer on the neck. He staggered back against the sink. Joe Ball quickly moved on him.

Surfer raised his hands, trying feebly to push him away but Joe brushed them aside and grabbed his head. Gripping each side, he smashed it against the edge of the tub.

Surfer's legs jerked spastically, then abruptly stiffened and relaxed.

Joe Ball checked to make sure he was still breathing. Satisfied that he was, he began to undress him. When Surfer was naked Joe Ball picked him up and threw him into the tub. Then he crouched over and turned on each of the faucets. While the tub filled, he carefully picked up Surfer's clothes and carried them into the bedroom. He found a laundry basket behind the door and put them in, then took a robe from the closet and hung it from the inside of the bathroom door.

The tub was half filled when he turned off the water, grabbed each of Surfer's feet and twisted him onto his stomach. For a moment there was no movement and then suddenly Surfer began to thrash violently.

Joe Ball held on and waited.

He put the bottle of Heineken in his pocket and rapidly went through the apartment. In a kitchen cabinet he found a coffee can stuffed with used twenty- and fifty-dollar bills. Shaking his head in disbelief, he used the sides of his wrists to move the can to the front of the shelf. He left the top off, allowing the money to be seen easily. He didn't want anyone to overlook it.

He found a quantity of blow in the dresser drawer beside the bed; alongside it was a hand mirror. He dusted the mirror lightly with some of the white powder, then left both objects on top of the bed.

Joe Ball returned to the bathroom and turned on both faucets. A few moments later he left the condo, locking the door behind him.

It took him almost an hour and a half to drive the forty miles back to his hotel room on Camora Island. He got stuck behind one of the ubiquitous elderly women that seemed to populate this portion of

Florida, who seemed to think that anything over thirty-five miles an hour was an affront against God.

Finally, seated in front of his patio window, Joe Ball opened his last can of Dixie and looked out at the Gulf. He had fourteen hours to go before he could catch his flight home. He glanced at the can sadly, thinking that next time he would definitely bring an extra case along. That there was going to be a next time he never doubted for a moment.

Gloria stood at the kitchen window looking out at the back yard. Elaine and Amy were at opposite ends of the badminton court. Amy, at nine, was four years younger than her sister. She moved gracefully across the lawn, swinging her racquet at the birdie with an energy and enthusiasm that her older sister lacked. Elaine, somewhat handicapped by the sudden onslaught of hormonal changes beginning in her body, swung awkwardly from one end of the court to the other.

Gloria leaned against the sink and watched them. Two years ago they had been inseparable. Their age difference had seemed inconsequential, but now Elaine, rapidly becoming more woman than girl, had begun increasingly to ignore her younger sister. Her time was spent with girls her own age and their conversations, from what Gloria had been able to overhear, revolved around boys, a subject that did not yet instill the slightest bit of interest in her younger sister Amy.

'That was out,' Gloria heard Elaine call.

'Was not.'

'Was too, wasn't it, Daddy?' Both girls turned to Charlie, who sat on a lawn chair watching them.

Gloria heard Charlie make his judgment. Elaine smirked at her younger sister and pranced up to the net.

She watched the girls play, noticing the disparity between their bodies. Amy, all lines and angles; Elaine, beginning to display curves where it seemed that only a week ago there had been nothing but the jut of bone and an indecipherable line between her waist and legs.

They continued playing, at times deadly serious, at others with a completely goofy abandon, which Gloria knew was for the benefit of their father. She shook her head wistfully, turned away from the sink and went out through the back door to join them.

153

She crept up behind Charlie's chair, planning on surprising him. She stopped directly behind him and was just about to bring her hands over his eyes when something about the way he held himself stopped her.

Startled by the sense of someone behind him Charlie whirled around fearfully.

Gloria quickly stepped back, then just as quickly moved towards him. 'Charlie, what is it?'

He turned away, bringing his hands up to his face.

'Charlie?'

'Nothing,' he muttered.

'What?'

'Not now, Glo.' He shook his head and sniffled.

Gloria turned to see both girls watching them curiously. She forced herself to smile. 'Why don't you two go inside and set the table.'

Amy smiled back at her, turned and raced into the house. Elaine held her gaze. 'What's wrong?' she asked quietly.

'Nothing, honey, just go in the house and help your sister. Okay?'

Elaine held her eyes for a moment longer, nodded reluctantly and turned towards the house.

Charlie pushed himself up from his chair and strode over to the side of the badminton net.

'Charlie, what's wrong?'

'It's nothing. It's just . . .' He stopped abruptly. He reached out and grabbed the aluminum pole.

'Charlie, you're frightening me.'

His hand tightened on the pole. She could see his knuckles whitening beneath his grip.

'You just do things sometimes, things that you think matter.' He turned to face her. She winced at the expression on his face and started to reach out to him. 'But it's all bullshit. All you're really doing is fooling yourself,' Charlie said and abruptly glanced away. He wiped at his eyes, then took a deep breath that shuddered through his throat.

'What is it?'

'I was watching the girls play,' Charlie said softly, looking out at the back yard. 'I was just watching the way they move. There's something about the way kids move that's so indescribable. It's like it's the most beautiful thing in the world.' Charlie turned back to her. This time he made no effort to hide his tears, but brushed at them angrily. 'I can't do this any more. I am not going to do this.'

'Charlie?'

'I'll be back in a little while. I have to go down to the office. There's something I have to do.'

She watched him straighten his shoulders. He came up to her and gently touched her arm. 'It's okay now, Glo. Really, it is.' He smiled, leaned forward and kissed her. Her arms, almost involuntarily, went around his shoulders and she held him tightly against her.

When he stepped back, despite the heat of the day, she felt a cold draught of air press against the length of her body. She walked up to the porch and stopped as she heard his car begin to back out of the drive in front of the house.

'Mom?' She glanced over at Elaine. 'Is everything all right?'

'Of course, everything's just fine.' She forced a smile, then, seeing the expression on her daughter's face, asked, 'Why? What's wrong?'

Elaine looked behind her, leaned forward and whispered, 'I think Daddy was crying.' Her eyes suddenly began to well up and Gloria quickly reached for her.

'No, it's nothing,' she said, hugging her daughter tightly, as she listened to the fading sounds of her husband's car.

'It's hot,' she explained, when she came out of the bathroom wearing only her bra and cut-off shorts.

Ryan, seated at the window table, looked at her closely. The small white brassiere seemed almost superfluous against her barely developed chest.

She moved without a trace of self-consciousness to the bed, sat on the edge and picked up her beer. She took a sip and crossed her legs. Ryan noticed a childish scrape on the heel of her knee.

'I like motorcycles,' she said, looking over the rim of her beer can at him. 'They make me hot.'

'I'll turn the air up a little higher.'

She giggled, shaking her head at him. She'd undone her hair and it fell in thick, dark strands along each side of her face. Her bangs were cut high on her forehead and accentuated the deep blue of her eyes.

155

She spilled some beer and began to smooth it along her thigh, glancing over at Ryan coyly. He returned her gaze impassively. She put her beer can down and leaned back on the bed, her small chest thrust forward. 'Why don't you come on over here for a while?'

'How old are you?'

'Old enough.'

'What does that mean?'

'I'm eighteen,' she said without any pretense of sincerity. She smiled enticingly, then patted the bed beside her. 'C'mere.'

Ryan rose and moved over to stand above her. She reached up to the front of his pants and began to undo his belt.

She unzipped his jeans, then wormed her hand along his stomach below his waistband until she touched him.

'Twenty-five for suck, and fifty for half and half,' she whispered, moving her hand along the length of him.

Ryan shook his head in amazement and smiled down at her. He reached for her hand and pulled it away.

'What do you want?' she whispered. Her tongue darted out to lick her lips in a childish parody of seduction.

'What else do you do?'

'That depends,' she said coquettishly.

She reached behind her, unclasped her bra and shrugged out of it displaying barely perceptible breasts.

'You do any hard stuff?' Ryan asked, watching her closely. He caught the quick flash of fear.

She sat forward, crossing her hands in front of her chest until she gripped each opposing shoulder.

'That's what I was really interested in.' Ryan smiled cruelly. 'I've got some stuff over there.' He nodded towards his duffle-bag.

She glanced at the bag and returned her gaze to his face.

'What d'you say? I'll make it worth your while.'

'Listen, mister, I'm only thirteen years old.'

'Thought you said you were eighteen.'

'I was lying.'

Ryan grinned. 'Doesn't matter. Eighteen, thirteen.' He shrugged. 'What's five years.' He reached for her.

She scurried across the bed until she was out of reach.

Ryan lunged at her and trapped her body beneath his. She opened her mouth to scream. He slapped his hand across his lips and leaned over her. 'One fucking word, and it's the last thing you'll ever say.' He watched her eyes dart fearfully towards the door, then back to his face. He released her when she stopped struggling, and glared down at her.

She swung her legs over the edge of the bed and stared at the floor. 'What do you want me to do?' she asked compliantly, sniffled and used the back of her hand to wipe her nose.

'Just stay there for a minute,' Ryan threatened and stalked into the bathroom. When he returned she was still in the same position.

He threw her shirt at her. It fell across her head. She jerked away in fear, then reached up frantically to pull it away from her face. She stared at it in confusion.

'Put it on,' Ryan ordered, stepping over to the window table and picking up his beer.

She hooked her bra and slid one arm into her shirt. She paused to glance over at him. 'Are you going to hurt me?'

She tried to meet his eye but her gaze kept slipping away.

'Just get dressed,' Ryan told her and looked outside at the parking lot. Heatwaves shimmered from the hoods of the cars, as the sunlight shafted blinding streaks of light off the chrome.

When he turned back to her she was seated primly on the edge of the bed, fully dressed.

'Are you a policeman?'

'No,' he answered and saw her fear again.

'Then who are you?'

'I'm the one who's going to ask the questions. Do you understand that?' He waited for her to respond before going on. 'What's your last name, Lailya?'

'Conally.' She didn't seem at all surprised that he knew her first name.

'How long have you been doing this?'

'About a year.'

'You working for yourself?'

She glanced up at him. Ryan met her gaze, then walked over to his duffle-bag and riffled through it. He threw her one of the photographs he had obtained from Caldwell's house. It struck her knee and fell to the floor.

157

In the photograph, Lailya was tied spread-eagled to a bed. Two men stood, angled towards its head with their backs to the camera. Each of them was masturbating over her face. A large rubber dildo had been inserted into her body. The cords of her neck were sharply defined as she twisted her head back in pain.

'Bring back memories?' Ryan said cruelly. He watched her examine the picture. Her hand began to shake. She suddenly shredded the photograph and threw it on the floor. She crouched over, wrapping her arms round her stomach and sobbing.

Ryan leaned back against the table and closed his eyes tightly.

He opened them abruptly to see the girl in the same position. He took a tentative step towards her, then almost involuntarily seemed to stop himself from completing the movement. 'There's more.'

She glanced up at him, her eyes red-rimmed and swollen. She reached up and rubbed at them with the side of her hands. The gesture made her look even younger than she was.

'Who are the men in the picture, Lailya?' Ryan asked softly a moment later.

Lailya glanced away.

'Who are they?'

'I don't know,' she sobbed.

'What is this bullshit. Who the fuck you think you're fooling with this little-girl crap?' She turned to him angrily. 'You've had more cocks in you than a fucking men's locker room.'

'No,' she screamed.

'Who are they?'

'I don't know.'

'Who the fuck are they?' Ryan asked, moving over until he stood directly in front of her.

'I don't know.'

'Bullshit.'

'I don't.'

'Then what the fuck *do* you know?'

'Nothing. I don't know anything,' she sobbed, then turned and flopped across the bed.

Ryan sat beside her. He lit a cigarette, turned to her and put his hand on her back.

She stiffened beneath his touch, but relaxed while he patted her as he would a child.

Ten minutes later, after she had composed herself, Ryan asked again, 'Who are they?'

The little girl rolled over on her side and pushed herself back against the headboard. She looked over at Ryan and closed her eyes tightly.

When she opened them she told him what he wanted to know.

Eighteen

Ryan closed his eyes.

'You ever think about it?' Zella asked. He laughed and shook his head. 'C'mon, Eddie, you must have at one time or another.'

Suddenly somber, 'No, never in any real sense,' Ryan answered.

'Why?'

Ryan all at once felt the need for movement. He pushed himself out of bed and over to the window.

'What is it?' He heard her ask and turned to look at her lying on the bed studying him.

He smiled softly. 'I just don't think I'd make a very good father.'

'I think you'd be a wonderful father.'

Ryan turned back to the window. A moment later he heard her rise and move towards him. Her arms came round his chest and he felt the length of her body press against his back.

'We could do it, you know,' she said softly into the crook of his neck. 'We could set up house somewhere and have a whole passel of kids.'

'Passel?' He smiled and turned to her, watching the sudden flush of color rise to her face. 'I don't think I know that word. Is that one of those things they say in Harlan?'

She thumped him on the shoulder. 'Don't change the subject by trying to embarrass me.'

Ryan grinned and took her in his arms. His hands went round her body, until they criss-crossed her back and rested on her hips. He felt the pressure of her breasts against his chest and her fine bones beneath his forearms. He held her tightly, closing his eyes, and for just a moment could actually see it, could feel what they might be able to give each other.

* * *

'Ryan.'

He jerked out of his reverie to see Gloria standing above him, offering him a cup of coffee.

'You get them to bed?'

'Yeah.' She nodded and wearily sat beside him on the porch swing. She began to rock gently. Ryan leaned back and rested his head against the ledge of the swing.

'What's it like in California?'

'Different.' Ryan shrugged.

'You ever miss Florida?'

'No, not really. It's been a long time since I've lived here.'

'It would be hard for me to leave here. I'd miss this,' Gloria said, nodding towards the front yard. The sun had disappeared, to be replaced with a slight breeze that rustled through the palms. A mocking-bird called from a bougainvillaea bush at the end of the property. 'I think this is one of my favorite times of the day. It always seems so peaceful now.' She looked at him. 'I'd hate to have to leave here, Edward.'

'I guess you shouldn't, then.' He smiled.

She returned his smile. 'No, I guess not.'

They both turned to look as a car came down the street, watching silently as it passed the house and disappeared into a drive further down the block.

Ryan lit a cigarette.

'Do you . . .' Gloria started, then stopped. 'Do you still miss her?' she asked softly.

Ryan looked out at the street. 'No,' he answered quietly. 'I don't think about her too much any more'

'That's good.' Gloria reached over to cover his hand with her own.

Charlie pulled into the drive. He paused for a moment as he saw Edward and Gloria sitting on the porch.

Gloria came down to meet him. She stopped at the foot of the porch and examined him hesitantly.

He smiled and reached out for her. Holding her, Charlie glanced over her shoulder to see Edward standing watching them. 'It's okay.'

'You sure?' Gloria asked, stepping back to look at him.

'Yeah. Everything's fine.'

They walked up to the porch together.

'Charlie.' Ryan nodded, and he nodded back.

'I'll get us some coffee.'

'Let me help you,' Charlie offered and followed her into the house.
He avoided Edward's eye as he passed him.

'I need to talk to Edward alone for a while,' he told her in the
kitchen.

Gloria continued to pour the coffee. 'Will you tell me what's
going on?'

'I will. Just let me talk to Edward first. Okay?'

'You promise?'

'I promise.'

She examined him closely. 'Okay,' she said.

Charlie stepped out onto the porch with the coffee and, without
saying a word, refilled Ryan's cup. He set the pot on the railing, sat
on the top step and swiveled round so that he faced the other man.

Ryan watched him and waited.

'What you said earlier.' Charlie paused. He glanced out at the
front yard. He heard the ticking sound of his car cooling in the drive.
'Well it was a little hard for me to hear.'

'Charlie, I didn't . . .'

'No, don't say anything, just let me finish,' Charlie interrupted. 'I
guess the hardest part was maybe realizing that you were right. You
see, things have been pretty good for us here. It's like what we used
to talk about when we were kids. Remember?' Charlie glanced over
at his friend. 'You know, the big picture. Having it all. I've got that
now, Edward. I don't know how the hell I did it, but I did. The kids,
Gloria, it's everything I've ever wanted, and I guess . . .' Charlie
suddenly stopped. He raised his cup and took a sip.

Ryan lit a cigarette. The sudden flare of his match highlighted his
face in a shadow of sharp angles.

'Well, I guess I didn't want to fuck it up,' Charlie said, turning to
Ryan and meeting his gaze.

'And now?'

'Now', Charlie grinned, 'I'm ready for whatever we have to do.'

Ryan smiled and reached out. Charlie took his hand and shook it.

Stutz drove home and changed clothes. He put on a pair of jeans and
a dark T-shirt, drove down to the pier and parked. Beach and pier

were crowded with people coming down for sunset. Many of them had brought lawn chairs and cocktails, and were comfortably seated on the sand, positioned so that they had a clear view of the western horizon.

Stutz surveyed the crowds along the beach front. The majority of them were elderly. They looked out at the water with expectant smiles on their wrinkled faces.

He walked out to the end of the pier and leaned on the railing and looked down at the water, watching it lick at the barnacle-encrusted pilings.

People milled around him. They clutched their cameras, waiting for the sun to begin its final descent. Stutz braced his forearms on the railing and watched as the sun slowly eased into the Gulf. For one instant, it seemed almost to liquefy as it touched the surface of the water. This effect lasted only a fraction of a second before it once again seemed to regain its solidity. It slid into the water, leaving a trail of wounded clouds in its wake.

Stutz turned as the last of the light faded from the horizon. He walked back to his car and pulled out of the lot.

He drove through Olde Siena and on into Royal Port. The houses rose extravagantly from their carefully maintained grounds. The lawns were verdant and lush, despite the day-long onslaught from the blazing sun.

He pulled onto a dead-end street and slowed, carefully examining the houses to either side of him, awed by the sense of opulence and graceful luxury they all seemed to display.

At the end of the road he made a U-turn and drove back towards the main street. At the intersection a Point Blank Security vehicle appeared. It slowed as the driver turned to scrutinize Stutz's car.

Stutz snorted disgustedly, turned quickly onto the main road and drove towards the Beach Hotel. He parked in the lot across the street and waited.

He spotted her coming out of a side entrance, accompanied by two other women. The three parted at the sidewalk. Judy crossed the street towards the parking lot and her car. Stutz caught up to her as she was reaching for the ignition.

'Bo, what're you doing here?'

'Just came by to see you.' He smiled.

'Great. Why don't we get a drink?'

'Maybe later,' he said, looking at her closely.

'What? What is it?'

'You remember what you were saying the other night?'

Judy glanced away.

Stutz leaned into her car. 'I need a name, Judy. I need it really badly.'

'Bo.' She shook her head. 'I can't do that.'

'Judy.' He waited for her to turn to him. 'Don't make this any harder than it has to be.'

She sighed. Her fingers began to tap nervously on the steering-wheel.

'Judy?'

'I don't have any name other than Surfer. That's the only way I know him.'

'Where does he live?'

'Del Mar Condos.'

Stutz reached in to touch her shoulder.

'Are you going to call later?' she asked, without looking at him.

Stutz smiled and tightened his grip until she turned to face him. 'As soon as I can,' he promised.

He watched her pull out of the lot, then quickly walked back to his car. He started it and turned onto the street leading him towards the Del Mar Condominium complex.

'I found her in Children's Services. They went in about two years ago to investigate an abuse charge,' Charlie said. He paused to glance at his notes. 'Nothing was proven one way or the other, but I got a hold of the counselor and talked to her about it. She said she definitely thought there was abuse taking place, but they just couldn't come up with anything to prove it.' Charlie sighed. 'They sent the kid back home. Jesus,' he shook his head in disgust, 'she was only eleven years old, Edward.'

Ryan nodded.

'What'd you find?'

'I found a thirteen-year-old-girl who was willing to give me a blow job for twenty-five dollars,' Ryan said brutally.

Charlie winced and glanced over at him.

Ryan took his time lighting a cigarette, then told him about Lailya Conally.

'She didn't know any of them?'

'No, not even Caldwell. She said she'd just get a phone call at work, telling her what time and where to be.'

'Who picked her up?'

Ryan smiled softly. 'That name I got.'

'Who is it?' Ryan raised his eyebrows at Charlie. 'We're in this together, Edward. I'm not bowing out now.'

'Okay.' Ryan nodded thoughtfully. 'Guy's name is Surfer. That's all she knows.'

'You know where he lives?'

'Del Mar Condos. You know the place?'

'Yeah, it's just a little north of here.' He looked over at Ryan expectantly.

Ryan shrugged and flipped his cigarette butt out into the yard. He watched it for a moment, then turned back to Charlie. 'Maybe we should take a ride over there.'

'Let me tell Gloria.'

Ryan stepped down to the lawn and waited.

'What about the houses she went to?' Charlie asked when he returned.

Ryan shook his head. 'Most of the time they took her to motels.'

'What about the other times?'

Ryan paused at the passenger door. He caught Charlie's eye over the top of the roof. 'They blindfolded her.'

'Jesus Christ.'

'All she knows is that the places looked rich.'

'What's rich to a thirteen-year-old?' Charlie said in disgust and slipped behind the wheel.

He pulled out of the drive, turning towards the main highway. At the first stop light he glanced over at Ryan.

'What?'

Charlie looked away. 'You know, none of this may have anything to do with Neal.'

'It has to.'

'Why?'

Ryan glanced out of his window without answering.

* * *

Before the lights had been turned off, the ostentatious display of art work and antique furniture decorating the room had been clearly apparent.

The three men, gathered for a private showing, sat on a Swedish wood-and-leather couch opposite a large-screen Sony TV. Each of them held snifters of cognac and cigars in their hands. The aroma of aged French cognac and Cuban cigars overlaid the subtle odor of wax and polish.

The videotape began to unwind across the screen and the men leaned forward excitedly. One of them burped softly.

A young girl appeared. She staggered into the frame, held up by a man, dressed only in shorts, on either side of her. She was naked.

As they led her towards the bed one of the men let his hand drift along her back to her buttocks. His hand tightened and dug viciously into the girl's flesh. When he released her the marks of his nails remained clearly outlined against her pale skin. A small trail of blood began to run from one of them. The girl seemed unaware of the injury.

The two men lowered her face down onto the bed, straightened and looked over at each other. They began speaking. Their gestures made it clear that they were trying to decide who would be first.

'We need to wire for sound,' one of the men in the room commented. The other two agreed enthusiastically. None of them glanced away from the screen while this exchange took place.

One of the men on the screen lowered his shorts and climbed onto the bed beside the girl while the other stepped back to the edge of the frame and watched.

The girl tried feebly to push herself up from the bed, but her actions seemed ill defined and awkward. The man seated beside her reached up and began to pet the back of her head. His other hand was buried between his legs, manipulating himself.

One of the onlookers laughed, as the man's attempts to excite himself became more frantic.

The other participant in the ménage stepped fully into the frame and spoke to the man on the bed. His words incited the other man to pull his hand abruptly from between the girl's thighs. He began to gesture wildly at his companion.

The man shook his head impatiently and removed his shorts. He slid onto the bed to the other side of the girl. His hand trailed along her back before it buried itself between her buttocks. His arm twisted sharply.

The girl's head jerked up from the pillow.

The other man pressed her back down, his gaze locked on what his companion was doing. He was now fully erect.

The two men turned the girl onto her side between them. She moved without any resistance. Her arm flopped carelessly across one of their shoulders. He grinned, then delicately picked it up at the wrist with two fingers and dropped it. The arm fell limply to her side, sliding off behind her back.

The man behind her turned the girl until the backs of her thighs and buttocks faced the camera. He crouched over and spread the cheeks of her buttocks. He spat, shifted and slowly eased himself into her anus. He paused and beckoned to the camera. The focus wobbled as the camera moved in for a close-up.

The man began slowly to ease himself in and out of her body. The camera zoomed in and captured each movement. The focus suddenly pulled back to include the other man in the frame. He was now crouched beside the girl's head. He fitted himself into her mouth and smiled widely towards the camera.

The watchers shifted nervously in their chairs. Cigar smoke swirled around them as they watched one of the men shudder, then thrust himself violently into the girl. He withdrew, quickly wiped himself off on the sheet and rose.

The other man continued to manipulate himself in the girl's mouth.

The girl's hands had now risen and were awkwardly trying to push him away. He slapped her on the back, leaving a red imprint of his hand on her flesh.

He grabbed the back of her neck, pulled her face into his groin and held her there. She moved sluggishly at first, then with increasing violence as she struggled to breathe.

The men in the room leaned forward. The harsh excited wheeze of their breath was the only sound.

The other man suddenly reappeared on the screen. He moved behind the struggling figure of the girl, grabbed her arms and trapped them behind her back. The man in front of her grinned at him, suddenly threw his head back and grimaced. He pulled back, then brutally thrust forward into the girl's mouth.

As he pulled out completely the girl's body convulsed, as she finally managed to draw an unimpeded breath.

The screen went dark.

'That was very good,' one of the men commented hoarsely, as he rose and moved towards the light switch.

'Just a minute. There's one more scene,' another said, motioning him back to his seat.

The screen suddenly lit up. The girl was tied across the back of a chair. The red outline of a hand, still clearly visible on her back, made it easy to identify her as the one in the previous shot. She was draped over the back of the chair. Her ankles were tied to the front legs, while her arms had been pulled over the back and tied below. Her back faced the screen. Her dark hair had fallen forward, leaving a pale strip of skin across her neck, which stood out in startling contrast to the rest of her tanned body.

The same two men stood beside the bound girl, alternately looking at her and then at the camera. They were both laughing.

One of the men pulled out a cigarette and lit it. He held it up like a magician preparing to do a trick, then slowly turned and pushed the lighted end between the girl's buttocks.

One of the men in the room leaned back and pulled a handkerchief from his breast pocket. He delicately patted his forehead, fastidiously refolded the cloth and replaced it. He took a small sip of his cognac and leaned forward intently to watch the remainder of the video.

Nineteen

There were two other condos on the sixth floor. Surfer's was situated in the south-west corner of the building. Charlie and Ryan stood outside his door.

'I hear water running,' Charlie whispered.

Ryan leaned forward and listened. When he straightened, he knocked loudly. The noise startled Charlie, who took a step back before he caught himself.

Ryan knocked again.

'I still hear the water.'

Ryan nodded thoughtfully and reached for the doorknob. He twisted it, forcing it in each direction.

'Give me your car keys.'

'Why?'

'Just give them to me. I'll be right back.'

Charlie handed him the keys.

'You keep knocking, but try not to disturb anyone,' Ryan said, nodding towards the other two condos.

Charlie turned back to the door after Ryan had disappeared into the stairwell. He banged on it, then listened carefully. All he could hear from inside was the muffled sound of running water.

When Ryan returned he found Charlie leaning against the side of the door.

'What'd you do?'

'Nothing,' Ryan said, motioning him to step away. Ryan ran his fingers along the molding of the doorway.

'What're you doing?'

'Alarms.'

'Why?' Charlie asked, then glanced down to see Ryan pull a

tire iron out of the waistband of his pants.

'C'mon, Edward, we can't.'

Ryan ignored him and fitted the tire iron into the door. Using his weight, he worked it in between the door and the frame, then gripping the bar with both hands, he jerked it towards him.

The sudden crack of splintering wood echoed loudly along the hallway. Ryan quickly slid the tire iron back into his waistband and grabbing Charlie by the shoulder, dragged him into the stairwell.

'Jesus Christ, Edward, what the hell are you doing?'

Ryan didn't answer, but peered out into the corridor.

A few minutes later he motioned for Charlie to follow him back out to the hall.

This time Ryan leaned in with his shoulder. He pushed off with his legs as he twisted the knob. The door splintered open.

'Edward, what the hell.'

Ryan grabbed him and pulled him in.

'This is the worst time. You're inside and you don't know what the hell's going on outside,' Ryan said casually, glancing around the room.

Charlie looked over sharply at his friend.

Ryan smiled, then winked. 'We'll know real quick if anyone heard us.'

'Where'd you learn how to do that?'

'Around.' Ryan shrugged, turned and moved quietly through the living-room.

'Where're you going now?' Charlie whispered.

Ryan motioned him to be quiet, then moved into a lobby leading towards the back of the condo.

Charlie watched him disappear round the corner and turned to survey the room. It was furnished expensively, but a little too garishly for his tastes.

He stepped over to the patio and looked out at the Gulf and froze when he heard the sudden scream of a siren. He listened carefully until it began to fade in the distance.

'You better come in here.' The sound of Ryan's voice startled him. Charlie twisted to see him standing in the hallway.

'Back here.' Ryan nodded and turned.

Charlie followed him down the corridor. He suddenly became

aware of the different texture of the rug beneath his feet. He glanced down curiously and noticed the moisture squeezing out from each side of his shoes. It grew thicker as he approached the bathroom door.

The sound of running water suddenly stopped and Charlie moved quickly round the doorframe. The floor was flooded.

Ryan stood inside the brightly lit room, staring into the tub.

It took a moment for Charlie to realize what he was seeing. 'Jesus Christ,' he gasped.

'Yeah,' Ryan grunted, as he crouched down and reached for the body.

'Don't touch anything,' Charlie warned him.

'Why?' Ryan turned to him.

Charlie returned his gaze blankly.

Ryan turned back to the tub. The body lay face down. On the back of its head was a three-inch gash, which cleanly parted the dark hair. Small tendrils of blood and flesh clung to the injury and bobbed in the water.

Ryan reached into the tub and turned the body. It flopped limply onto its back. He glanced up at Charlie as he heard him retch.

'Don't,' he cautioned, then waited for Charlie's nod before he turned back to the corpse.

The man's eyes stared blankly up through the water. His mouth was stretched open in a soundless scream. His tongue was swollen and thrust out darkly from between his bloodless lips.

'Shit,' Ryan said disgustedly, pushed to his feet and stepped round Charlie into the bedroom across the hall.

'Look at this.'

Charlie pulled himself away from the bathroom and joined him in the other room.

Ryan stood by the closet with a pair of pants in one hand, holding out a wallet to Charlie with the other.

Charlie examined the driver's license. 'It's his face and address.'

'Thomas Langley, better known as Surfer,' Ryan said softly and looked around the bedroom. 'It's fucking perfect.' He shook his head in disgust.

Charlie looked over at the bed and saw the mirror and plastic bag of powder beside it.

'Guy runs a few lines, takes a bath, slips and falls. He's all fucked up. He doesn't know what he's doing.' Ryan turned to Charlie. 'The perfect accidental death,' he said sarcastically.

'It happens.'

'Yeah, it does, but the timing sure is neat.'

Charlie glanced over his shoulder at the bathroom door and back to the bed. 'What're we going to do?'

'Look around.'

'And then what?'

Ryan met his gaze. 'Then we're going to get the fuck out of here.'

Charlie held his eye and nodded reluctantly.

'You take the kitchen. I'm going to start in here.'

'What're we looking for?'

'Anything that connects him to the girls or Neal,' Ryan said, refusing to acknowledge Charlie's skeptical glance at the mention of his brother's name.

Ryan went through the closet. He started at the top and worked his way along the shelf, then began to search through the man's clothes. He heard Charlie in the front of the condo, opening and closing cabinets.

Charlie was stooping down to examine the cabinet beneath the sink when he heard the noise. At first he thought it was Edward, then he heard him in the back room as well as the sound at the front door.

He raced into the bedroom. 'Someone's at the door,' he gasped.

Ryan glanced over at him sharply, reached into the waistband of his pants and pulled out the tire iron.

'Jesus Christ, Edward, what the hell do you think you're going to do with that?'

Ryan stepped quietly over to the doorway. He glanced over his shoulder. 'Get some answers,' he said and slipped into the hall.

Charlie started to follow. He walked to the door, then stopped as he heard the front door opening. A moment later there was the unmistakable click of a gun being cocked. He quickly pulled back and pressed himself against the wall. He listened carefully but couldn't hear anything other than the sound of his own heart, thudding painfully in his chest.

* * *

'Quite good,' one of the men said, as he rose to turn on the lights. Another of the group stepped over to rewind the video. The third man leaned back in his chair and puffed contentedly on his cigar.

'You could have a career in Hollywood, Allen,' the man crouched before the TV commented.

Allen beamed at the other man from the comfort of his chair.

Leonard turned on the lights and walked over to the oak sideboard. He picked up a bottle of cognac and offered it to the two other men. Allen held his glass up for a refill.

The other man shook his head. 'I want to keep a sober head,' he explained.

Both Allen and Leonard smiled as the man in front of the TV set eased himself to a standing position.

'You think that's the problem, Robert?'

'We'll find out soon enough.' He grinned, then grimaced as he pushed a hand into the small of his back and began to massage his hip. 'I think I pulled something.'

'I know just the thing to make you forget all about that,' Allen teased.

Robert returned his smile and limped over to his chair.

'Maybe we should adjourn to the other room,' Leonard said.

Allen pushed himself enthusiastically to his feet.

Robert rose more slowly, his hand still pressed against his back.

Leonard led the two men through the hall to the small elevator at the end.

'Where's Emily this evening?'

'Some charity for the underprivileged,' Leonard responded and snorted disdainfully.

The house was two storeys high. The elevator rose to the second floor. Leonard led the men to a bedroom at the end of the hallway, then, with a flourish, opened the door.

Inside the room, tied spread-eagled across the bed, was a young girl. She wore only two articles of clothing. The first was a black mask that covered her eyes, the second a red leather muzzle. The muzzle was tied round the back of her head and rigidly forced her mouth open.

The three men paused by the door and examined her carefully.

The barely discernible swell of her breasts rose from between the clearly defined bones of her ribs. Her genital area was devoid of all hair.

'Is she drugged?' Robert whispered.

The sudden gasp and clenching motion of the girl's body answered Robert's question before Leonard could.

Allen stepped over to the side of the bed and ran his hand over the nascent swell of her breasts.

The girl froze at his touch, then, as it continued, tried to pull away.

'You are a sweet one,' Allen cooed, as he leaned over and ran his tongue down the front of the girl's body.

'Allen!'

He turned to Leonard, who shook his head at him and nodded to Robert.

Robert grinned at both men and limped over to the side of the bed. He looked rapaciously down at the girl and glanced over at Leonard. 'Who is she?'

Leonard smiled proudly. 'A runaway.'

Robert nodded happily and turned back to the girl. He scrutinized her, then reached up and began to unbutton his shirt.

When he was naked he started to move onto the bed. In mid-movement, he suddenly grimaced and clutched his back. He looked imploringly over his shoulder at the two other men watching him.

With a sigh Leonard stepped over and helped him onto the bed. As he walked back to his chair he heard the excited, phlegmatic sound of Robert's breath behind him.

Stutz eased himself into the condo. He noticed the disarray, and pulled his service revolver. He crept into the living-room and paused. He heard the steady sound of dripping water coming from somewhere at the back and moved silently across the floor.

He stepped into the hallway and froze abruptly as he became aware of a motion behind him. Hearing a voice, he whirled round wildly with the gun pointed in front of him. He saw the figure rising from behind the kitchen bar and crouched forward, aiming his revolver. His finger began to tighten on the trigger.

'Take it easy.'

Stutz glared at the other man and slowly straightened. He kept his revolver trained on the man's chest.

Ryan stood before him, watching the policeman carefully. He held his hands out in front of him.

'Let's just take this slowly,' Stutz told him, moving forward as he reached behind his belt for his handcuffs. 'Let's not do anything stupid here.'

Stutz grabbed Ryan's hands, wrenched them behind his back and cuffed him. Only then did he holster his revolver.

'You want to tell me what's going on?'

'What're you doing here?' Ryan asked, ignoring his question.

Stutz held the other man's gaze for a moment, shook his head and walked over to the phone. He picked it up without taking his eyes off Ryan.

Ryan returned his gaze impassively.

'Bo.'

Stutz jerked round to see Charlie Benning step out of the hall.

'Don't call. Not yet. Okay?'

Stutz glanced at them both, his gaze settling on Charlie. 'Why not?'

Ryan shook his head imperceptibly.

'Just let me talk to you for a moment,' Charlie said, avoiding Ryan's glance.

Stutz examined the other man thoughtfully and with an abrupt nod replaced the phone. 'This better be good, Charlie. Because you and your friend are going to have to have one hell of an explanation to get out of this.'

'No one's trying to get out of anything,' Ryan said, turning to glare at the policeman.

'You shut up,' Stutz retorted, then eyed Charlie. 'You want to explain what's going on here?'

Charlie looked over at Ryan, then back at Stutz.

'Charlie, you either talk to me now, or you talk to me later at the station.' Stutz shrugged. 'Either way, you are going to talk. It's just a matter of where.'

Charlie sighed and came into the room. 'First you'd better take a look in the bathroom, Bo.'

Stutz looked at him suspiciously.

'Don't worry, we're not going anywhere,' Charlie said and sat down on the couch.

177

Stutz examined him closely and walked into the hallway. He heard Ryan whisper something quickly to Charlie, but couldn't make out the words. The rug squished beneath his feet. He glanced down at it curiously, moved to the end of the hallway and into the bathroom.

'Surfer?' he asked the two men when he returned to the living-room.

'We think so,' Charlie answered.

Ryan remained quiet. He was seated awkwardly on the arm of a chair, his gaze focused intently on the policeman.

Stutz looked at the two men, nodded and sat down across from them. 'Accident?'

'Looks that way.'

'Does, doesn't it,' Stutz answered, examining Charlie's face. He turned to Ryan when he heard his impatient snort of disgust. 'What's your problem?'

'I don't have one.' Ryan paused. He looked at the other man appraisingly and added, 'But maybe you do.'

'Yeah,' Stutz challenged, 'and why is that?'

Ryan smiled. 'What are you doing here?'

'My job.'

'Plainclothes?'

'I was promoted,' Stutz responded dryly.

'I don't think so.' Ryan shook his head.

'What're you getting at?' Charlie asked.

Ryan nodded towards Stutz. 'He's either a part of it, or he's trying to find out the same thing we are.'

Charlie glanced over sharply at Stutz. 'Find out what?' He turned to Ryan, then back to the policeman. 'What are you doing here?' he asked.

'That's it,' Stutz said, rising and moving towards the phone. He picked it up, paused and looked at the two men. He felt Ryan's eyes boring into him. When neither man made any response, he dialed. He straightened, waiting for the connection to be made.

'Charlie, go over and listen.' Ryan nodded towards the phone.

Charlie stepped over beside the policeman.

Stutz calmly met Ryan's gaze, then held the phone out to Charlie. 'It's the dispatcher.'

'Hang up, Stutz,' Ryan told him.

'Do it, Bo. Just listen to us for a minute.'

Stutz sighed, then hung up without responding to the voice at the other end. He sat down on the couch and looked up at the two men expectantly.

'Take these off,' Ryan asked, twisting round and offering his hands to the policeman.

'Not just yet.' Stutz turned to Charlie. 'Go ahead. Tell me what you're doing here.'

Charlie leaned forward and began to explain.

'Who's on tonight?'

'Ray,' Leonard answered, then motioned the other man to be quiet as he spoke into the phone.

Allen stepped over to the window looking out at the pool.

'He'll be here in a minute,' Leonard informed him, as he joined him.

They both turned when Robert entered the room. His hair was still wet from his shower.

He grinned proudly at the two men. His limp was more pronounced.

'Didn't think I had it in me, did you?' he said gleefully.

Allen smiled and shook his head.

'Takes a little longer, but it's all still there and working just as good as it ever did.' Robert cackled and slowly lowered himself into a chair. He leaned back and sighed heavily.

'Ray's on his way over.'

'That's the boy with dogs, isn't it?'

'Yes.'

'I like that boy. I think he shows promise.'

Allen stepped over to the sideboard. He poured himself a half jigger of cognac and carried it over to the couch. He leaned back wearily. 'I'm getting too old for this.'

Robert snorted sarcastically. 'You've got another thirty years ahead of you.'

'I don't know. It seems as if . . .' He stopped abruptly at the sound of the doorbell.

Leonard met the Point Blank Security Guard at the front door and led him to the elevator. They rode up silently to the second floor.

Leonard pointed to the bedroom door.

'In there,' he motioned, 'and try not to make a mess.'

Ray nodded and stepped into the room. On top of the bed was a small bundle, encased in a rubber sheet. At the edge of the sheet, dripping onto the exposed mattress, was a little puddle of blood.

Ray hoisted the bundle easily onto his shoulder. He took the elevator down to the first floor and carried it out to his truck. He threw it into the bed of the truck, turned and went back to the house. Leonard met him at the door and handed him an envelope.

'Thank you, sir.'

Leonard dismissed him with an imperious nod and closed the door.

Ray pulled out of the drive and headed out to the main highway.

He drove thirty miles out of town, then took a dirt road leading off into the expanse of Big Cypress Swamp. He drove another five miles before stopping.

He took a police flashlight from the glove compartment, pulled the body out of the truck and carried it to the edge of a canal. As his light flashed over the turgid water, he saw a number of gleaming eyes glinting back at him.

He threw the bundle onto the ground and unrolled the body. He flashed his light over the tortured face of the little girl and shook his head in a combination of disgust and admiration.

'Weird old fuckers,' he muttered, lifting the girl in his arms and throwing her into the canal. The splash was swiftly drowned out by the hurried rush of movement from each side of the canal. The noises quickly converged on the body, bobbing gently in the swampy water. Suddenly it jerked and a moment later disappeared beneath the surface.

Ray climbed back into his truck. He turned on the dome light and peered into the envelope. It was thickly packed with twenty-dollar bills. He shoved it into his pocket, started up the truck and headed back into town.

Twenty

Richard took the call at ten thirty. He was seated in his living-room with his nightly cup of Earl Grey. He had picked up the habit ten years before on a business trip to London. In the two weeks he had been there, he had found the diurnal cup of tea tremendously beneficial in insuring a sound night's sleep.

Seated before the wide expanse of glass looking out at the Gulf, Richard savored each sip of tea. He heard the ring of the phone coming from the other room. He paused, holding his cup midway to his lips, until he heard footsteps approaching the door of the den.

'Sir?'

Richard turned to the voice. David stood politely at the door. 'A call for you, sir.'

'Who is it?' Richard asked in annoyance.

'Mr Logan, sir.'

Richard nodded curtly and dismissed him. He picked up the phone. 'Yes, what seems to be the problem?'

'You asked me to keep you informed of things, sir.' The man at the other end of the line paused.

'Yes?' Richard demanded impatiently.

'Well I thought I should let you know that I did a little job for Leonard tonight.'

'What kind of job, Ray?' Richard asked softly, without any trace of his previous annoyance.

'The usual, sir.'

'Thank you, Ray. I'm very grateful that you called. I'll see that your assiduousness is amply rewarded.'

'That's . . .'

Richard hung up on the other man. He stood, stalked over to the window and stared out thoughtfully at the water. His shadowed reflection shimmered grotesquely across the glass in front of him.

'Sir?'

Richard turned to see David entering the living-room. 'Would you like another cup of tea?'

'No, I think a brandy might be nice.'

Richard waited for David to return with his drink before he seated himself by the phone.

'Leonard, my friend. What is this I hear about your activities this evening?' he asked pleasantly.

'Richard?'

'Yes, Leonard, it is. Now what is this I've heard about you and your friends tonight?'

'C'mon, Richard, it was no big deal. We simply . . .'

'Simply what, Leonard? Ignored the majority ruling of the group? Jeopardized everyone's welfare?' Richard paused. 'Is that what you were going to say?' he asked quietly.

He waited for a response. When none was forthcoming, he asked, 'Why don't you tell me exactly what transpired this evening? And, Leonard, don't leave anything out, no matter how inconsequential it might seem.'

Leonard began to talk. Hesitantly at first, then with increasing enjoyment, he outlined his, Allen's and Robert's evening.

'Explain about the girl again, please?' Richard asked politely, after Leonard had concluded his version of the night's activities.

'Reynolds located her over at the . . .'

'No, not that one, the initial one you attempted to reach.'

'She wasn't available. Allen tried to get a hold of her, but she was out or something.'

'She was out or something,' Richard repeated slowly.

'Well that's what we were told,' Leonard responded. 'Why, what's wrong with that?'

'Did it ever occur to you, or your friends, that there was a very definite reason to forestall all the group's activities?'

'But . . .'

'You have put all of us in jeopardy.'

'C'mon, Richard, you're over-reacting. We didn't do anything that we haven't done before.'

'That's certainly true, Leonard. But you did it at a time when we are under close scrutiny.'

'I don't think it's . . .'

Richard interrupted again. 'That's exactly correct, Leonard. You don't think. There is a reporter, and also Neal's brother, who would both just love to know what we have accomplished here.'

'We were very careful,' Leonard protested.

'Were you?'

'Yes, we were.'

Richard smiled. 'Let me ask you one question. The girl you attempted to reach earlier this evening. Has she ever been unavailable at that particular time before?' he asked and listened to the silence at the other end.

'You don't think she was . . .?'

'Of course, that's exactly what I think. And, if you ever took the time to do the same, the identical conclusion would be inescapable to you.'

'What are we going to do?'

Richard nodded in satisfaction at the sound of capitulation in the other man's tone. 'I'll take care of it this time. But no more, Leonard. Not until it's been decided that it's safe to continue.'

'Thanks, Richard. I won't forget this.'

'You'd better not,' Richard responded and hung up.

He leaned back in his chair, immensely satisfied with the conversation. He allowed himself a moment to savor his sense of victory before he reached for the phone. 'We have a slight problem. I want you to look into it,' he said into the receiver.

There was no need for him to identify himself. The man at the other end had quickly come to know the sound of his voice.

'What d'you think?' Charlie asked, once they stepped inside Ryan's motel room.

'I don't know.' Ryan shook his head thoughtfully and walked over to the window. 'But I guess we'll find out in a few minutes, one way or another.'

'Christ, this whole thing is out of control.'

Ryan turned to look at him. 'No, it isn't. We're just starting to get control.'

183

After a moment Charlie nodded, then stepped over beside him. They looked out silently at the brightly lit parking lot. Charlie's car was parked in front of the room beside Ryan's motorcycle.

Charlie straightened as he saw a car pull into the lot. The headlights flashed briefly across the window and flicked off.

Ryan opened the door and waved Stutz inside.

'I stopped and called it in.'

Both Charlie and Ryan looked at him.

'I did it anonymously,' the policeman said, throwing a disgusted glance at both of them. He went over to the table by the window and sat down. 'You got a beer?'

Ryan pulled three cans from an ice-bucket beneath the bar and passed them out.

Stutz took a sip before he looked over at Ryan. 'Let's see what you've got.'

Ryan pulled the pictures and catalogues from his duffle-bag and put them on the table. He stepped back and watched as Stutz leaned forward to examine them.

'Jesus Christ,' he said in disgust. 'They're just kids.'

'Not any more,' Ryan commented quietly.

'You talked to one of them?'

'Yeah, this afternoon.' Ryan pulled out a cigarette. 'She was thirteen years old.'

'She tell you anything?'

'Just that whoever's running this has got a system down that's pretty smooth.'

'Tell me about it.'

Ryan sat down on the edge of the bed and outlined what he had learned from Lailya. He told Stutz about the blindfolds, the timed phone calls and the meeting places.

'She's never seen any of them?'

'Only Caldwell and I don't see that he's going to be too much help,' Ryan said dryly.

'What about you? What you got?'

'Nothing, really.' Charlie shrugged. 'I discovered one of the girls' names.' Charlie pulled out his notebook. 'Debbie Cox. She lives out on the north side of town. I found her through Children's Services.'

'What about these others?' Stutz asked, waving to the photographs spread across the table.

Charlie shook his head. 'Nothing. They're all just kids. No records.'

Stutz nodded reflectively. 'So they're not using a source connected with the city?'

'How do you know that?' Ryan asked. 'Maybe they're covering it up somehow?'

'No.' Stutz shook his head. 'If they were, this girl wouldn't have been included.'

'What about Surfer?'

'I don't know. It could have happened the way it looked. I think we're better off waiting for the ME's report.'

'Stutz,' Ryan said and waited until he had the other man's attention. 'We've told you what we think. What about you? What do you have?'

'Not much, just a lot of suspicions.'

'Such as?' Charlie asked, glancing down at the pictures and quickly looking away.

'Well, it's obvious that something's going on. What I can't figure out is exactly where it starts,' Stutz said and began to tell them about his confrontation with the Point Blank Security people and his subsequent talk with Judy. 'According to her, everyone seems to know that just about anything's available for a price in this town. The only name she could give me was Surfer's.'

'And Surfer's dead. Sure is convenient for someone,' Ryan commented wryly.

'Yeah, it is,' Stutz agreed, lifting his beer. He glanced down at the pictures, suddenly leaned forward and began to study them more closely.

'What is it?'

Stutz ignored him and started to sort the pictures into piles. When he was done, he had two stacks. 'Look at these.' He handed one stack to Ryan and the other to Charlie. 'Tell me what you see.'

Both men shuffled through the prints.

'They're all of Caldwell.'

'What about yours, Charlie?'

Charlie grimaced. 'I hate these damn things,' he said, placing them face down on the table.

Stutz picked them up and passed them to Ryan. 'What do you see?'

'Just the girls.'

'What about the man?'

'It's Caldwell.'

'Look closer.'

Ryan examined one of the pictures that clearly displayed Caldwell. He compared it with another where the man's back was turned to the camera. He forced himself to concentrate on the man and ignore the girl.

Caldwell was naked in both photographs. Ryan examined him carefully. 'It isn't him, is it?'

Stutz shook his head. 'What else do you see?'

Ryan went back to the photos. 'Oh Christ.'

Stutz nodded knowingly.

'What is it?' Charlie asked.

'None of these is Caldwell. They're all different men,' Ryan said, holding up the larger stack.

'I don't get it. What does that mean? We already know there had to be at least two of them. Somebody had to take the picture.'

'Look at this,' Ryan said, stepping over to him. 'Just shut out the girl and look at the man.'

Charlie examined the photographs carefully and glanced up in confusion at Ryan.

'You don't see it?'

'See what?'

'The men,' Ryan said. 'That's why we thought all of them were Caldwell. They're all old.'

'Something else we might want to think about,' Stutz interrupted. 'If this thing with Surfer wasn't an accident, then these people, whoever they are, moved pretty damn fast.'

'So, what's your point?'

'My point, Ryan, is that all of us were on our way to see Surfer when he bought it. So one of us – if not all of us – is probably being watched.'

'The girl,' Ryan said abruptly, pushing himself off the bed.

'Yeah.' Stutz nodded.

Ryan moved towards the door. 'I'll go get her.'

'They might be following you,' Stutz warned him.

'Not on the bike.' Ryan grinned and hurried out of the door. A moment later the two men in the room heard the deep roar of the engine starting.

When it faded, Charlie turned to Stutz. 'What's going on, Bo?'

'I don't know exactly.' Stutz shook his head. 'But I sure the hell want to find out.'

'You think this has anything to do with Edward's brother?' Charlie asked quietly.

'It's hard to believe that it doesn't. Maybe he found out something and was going to talk.'

'We should try to see Burdick again?'

'He'd certainly be one person to talk to.'

'What about Rainey? You think he's a part of this?'

'I don't have any idea.' Stutz shook his head. 'But someone down there is. That security guy knew exactly what he was doing that night.'

'Jesus, who the hell do we trust?'

'I don't know, Charlie,' Stutz said and glanced over at the other man thoughtfully. 'What about Ryan?'

'What d'you mean?'

'I pulled his file today.'

Charlie looked out of the window.

'The guy's been around. You know he used to ride with both the Jokers and the Angels.'

Charlie shook his head without turning.

'I also pulled up his juvie records,' Stutz said quietly. Charlie glanced over his shoulder at the other man. 'You want to tell me about that?'

'It was a long time ago, Bo. It's water under the bridge.'

'Not if I'm going to be putting my trust in him it isn't. I want to know what that was all about.' Charlie shook his head wearily. 'Tell me?'

'I don't know it all.' Charlie sighed and turned to face the policeman. 'I only know some of it. I know that Edward's father was a drunk.' He paused and turned back to the window. 'I remember one time the three of us went skinny-dipping together. Both Neal and Edward had burns all over their legs.' Charlie turned to Stutz. 'They were cigarette burns, Bo,' Charlie said softly, shaking his head in

187

disbelief. 'None of us was much older than eight or nine then. Their mother, along with just about everyone else in town, was terrified of the man. He was one of those old-time fishermen who thought the only way to get rid of the feel of the water was to drink it away. He was one mean son-of-a-bitch, drunk or sober.'

'So what did happen that night?'

'I don't know. Edward's never talked about it and I've never asked him.'

'Do you think he did it?'

'I don't have any idea. And to tell you the truth, I don't care,' Charlie said, holding the policeman's gaze.

Stutz nodded and looked away.

'Why don't we just concentrate on what we're going to do now.'

'Fair enough.' Stutz nodded. 'I'll see what I can pull up on the computer. Maybe some of these girls will show up somewhere.'

'I'll work Caldwell, see if there's anything I've missed. What about Burdick?'

'Why don't we hold off on him for a little while, until we know more.'

Charlie pushed himself to his feet and started towards the door.

Stutz gathered the photographs and followed him.

'I'll let you know in the morning what I hear from Ryan.'

'Call me at home.'

Charlie glanced at him curiously.

Stutz shrugged. 'I don't know if I'm just being paranoid or what, but I want to be real careful about what we're doing here. There seems to be too much going on to get careless.'

Charlie agreed and went to the parking lot. He pulled out to the street as Stutz climbed into his car.

On the drive home, Charlie kept glancing nervously into his rear-view mirror at a pair of headlights that seemed to mimic his every turn.

Stutz pulled out a can of beer from the refrigerator and carried it over to his kitchen table. He sat down and began to examine the pictures carefully.

He rose once to get a magnifying glass from the bedroom, using it to scrutinize the men.

When he was finished, he had discovered that he could differentiate physically between four separate men. The only single aspect they had in common was that all of them had to be in at least their sixties. That, and the fact that the girls they enjoyed were fifty years younger or less, were the only two conclusions he could honestly reach.

Joe Ball was not happy. The call he had received earlier that evening had not improved his mood one iota. Even with the added incentive of an extra five bills he was still not pleased.

The voice at the other end had not even asked if he would be interested in the assignment. It had simply stated what had to be done and assumed that he would do it.

His acceptance of the assignment had been with the realization that he had no other choice. He knew this, and the way the voice had commanded him imperiously let him know that the man at the other end of the line was also aware of this fact.

It was not a position that Joe Ball enjoyed.

He had not even requested the additional five thousand. It had been offered as a consolation for his inconvenience.

He had decided, after hanging up, that it was time to disappear. He would complete this last brief and that was it. He had planned carefully for this eventuality. He had IDs and money stashed in a San José safety deposit box. All he had to do was buy himself enough time to get out of the country to collect them.

Joe glanced at the directions he had written across the hotel stationery. They had been given precisely and he had noted them down meticulously.

He figured he was no more than two to three miles from the house. He wasn't quite sure what to expect once he arrived. The voice had told him that there would be no more than two people at home. He was to remove one of them, or take out both if there was no other way. It was imperative, the voice had told him, that the designated brief be removed as quickly as possible. Then it had paused abruptly, leaving the threat unspoken, but clearly evident.

Joe Ball turned off the highway and began to make his way through a residential district that would eventually lead him to the dead-end street he sought. The house was at the end of it, he'd been told. The nearest neighbors were a block away.

Joe turned onto the road that, according to his directions, would take him to the street he wanted. He was blinded momentarily by a single headlight speeding up behind him.

A motorcycle whizzed past. Joe watched the tail light take the curve ahead and disappear from sight. As he entered the curve, the sound of the bike died abruptly. The sudden silence seemed to close in around him ominously.

Twenty-One

It was a small, single-storey house set on a third-acre plot of land. A lone dwarf palm-tree, along with an old gutted pick-up truck, decorated the front yard.

The house was well lit. Through the kitchen window a man could be seen, seated at a battered formica table. A black-and-white TV set was perched across from him at the other end of the table. The empty beer cans strewn across the floor made it clear that the one he was drinking wasn't his first. Ryan walked up to the door and knocked.

'Yeah, what d'you want?' The man leaned against the doorframe, glaring at Ryan through the screen. His white T-shirt was stained and torn across the front. From his unshaven face his bloodshot eyes looked at Ryan warily.

'I'd like to talk to Lailya,' Ryan requested. He was surprised when the man nodded glumly and turned away, motioning for Ryan to follow him.

'She's back there.' He nodded curtly towards a door leading off from the kitchen and returned to his chair in front of the TV.

Ryan stepped into the living-room. He heard the pop of a can being opened behind him and, after a moment's silence, a throaty burp.

'What do you want?'

'To talk,' Ryan said.

She shrugged, turned and motioned him inside.

Compared with the rest of the house, her room was neatly made up. A single bed stood against one wall. It was covered by a clean white sheet. Sitting on top of it was a stuffed rabbit. Alongside the opposite wall was an aluminum rack, with clothes stacked neatly

191

on each of the shelves. Above her bed was a poster of a snow-covered mountain.

'Makes me think it's cool,' she explained, noticing the direction of Ryan's gaze. She sat down on the edge of the bed and looked up at him expectantly.

Ryan turned to her.

'What d'you want?'

'More than what you've told me.'

'I already told you everything I know.' She shrugged and scratched her left elbow.

Ryan saw a small smear of blood open up on her flesh. 'Why didn't you tell me the men were old?'

'You didn't ask.'

Ryan stared at her until she glanced away. 'This isn't a game, Lailya. You remember Surfer?'

'You talked to him!'

'No.'

She sighed in relief and sprawled across her bed.

'I couldn't,' Ryan said abruptly. 'He was dead.'

'What?' She jerked forward.

'He's dead. That makes three so far. You could be the fourth.'

'That's nuts, no one would want to kill me.'

'They might.'

'Yeah, why would they?' she smirked.

'Maybe because they think you've been talking to me.'

'No way.'

'You don't think so?'

'No, they're just a bunch of old farts. They're not running around killing people. Especially me. They like me.'

'Not all the time,' Ryan said pointedly.

Her eyes dropped. 'That's just how they get off. It doesn't mean anything.'

'Tell that to Surfer.'

She shook her head. 'You're just trying to scare me.'

Ryan looked over at her appraisingly. After a moment he shook his head sadly and said, 'No, I'm not trying to scare you.'

'Good, because you aren't.' She smiled, leaning back against the bed, but her smile faltered as Ryan crouched in front of her, until his face was only inches from hers. 'Now you listen to me, Lailya, and you listen close.' Ryan reached out to grip her shoulders, forcing her to face him. 'We're getting out of here right now, and then you're going to tell me everything you know.'

'Let go, that hurts,' she whined, trying to twist out of his grip.

Ryan leveled his gaze on her and shook his head.

'I'm going to scream.'

'Go ahead, scream,' Ryan invited.

Abruptly she swung her nails at his face. Ryan easily batted her hand away. She threw her head back and screamed.

'What the fuck's going on in there?' the man called from the other room.

'This guy's trying to rape me.'

'Well don't be breaking up the whole goddamn house doing it,' the man yelled back.

The girl suddenly grew still. Her glance quickly shifted away from Ryan's.

'C'mon,' he said gently. 'Let's get out of here.' He released her arms as he saw her eyes begin to well up. She followed him meekly to the front door.

'Where you going?' her father demanded as they passed the kitchen doorway.

Lailya ignored the question and went out with Ryan to his motor- cycle. As they climbed on, they both looked back at the house. The man was still seated before the TV screen with a beer in his hand.

Ryan started up the bike and wheeled out onto the street. Her arms crept round his waist and held on tightly.

He took the first curve and followed it round. As he came out of it, Ryan became aware of a car coming up behind him. He watched in his rear-view mirror as it started to pass him. As it came up on his left, he glanced over to see a newer model white Cadillac with a man seated behind the wheel. He looked back at the road as the Caddie moved a little ahead swinging abruptly in front of him. Ryan heard Lailya's scream as he turned to the shoulder and eased on both rear and front brakes. He felt the rear wheel going out on him and threw his weight to the side, pulling Lailya along with him. The front wheel hit the dirt shoulder and skidded out. Ryan quickly shifted his weight and brought the bike back under control.

He eased back onto the street and glanced up to see the Cadillac parked in the center of the road, half a block ahead of them. 'What the . . .' he growled, then stopped as he saw its back-up lights flicker on.

The Cadillac shot backwards.

Ryan quickly wheeled the bike round and took off.

'Who is that? Why's he trying to . . .'

'Shut up,' Ryan yelled. 'Just lean with the bike.'

He ran it up into fourth before he chanced a quick look back. He saw the Cadillac just coming round a corner and shooting towards them.

He kicked down into third and swung into a turn, leaning the bike almost parallel to the road. He felt Lailya's arms tighten stiffly round his waist as she fought the turn. Her weight wobbled the front wheel. He concentrated on the bike and just barely managed to bring it out of the turn. 'You've got to lean into it,' he yelled over his shoulder, hitting the gears, tearing it back up into fourth.

He glanced into the rear-view mirror to see the Caddie coming out of the turn, a good fifty feet behind. He kicked it up into fifth, then down as he approached another turn. This time he felt Lailya's weight riding with the bike.

Coming out of the corner, they picked up another ten yards on the Cadillac. He kicked into fifth, making another fifteen yards on the car behind.

Ryan desperately searched the road ahead, trying to find a way out to the highway. He knew he could out-accelerate the Cadillac, but on a straight-way the other vehicle would eat him up. Their only chance was to outmaneuver it, or to get to a place where there was more traffic.

'Where the hell are we?' he shouted, glancing ahead at the unfamiliar roads.

'The highway's over that way.'

'Where does this road go?'

He looked into the mirror. The Cadillac had picked up twenty yards and was closing fast.

'Nowhere, it just circles round.'

'Aren't there any roads leading off this?'

'No, it's all straight.'

The headlights flashed across his rear-view mirror, momentarily blinding him. He crouched over the gas tank, pulling Lailya along with him, and accelerated. The bike shot forward, picking up a few yards on the car behind. The gain quickly disappeared as the steady roar of its engine began to eat up the distance separating them.

The shoulders to each side of the road were thick with mangroves and scrub pine. Trying to pull off at the speed they were traveling would be suicidal. They wouldn't get five yards before they lost the bike, which would be only half the problem, the other half being the man behind them. Ryan had a feeling he might not give up so easily.

The Caddie moved up to within fifteen yards of them. Its headlights pinned them to the road.

Ryan began to swing from side to side, trying to throw the man off. But the car didn't even budge. It stayed dead center in the middle of the road and followed, seemingly knowing that the end was inevitable.

'There's got to be something up ahead,' he yelled hoarsely, bent over the handlebars, desperately searching each side of the road.

Lailya leaned forward and buried her face in his back. Ryan felt her shake her head without answering.

The Caddie moved inexorably forward, gaining on them.

Ryan hit the throttle. It responded with a short burst of speed that increased the distance between them by only a yard or two. He cursed wildly, squinting at the road ahead, looking for anything that could take them out of the path of the car behind.

'There,' Lailya suddenly shouted. She removed her hand from his waist and pointed directly ahead. 'There's a bridge up there.'

'Where?'

'Straight ahead, off to the right. It goes over a sewage ditch.'

'I can't see anything,' Ryan yelled, catching sight of the Caddie moving forward. Only a few feet separated them. At the speed they were traveling, the slightest nudge would send the bike careening out of control.

'It's right up there. Can't you see it?' Lailya screamed.

Ryan searched the road ahead of him. He swung the bike from side to side, then suddenly caught sight of a small pathway cut into the mangroves, about fifty yards in front of them. 'Where's the bridge?'

'It's there.'

'How far from the road?'

'I don't know, it's at the end of the path.'

Ryan glanced into his rear-view mirror. He saw the dim shadow of a man, hunched forward over the steering-wheel.

'Go for it,' Lailya screamed.

Ryan squinted into the darkness, trying to make out a trace of the pathway. He raced forward and suddenly it flashed before him. He swung the handlebars towards the path. He felt Lailya's arms jerk tightly across his chest and a moment later her face pressed fearfully into his back.

The Caddie shot forward just as Ryan hit the shoulder. The loose dirt tore at the front wheel. It wobbled precariously, then straightened and shot them along the path.

Mangroves slapped and tore at his legs. He couldn't see anything in front of him. He heard the squeal of the Cadillac's tires on the road behind, then suddenly saw a wooden bridge rising up before him. 'Go with the bike,' he screamed back at Lailya, as the front tire hit the wooden planks.

The bridge rose two feet in the air. Ryan hit it at fifty-five miles an hour. At the first rise in height, the bike left the ground and shot into the air.

Lailya screamed.

Ryan clung to the bike, trying to keep his weight, as well as Lailya's, evenly distributed over the front fork.

The bike began to descend. Ryan desperately tried to see the ground, but lost it for a moment. The front tire slammed into the dirt. Lailya smashed into his back, almost throwing him over the handlebars. Quickly he pulled back, then felt the rear wheel skidding out on him. He threw himself into it, pulling Lailya with him. The back wheel wobbled, caught dirt and kicked out again.

Ryan leaned into it and rode it down.

The motorcycle slid onto its side, dragging them both across the ground. He felt something tear into his calf and thigh and tried to kick off, but his leg was trapped beneath the weight and motion of the bike.

The motorcycle skidded along the path crashing into the mangroves. The engine cut off abruptly as it came to rest against the trunk of a banyan tree.

The sudden silence was broken only by the ticking of the cooling engine. A moment later the swamp again began its nightly chorus. Cicadas and the deep croak of frogs echoed across the marsh.

Ryan felt the pain in his leg. The bike was sprawled on top of him. He closed his eyes tightly, and for a moment, felt the drift moving in on him. He fought it, forcing himself to crawl out from beneath the machine.

His left pant-leg was torn. He couldn't tell how badly he was hurt, but he could feel blood trickling along his thigh and calf. Gingerly he took a step, easing his weight onto the leg. It held him. He glanced around, searching for Lailya and spotted her sprawled across the ground, a few feet from the bike. He limped over to her. She was on her back, staring up at the sky.

'You okay?'

'What?' she asked, looking up at him in confusion.

Ryan ran a hand along her body. Her right arm and shoulder were scratched and bleeding, but other than that she seemed to be fine.

'Can you sit up?' He gently put a hand behind her back to help her.

Suddenly, he heard a crashing sound in the underbrush coming from behind and looked over his shoulder towards the road. In the bright glare of headlights he saw a crouched figure moving across the bridge. An object in the figure's left hand glinted dangerously against the light.

'C'mon, we've got to move.' Ryan helped her to a sitting position.

Lailya shook her head weakly, unexpectedly leaned forward and vomited.

'Lailya, he's coming. We've got to get out of here,' Ryan whispered urgently.

'I don't think I can,' she answered slowly. She seemed to have trouble enunciating her words. She retched again.

Ryan glanced at the man closing in on them and turned back to Lailya. He put his arm round her shoulder and eased her into the mangroves. 'Quiet,' he gasped, as she began to protest.

197

He dragged her deeper into the marsh. He heard something slither ahead of him through the swamp grass and paused. He glanced back to see the man now standing where the motorcycle had gone down. He was studying the ground carefully.

Ryan moved a few more feet away from the bridge. He smelled the stench of sewage and kept crawling forward, carrying Lailya along with him.

He grabbed at the ground ahead. His hand closed around a tuft of sawgrass. Something hissed, then slithered out from between his fingers into the swamp. Involuntarily, he jerked back, glancing quickly over his shoulder to see if his movements had given them away.

The man was walking away from the motorcycle towards the path they had taken.

Ryan began to move more quickly away from the road, deeper into the swamp. He paused when he heard a vehicle come up on the street behind them. It slowed, then quickly picked up speed and disappeared.

Ryan watched as the man rose from where he had hidden himself. He eyed the swamp, then turned and moved back to the road. A moment later Ryan heard the sound of the Caddie starting up and pulling away.

'He's gone.'

'That's nice.' Lailya nodded slowly.

Ryan examined her.

'I don't feel so good,' she said, struggling to sit up. Ryan reached for her. Suddenly she sagged and slumped across the ground.

Ryan put his arm beneath her knees and shoulders and lifted her. He paused when he felt the dampness against his left palm and carried her quickly towards the bike. He flicked the key and the headlight came on.

He examined Lailya beneath its glare. The back of her hair was matted with blood. He laid her down gently on the grass and crouched over the bike. He righted it and had just settled on top of it when a vehicle pulled up on the road behind him.

Ryan dived off the bike into the mangroves.

A moment later a spotlight flashed over the swamp. Ryan gave a sigh of relief and stood up.

'Just hold it right there. Keep your hands in sight.' The voice from the loudspeaker shattered the silence.

Ryan blinked against the bright light and raised his hands.

'Somebody's hurt here,' he called out.

'Don't move,' the voice warned. The side door opened and a policeman stepped cautiously out of the car and started towards him.

'I've got somebody hurt over here,' Ryan shouted.

The policeman walked across the bridge. His partner remained at the foot of it. Both men had their guns drawn and pointed in Ryan's direction.

'Here,' Ryan said, motioning towards the ground.

The policeman approaching him immediately froze and jabbed his gun in Ryan's direction. 'Don't fucking move,' he threatened.

Ryan slowly brought his hands back in sight.

The policeman came over to him, wrenched his arms behind his back and cuffed him.

His partner walked over and stooped down beside the girl.

'How is she?'

'It's her head, she . . .' Ryan started to answer.

'Shut the fuck up.' The policeman glared at him.

'Listen, what the hell is this?' Ryan retorted angrily.

The policeman turned to him. 'You been drinking?'

'For Christ's sake.'

'Had a few tonight, have you?'

His partner moved over to the patrol car.

Ryan could hear him calling in for assistance. 'Some guy tried to run us off the road. He was driving a Cadillac and he . . .'

'Yeah, we know all about it,' the cop said, shaking his head wearily.

Ryan stared at him in astonishment.

'He stopped us a few miles back, said you were wobbling all over the place and almost ran into him.'

'That's not the way it happened. This guy tried to run us off the road.'

The policeman examined him closely. He looked at Ryan's Harley T-shirt and the torn jeans, then down at the girl. He turned back to Ryan with a knowing smile. 'How old's the girl?'

Ryan glared at him and turned as his partner walked over.

'Five minutes,' the other man said and glanced down at Lailya.
'What's the story?'

'Drunk,' the policeman said, then snorted in disgust and turned to
Ryan. 'You have the right to remain silent, any . . .'

Joe Ball went out to the airport immediately and dropped off his
rental car. He picked up a new Chevy Caprice and drove to a motel
off the main highway in North Siena. He checked in under the same
name he had used to rent the car. Grudgingly he picked up a six-pack
of Miller Genuine from a nearby 7–11 and carried it into the motel
room with him.

He turned on the air, popped his first beer, sat on the edge of his
bed and drank it. He went through two more before he felt calm
enough to undress and crawl into bed. He set his watch alarm for
seven o'clock the following morning.

It took him a little while to fall asleep. Every time he closed his
eyes, he kept seeing the harsh glare of his headlights, pinning the two
wobbling figures on the motorcycle to the road ahead of him. He still
couldn't understand how he'd blown it.

He rolled over on his back, thinking maybe it was time he gave
it up. Before he did that, he finally decided, he'd go out as a
professional.

Satisfied with this decision, he turned over on his side and fell
asleep.

It was past two o'clock in the morning when Richard was woken by
the phone. He identified the voice at the other end immediately.

Marjorie rolled over restlessly. Richard could smell the stale scent
of alcohol surrounding her sleep-warm body.

He hurried from the bedroom and took the call in his den.

'We've got the girl. She's in the county hospital.'

'Where was she?'

'You were right. She was with the brother.'

Richard paused thoughtfully. A moment later he asked, 'And the
brother?'

'DUI.'

Richard smiled in satisfaction. 'You will take care of the girl.'

'I don't do that sort of thing.'

'Oh, yes, that's right. You don't, do you?' Richard answered sarcastically.

'I got to go. My partner's out in the squad, waiting for me. If you want her, she's in room 410,' the voice at the other end wearily concluded.

Richard hung up without responding. He dialed Joe Ball's number. After the fifth ring, he hung up. He leaned back in his chair reflectively.

An hour later, satisfied with his conclusions, he climbed quietly into bed beside the sleeping body of his wife and quickly turned away from her. Her smell disgusted him. It was a mixture of stale alcohol and age. One he could tolerate. The other, Richard had long ago decided, was unforgivable.

Twenty-Two

When he woke, he found Gloria seated on the edge of the bed. She sat, staring blankly across the room. Charlie watched her for a moment longer, before he reached out to her.

She turned at his touch.

'What? What's wrong?'

She tried to smile, then shook her head and glanced away.

'Glo?'

'It's Elaine,' she sighed.

Charlie felt a stab of panic. 'What is it?' He swung his feet off the side of the bed.

'She wanted to go out to the mall.' Gloria met his glance. 'I wouldn't let her. My God, Charlie, I was terrified to let her go alone. What's happening?'

'I don't know,' Charlie murmured, putting his arm round her shoulder and pulling her against him.

'What kind of men would do something like that?' she asked quietly.

'I don't know.' He shook his head.

'Dad?' Amy leaned in through the doorway.

'What?'

'You've got a phone call.'

'I didn't even hear it ring,' he complained.

'Maybe you weren't listening,' she smirked and quickly disappeared round the doorframe.

Charlie grabbed the phone.

'They picked up Ryan last night on a DUI.'

'What?' Charlie exclaimed, still not fully awake. He was aware of Gloria's eyes on him.

203

'He's in the city jail. The girl's in the county hospital.'

'What happened?'

'I don't know, all I *do* know is he went down on his bike. Nothing else,' Stutz answered. 'I haven't had time to look into it. I don't want anyone to think I'm too interested.'

'How bad's the girl?'

'I'm not sure. Like I said, I haven't been able to find out too much about it yet.'

'We need to get Edward out.'

'He's the one who's going to have the answers. Can you do it?'

'Sure, no problem.'

'By the way, the ME's report on Surfer came in today. They didn't find any cocaine in his body.' Stutz paused, allowing Charlie time to digest this piece of information.

'That means it wasn't accidental, doesn't it?'

'Yeah, that's what I would have to think. It was a set-up. Whoever it was just got a little too cute.'

'Are they looking into it?' Charlie asked and heard a disgusted sigh from the other end of the line.

'No, they're going with it as an accident. There's also something else about this whole thing that's kind of interesting.'

'What's that?'

'Not now. I've got to get back on patrol. You get Ryan out and talk to him and I'll get in touch with you later this afternoon. There's a few things I want to look into first, before I say anything.'

'Bo?'

'Yeah.'

'Be careful, all right? This whole thing is getting a little scary.'

'Tell me about it,' Stutz answered wearily and hung up.

Charlie caught Gloria's inquisitive glance. 'Edward's in jail. He was in some kind of accident last night and they picked him up on a DUI.'

'Is he all right?'

Charlie glanced away.

'Is he?'

'I didn't even think to ask.' He turned to face her. 'I never even thought about it.'

Gloria touched his hand. 'It's all right. I think it's just a matter of knowing who he is.' She smiled. 'He seems like one of those people who's never going to get hurt.'

His eyes caught hers. When she looked away, he knew without having to ask that the memory they had both briefly shared proved her wrong.

'Dad?' Elaine pleaded.

'It's up to your mother,' Charlie said, gulping a cup of coffee as he tried to button his shirt with his free hand.

'But I just want to go up to the mall,' she said, glaring up at him impatiently.

Charlie looked at her, discerning the beginning swell of her breasts and the curve of her hips. It frightened him that she was so quickly becoming a young woman, or rather that physically she was becoming a woman, while emotionally she was still so much a child.

He thought of the photographs. 'No, you do what your mother's told you.'

'Oh, Dad,' she groaned and stomped out of the room.

Charlie turned and caught Gloria's eye. He glanced away when he saw the fear he felt reflected in her gaze. 'I'm going to get Edward. I'll call you later.'

'Bring him back with you, okay?'

'I will,' he promised and went out to his car.

He pulled onto the highway and quickly turned towards the police station.

Ryan let the drift take him. He watched the scene redevelop, until it began to unwind before him without any conscious effort on his part.

'Fucking kids,' his father muttered, as he staggered across the living-room. He held a half empty bottle of Jack Daniels. A cigarette dangled from his lips. Ryan watched the ash slowly topple down the front of his father's greasy T-shirt.

'You fucking kids never do anything you're supposed to do,' his father ranted, swinging around drunkenly to glare at the two of them.

Neal sat beside him on the couch. Ryan could feel his leg pressed against his own. He felt it quivering uncontrollably.

'If just once, just one goddamn time, you'd do what you're supposed to do, none of this, not one fucking bit of this shit,' his father screamed, waving his arms to encompass the house, his wife, and seemingly his whole life, 'would be the way it is.'

His father suddenly paused. He swayed precariously then caught his balance. It took him two attempts to capture his cigarette from his lips. He glared at the burning end, then slowly began to smile. He turned his gaze on the two boys seated in front of him.

Ryan tried to hold his father's glance. He quickly looked away. His eyes fell to his brother's bare legs. Crisscrossed along the top of Neal's thighs were a series of welts. Some of the welts had scabbed over. A few of them still bled.

'It's all your fault,' his father suddenly shouted, whirling around to glare at his wife.

Elsa flinched and raised her arms protectively in front of her chest.

'I told you. No goddamn rug rats, but no, you fucking bitch, no fucking way.' His father raised the bottle.

Ryan watched his adam's-apple bob as he drank. He put his arm around his brother's shoulder. Neal sniffled softly and turned his head into Ryan's side.

'You little faggot,' his father sneered, turning on Neal.

'Leave him alone.'

'Why, what're you going to do about it?' his father taunted his elder son.

'Just leave him alone.'

'Eat shit.' His father reached out and slapped the back of Neal's head.

Ryan tried to bat the hand away as it swung out at Neal.

'Faggot.'

'Leave him alone.'

'Fuck you, too, you little pansy asshole.' His father took a drag of his cigarette, then carefully examined the burning end. He swayed, then leaned over Neal. The fiery end of the cigarette descended towards Neal's neck.

Ryan jumped off the sofa. He heard his mother's startled gasp as he slapped his father's hand away. For a moment his father's eyes glared back at him soberly. He found this more frightening than the drunken gaze.

'You want some, big boy. You want some of this,' his father threatened, taking a step back and raising his fists.

Ryan held his ground.

His father threw the Daniels bottle at the wall. It smashed to the floor. The smell of sour mash swamped the house, overriding the other odors of must and sweat.

'Well here we go, big man. Let's see what you got.'

Ryan attempted to duck the first punch, but it caught him on the top of the head and knocked him to the floor. Dazed, he tried to push himself to his feet, but his father's boot quickly lashed out and thudded into his chest.

Ryan rolled away, remembering the pain of the broken ribs, and the length of time it had taken for them to heal.

'C'mon, you little fuck, what're you going to do now?'

'Abner, don't,' Ryan heard his mother wail as he struggled to his feet. He glanced over to see Neal lying face down across the couch. He could see his brother's head shaking back and forth. 'No, no, no,' he heard his muffled voice chanting, and then his father kicked him in the crotch.

The pain was like nothing he had ever felt before. It went beyond the cigarettes, the belt and the whiplash razor sharpness of the bamboo. It was a dull, expanding pain that worked its way through his whole body and left him gasping for breath, unable even to moan.

'Fish fuck,' his father sneered and wheeled round.

Ryan clutched his knees to his chest, listening to his father's footsteps retreating to the front door. When it crashed closed his mother hurried over to him. He felt her hand on his back. He heard her sob and opened his eyes to see Neal sitting on the couch, rocking back and forth. His eyes were tightly shut and his mouth was twisted into a wretched grimace. 'Neal,' Ryan gasped and fell back to the floor. He heard the sound of his father's truck start up and pull out of the yard.

'He's gone now,' his mother sighed.

And Ryan knew, even as the noise of the engine faded into the distance, that it wasn't enough, because his father was always going to come back.

'Edward Ryan?'

Ryan jerked up from his bunk. It took him a moment to realize where he was. He rose and stepped towards the front of the cell.

'You got a friend,' the jailer told him and unlocked the door.

Ryan followed him down a concrete hallway. They both waited for the release buzzer to unlock the entrance door.

He saw Charlie standing by the sergeant's desk and nodded to him. He caught the direction of Charlie's gaze and glanced down at himself. His Harley T-shirt was torn and stained. The left leg of his jeans was shredded along the side and caked with dried mud and blood. He glanced back at Charlie and shrugged.

'Check your stuff and sign.'

Ryan picked up his wallet, belt, cigarettes and pocket change, and signed the sheet. He was handed a receipt for his personals, along with a ticket informing him of the charges brought against him.

'You okay?'

'Yeah, let's just get the hell out of here.' Ryan moved quickly towards the door. He welcomed the sudden rush of humid air.

'You look like hell.'

'How's the girl?' Ryan asked, brushing aside Charlie's concern.

Charlie shrugged. 'I don't know. Stutz called me a little while ago and told me what happened. As far as he knew, she was all right,' Charlie said, examining his friend closely. 'Why don't we swing by your motel and get you some clothes and I'll tell you what's going on.'

Ryan nodded.

'You first,' Charlie said, after he started his car.

Ryan pulled a cigarette and lit up. He inhaled deeply. 'First non-smoking jail I've ever been in. Your town sure has some weird priorities, Charlie,' he commented and began to outline what had happened the night before.

'I don't know if the guy was watching her or me, but he sure the hell was there,' Ryan finished, as they pulled in and parked in front of his room.

'Did you get a look at him?'

'No, just the make of the car, and that didn't do me too much good. I don't think they even listened. They took one look at me and that was it.' Ryan opened the door to his room and stepped inside. 'Comes down to me or a citizen, it's usually the other guy who wins.'

'You're the one who made that choice.'

Ryan paused and turned to stare at his friend. 'No,' he said quietly, 'that was a choice that was made for me a long time ago.'

He grabbed some clothes and disappeared into the bathroom.

Charlie sat on the edge of the bed and listened to the sound of the shower coming from the other room. He pulled the photographs from Ryan's duffle-bag and forced himself to examine them.

When Ryan stepped out of the bathroom toweling his hair, he found Charlie leaning over the prints. 'You find anything new?'

'No, nothing.'

'If we just had one clear shot of a face it would give us somewhere to start.'

Ryan sat and lit another cigarette. 'Tell me what Stutz said.'

Charlie repeated their conversation. He finished as Ryan pulled on his boots.

'He also mentioned he found out something about Surfer, something he wanted to look into a little more closely before he said anything.'

Ryan stared over at him.

'I don't know.' Charlie shrugged. 'He wouldn't say anything more about it.'

Ryan nodded. 'Let's get out to the hospital.'

'What did they end up charging you with?'

'DUI, reckless driving and endangerment.'

'Christ, what would they have done if you'd been hurt badly?' Charlie said in disgust.

'Probably added attempted suicide,' Ryan commented dryly.

Stutz was scared. Up until that morning he hadn't completely believed what he suspected. He had felt that the Point Blank Security incident could have been an isolated situation. Even Surfer and the photographs hadn't actually frightened him. They had angered him, but he hadn't felt truly threatened by either discovery.

This morning he had read the ME's report. The lack of cocaine in the man's system made it clear that whoever had set it up had wanted it to look like just another drug death. Stutz hadn't been too surprised by this. The way the force had decided to handle the case also seemed fairly predictable to him. The death of one more druggie, especially one without any relatives to stir up the water, was not something the police force was going to examine too closely. It was this line of thinking that had led him to run Surfer's prints.

Within fifteen minutes, a positive ID had come back from Tallahassee.

Thomas Langley, a.k.a. Surfer, was wanted on three separate drug warrants in Dade, Hillsborough and Nassau counties. Along with these warrants there was an additional one for armed robbery out of Alachua county.

Stutz had then checked the back files. He found a file, marked closed, listed under the name Harold 'Surfer' Thomas. Surfer had been picked up six months ago for procurement. He had been arrested, booked and kept overnight. The following morning the charge had been dropped due to lack of evidence, and Surfer had been released.

It was this final piece of information that terrified Stutz.

Surfer had been finger-printed. What had happened to the prints?

Stutz quickly checked out a car and left the station. He drove up to the county hospital. He wanted to talk to the girl as soon as possible, and he wanted to do it before Ryan had a chance to see her. He still wasn't sure about Ryan.

He pulled into the county lot and climbed out at the entrance way to the emergency room.

'I'd like to check on', he pulled out his notebook from his back pocket and read, 'Lailya Conally'.

The woman behind the desk directed him to the fourth floor.

Stutz took the elevator and stepped out into the cool antiseptic atmosphere of the hospital. He walked down to the nursing station.

'Lailya Conally?' The nurse glanced up at him sharply.

'What is it?'

'Well, I'm sorry, officer, but Miss Conally passed away this morning', she glanced down at her notes, 'at nine sixteen. If you'd like to talk to the attending physician . . .?'

Stutz shook his head in stunned silence. He backed away from the desk and took the stairs down to the street.

As he climbed into his patrol car, he heard his call sign and checked in.

'. . . wanted for vehicular homicide, approach with all caution,' he heard and signed off.

'Shit,' Stutz muttered and slammed his fist against the wheel.

He started up his squad car and quickly pulled in front of the hospital. He eased into a parking place between a Chevy van and a pick-up truck. The two other vehicles successfully hid his car from casual sight.

His parking place gave him a clear vantage point from which he could view the hospital entrance. He leaned back and waited. He knew they'd show up soon.

Twenty-Three

By eight o'clock that morning, Joe Ball had discovered the where-abouts of the Conally girl. Fifteen minutes later he had stepped up to the admission desk at the county hospital.

His perseverance in completing the brief was now more out of fear than any sense of professionalism. The voice knew too much about him. Joe wanted to close the brief out as quickly as possible and begin the complicated journey that would eventually lead him to South America and a new identity.

At the hospital he had been informed of the girl's death earlier that morning. Joe Ball was considerably cheered by this piece of information. Ingratiating himself with one of the nurses' aides, he had also discovered that the man responsible for the accident was incarcerated in the city jail.

An hour and a half later, he pulled up to the side entrance of the Radisson Hotel on Camora Island. He left his car in a waiting zone, entered the hotel through a side door and took the elevator up to his floor. He had just unlocked his door and stepped inside when he heard the buzz of the phone.

Without thinking, he quickly picked it up. Only later would it occur to him how perfect the timing had been. Almost as if someone had known the exact moment he would get to the room.

'Mr Ball.'

'Yes.' He recognized the voice immediately.

'You did quite well with the girl. I am pleased. But there has been a slight problem.' There was a pause.

Deciding not to enlighten the voice about his part in the girl's death Joe Ball waited for the rest of it.

'The girl managed to identify you before she died.'

213

'How the hell could she? She never even saw me. She wasn't anywhere . . .'

'I have no idea. I only know that an identification was made,' the voice interrupted. 'I suggest that you leave the area at once. I will keep you informed of any further developments. Thank you.'

Joe Ball stared at the dead receiver, hung up and packed the remainder of his belongings. He took the elevator to the ground floor and hurried out of the side door to his car.

He threw his suitcase into the back and placed a .22 Woodsman on the seat beside him. He covered it with his windbreaker and started up the car. He wanted the gun within easy reach so he could dump it as soon as he found a reasonably safe place to do so.

He took the turn-off to the Camora Island shuttle service. Coconut palms lined each side of the residential street. Bougainvillaea bushes bloomed in lush scarlet colors along the edges of the properties. Ahead of him, he saw a prop-driven airplane shoot across the implacable blue sky.

He looked in his rear-view mirror at a squad car coming up quickly behind him. He forced himself to keep within the speed limit as he watched it grow larger. He glanced ahead. He was only twenty yards from the entrance to the shuttle service. Once on the plane, it would be an easy jump to Tampa, then up into Georgia. From there he could be out of the country later tonight or early tomorrow morning.

The sudden shriek of a siren drew his eyes to the mirror. The squad was directly behind him, its lights flashing.

Joe Ball glanced anxiously at the entrance way, only ten yards ahead, and reluctantly pulled off to the side of the road. He forced himself to remain calm as he turned to watch a patrolman climb out from the driver's side of the squad. The man's hand was on the butt of his service revolver. Joe Ball swiveled round to see another policeman ease out of the passenger door. They approached cautiously.

'What can I do for you?' Joe Ball smiled.

'Sir, would you please step out of the car.'

'Why? What seems to be the problem?'

'Please get out, sir.'

The two patrolmen stood a short distance from his door. The one speaking was the closest. The other stayed a few feet away to the side of his partner's right shoulder, with his gaze locked on Joe Ball.

'Out,' the patrolman ordered, his hand tightening on his service revolver.

Joe Ball nodded. He reached for his doorhandle, throwing a quick glance towards the airport. It was within walking distance.

He fumbled at the handle, using the motion to cover the movement of his other hand. He opened the door and got out.

'Put your hands on the roof.'

Joe Ball looked at the two men. Neither of them was much older than twenty-five. He smiled and shrugged. He started to turn, then quickly spun round bringing his gun up to bear on the two men. 'Nothing. Not a fucking sound.'

The policeman directly in front of him froze in place. The other one moved.

Joe Ball shot him in the chest. The blow staggered him. He lurched back, grabbing his chest, and fell to the ground.

His second shot clipped the other patrolman in the shoulder and spun him completely round. The movement threw Joe's third shot wide. By this time the policeman had managed to level his own gun. Joe Ball's next shot caught him in the stomach. The blow doubled him over. His finger jerked against the trigger and his gun went off. The shot hit Joe in the neck, traveled upwards through his jaw and into his brain.

Joe Ball staggered back against the car door. A gushing arc of blood spun out into the sunlight. It seemed momentarily to hang in mid-air, with all the evanescence of a rainbow, before splattering across the pavement.

Joe Ball slowly slid to the ground, then toppled over onto his side.

'You ever dream about Daddy?' Lisa asked softly.

Ollie squinted up at her from where he was crouched over her shoe.

'Daddy,' he said thoughtfully. 'Daddy went away.'

Lisa nodded and watched as Ollie went back to her shoelaces. She was trying to teach him how to tie a bow.

'Daddy's coming home in June,' Ollie said abruptly, tugging on her laces, trying to figure out what went where.

'Do you ever dream about him sometimes?'

Ollie's tongue was stuck out of the side of his mouth in concentration. He moved it to the middle and shook his head.

'Never?'

'Daddy's coming in June,' he said angrily and jerked on her laces.

'Hey, that hurts.'

'In June,' Ollie shouted, suddenly standing up and glaring at her. 'He's coming home in June.'

'In June,' Lisa agreed softly.

Ollie examined her closely, grinned and began his noises. He raced down the porch and zigzagged across the front yard.

Lisa crouched over and tied her shoe.

'What're you doing, hon?'

She glanced over her shoulder at her mother. 'Nothing.'

Maggie came and sat beside her. She put her arm round her daughter and looked at her son running around in circles on the front lawn. She shook her head, smiling with fond exasperation.

'Ollie thinks Daddy's coming home in June,' Lisa said quietly.

Maggie glanced over at her quickly, but Lisa wouldn't meet her eye. She smoothed the back of her daughter's hair. 'Does he?'

'Yes.' Lisa turned to her mother. Maggie wanted to look away, but forced herself to meet her daughter's serious gaze. 'He isn't coming home, ever again, is he?'

'No, hon, he isn't.'

'He's dead, isn't he?'

'Yes.' Maggie sighed.

Lisa nodded solemnly. She looked at Ollie who paused to smile up at them. 'Are you going to tell Ollie?'

'Yes.'

'When?'

'When he'll understand,' Maggie said. 'When do you think would be a good time?'

Lisa shrugged and turned away. She wiped at her eyes and stared out at the front yard. 'I don't want Daddy to be dead,' she said quietly, and Maggie turned and took her in her arms. She listened to the sounds of her daughter crying, as she heard her son's engine noises circling the house.

Maggie sat at the kitchen table with her magazine in front of her. She turned the pages listlessly, without seeing anything but the garish photographs displayed inside. None of it seemed to make any sense to her. How could all this still be in existence, when her own life no longer seemed to share that same existence.

She leaned back and picked up her coffee cup. Ollie was taking a nap upstairs and Lisa had gone next door. Maggie listened to the quiet house and found the silence threatening. She stood up abruptly and turned on the radio. She turned it to a local, easy-listening station and refilled her coffee cup, carrying it back to the table and her magazine. She turned to an article she had been trying to read the other day, which was marked with the envelope she had found. It was still unopened. The name Edward Ryan, printed in blue ink, was in sharp contrast to the aged paper. She picked it up and held it to the light, then replaced it a moment later and closed the magazine.

'Police authorities identified the body as Joseph Leland Ball of Leslie, Georgia. Ball, a reputed contract hit man, has been linked to the deaths of local banker John Caldwell and Neal Ryan. Both men were shot down earlier this month. Police . . .'

Maggie closed her eyes tightly and leaned over the table, her hands pressed against her stomach as if trying to keep the pain in place. It welled out of her. She sobbed and, unable to stop herself, leaned forward and cried.

Charlie pulled up to the emergency room of the hospital and parked.

Ryan glanced pointedly at the 'no parking' signs liberally posted around the area.

'Power of the press.' Charlie winked and climbed out of his car.

Ryan followed him into the emergency room. The admitting nurse sent them to the front desk. They took the stairs up to the first floor and stepped out onto the lobby of the hospital. Near the information desk was a young woman holding a microphone. Standing behind her an older man aimed a camcorder at her, and another man stood beside her with both hands over his face.

'What the hell's that all about?'

'That's Jean Riley, Channel 7 News,' Charlie answered, moving towards the three people.

'Mr Conally, the man you saw last night, was he your daughter's boyfriend?'

The man pulled his hands away.

Ryan stopped and stared at him. He had shaved and changed into a clean pair of jeans and shirt, but his eyes were still the same bloodshot color as the night before.

'She was my little girl,' the man wailed. The cameraman moved in closer. 'She was all I had and someone took her away from me,' he cried. 'I did everything for her, everything she ever wanted she had. I just can't . . .' The man suddenly stopped, burying his face in his hands.

Charlie stepped up to another newsman standing beside the cameraman. The man greeted him and passed on the news of the girl's death, earlier that morning.

'Doctor Allen Firth was the attending physician. Dr Firth,' the newswoman said, turning to a dapper-looking elderly man standing behind her, 'could you explain what happened?'

Dr Firth nodded solemnly to the camera. 'The girl was admitted late last night. She had been the victim of a motorcycle accident. There was a head injury and she was disoriented and severely traumatized by the injury. We immediately stabilized the patient and began treatment.' The doctor paused. He looked at the camera sadly and shook his head. 'We just do not have the necessary facilities to take the proper precautions in cases such as this. If the previous tax referendum had been passed this unfortunate occurrence never would have taken place.'

Charlie turned and quickly made his way back to Ryan. 'Let's get out of here.'

Ryan nodded and started towards the door. As he turned he caught the doctor's eye. The momentary flash of recognition that crossed the other's face surprised him.

'C'mon, we've got to move.'

'Why?' Ryan asked.

'There's a warrant out for you.'

Ryan looked over at him sharply.

'They're calling it vehicular homicide.'

They started down the front steps of the hospital.

'Hold it right there.'

They halted and saw Stutz standing a few feet in front of them.

'Jesus, did you hear what happ . . .' Charlie stopped abruptly as he saw the gun leveled in Edward's direction.

'This way.' Stutz motioned them towards his squad car.

'What are you doing, Bo?'

'C'mon. Now,' Stutz ordered.

Ryan held his gaze and, with a shrug, turned and moved towards the car.

'Bo, just what the hell do you think you're doing?'

'Just shut up, Charlie, and move.'

Stutz trailed a few feet behind them. He hid his gun from sight, but kept it pointed at their backs.

'What now?' Ryan asked insolently as he stopped by the side of the car and turned to face the policeman.

Stutz reached backwards and pulled out his handcuffs. 'You know the position. Take it.'

Ryan snorted in disgust, turned and put his hands behind his back.

'Judge Roland Wilson had informed local authorities about the blackmail demand earlier this morning. "The man called me at my home and demanded twenty thousand dollars in cash to be delivered at some unspecified location. He said if I did not deliver the cash I would suffer serious consequences." Judge Wilson, through a bit of detective work of his own, was able to ascertain Ball's location through his answering service. He called the authorities who intercepted Ball on his way to the airport. Services for Patrolman Sorenson, who was killed in today's shooting, will be held Thursday afternoon. Patrolman Honewell is still listed in critical condition at Collier County Hospital. Now on to the weather.'

Richard smiled as he reached over and turned off the radio. He leaned back wearily and looked out at the placid surface of the Gulf. He'd had an exhausting, albeit successful, morning.

He picked up the phone on the first ring.

'Did you hear it?'

'Yes, I did, Roland. I congratulate you on your detective work.'

Roland laughed, then began to cough. When he had managed to recover himself he said, 'I rather enjoyed that part of it.'

'You did very well. I think we have put everything in its proper place now.' Richard paused to pick up his orange juice. 'Will there be any problem with the brother?'

'No, I'll have it assigned to my docket. No one will think anything about it,' Roland assured the other man.

'If there is, we can always call Robert.'

'No, no problem, Richard. I can take care of it through my office.'

'Excellent.'

'Richard?'

'Yes?'

'Are we all right now?' the other man asked hesitantly.

'Yes.' Richard smiled contentedly. 'We're just fine.'

Richard took Allen's call later that afternoon. The doctor was buoyant about his appearance on the Channel 7 afternoon news.

'I saw Ryan at the hospital.'

'Yes?'

'He was with that reporter.'

'It's only a matter of time before he's picked up.'

'And then?'

'Then his case will be assigned to Judge Wilson.'

'Ah, that works out rather well, doesn't it?' Allen said happily.

'Yes, it does,' Richard assured him.

Late that afternoon Richard took Marjorie to a cocktail party at the Royal Port Country Club. He mingled with the other guests. All the members of the group were there and throughout the afternoon Richard made it a point to stop by each of them and inform them of its current status. He reassured them that everything was going according to plan.

He found Robert standing in a corner off from the rest of the party, glumly sipping his drink.

'It's only a few weeks.'

Robert glanced up disconsolately. 'I'm seventy-four years old, Richard. A few weeks can be a long time.'

Richard gripped his shoulder warmly. 'Robert,' he shook his head fondly at the other man, 'you've years left to spend in pursuit of the finer things in life.'

Robert snorted. 'Easy for you to say.'

'I'm sixty-eight years old, Robert. Leonard's seventy, Roland's sixty-nine. None of us is a young man any more.' Richard paused and smiled conspiratorially. 'But we've all learned the secret of eternal youth.'

'And what's that?'

'That age is merely a matter of sustaining interest. If one can learn how constantly to pique that interest one can be young for ever.'

'Councilman Raynor?' They both turned as a local contractor made his way over to them. 'I've been meaning to talk to you about the upcoming impact fees the city's talking about passing.' Robert turned to the man. 'It would damage the local economy drastically. I was hoping we might be able to get together on this.' The contractor shot a suspicious glance at Richard.

'Excuse me, gentlemen.' Richard moved away. He caught Robert's eye. The other man winked at him and turned to the contractor. His hand came up and warmly gripped his shoulder. 'Well, you know, there might just be something we can work out.' Richard heard Robert say smoothly, as he manipulated the contractor towards a room off from the main party.

Richard watched them disappear. He tried to calculate what the contractor's worth might be to the group, but then shook away from the thought as a waitress passed by. He grabbed a glass of champagne and carried it over to the window overlooking the beach.

There was a huge multicolored blanket spread across the sand. Lying on top of it were three young girls, none of them older than thirteen. He became aware of someone else standing at the window and saw Allen avidly eyeing the girls. He moved down and stood beside the other man. 'Don't even think about it, Dr Firth.'

Startled, Allen whirled round, spilling some of his drink. Recognizing Richard, he relaxed.

'I'm serious, Allen. We can't afford any mistakes at this point. Everything is being arranged. Another two or three weeks will see us clear of all this.'

Allen looked out of the window at the girls, then, with a dismayed sigh, turned back to survey the room.

Richard moved across the floor to join Marjorie. She held a full glass of amber liquid. Richard could smell the pungent odor of bourbon surrounding her.

'Ah, Richard,' she smiled gaily, 'I was just telling Harriet how you used to be such a hot-shot commodities trader.'

Richard turned to the woman standing beside his wife. She was in her late fifties. She wore a short white sun-dress that left her shoulders bare and also offered a generous display of leg. Her face was unlined and flawlessly made-up. Her blue eyes focused intently on his.

'My late husband was in securities,' she said, arching one dark eyebrow.

Richard sensed her interest in him. He examined her carefully. When he spotted the faint, tell-tale scars at the edge of her hairline he smiled charmingly. 'How interesting,' he said, without the faintest hint of sincerity.

The woman's gaze faltered for a moment. She was not used to being dismissed so readily. She recovered quickly and asked, 'Have you lived here long?'

'We have,' Richard answered without elaborating.

Marjorie anxiously signaled to a waiter with her empty glass. The woman glanced over at her, then turned her gaze back to Richard. She cocked her head slightly, as if waiting for him to make a comment.

Richard ignored her and moved away, enjoying the woman's startled expression. He felt her eyes follow him as he drifted across the room. He enjoyed rejecting her almost as much as he felt insulted that she had the audacity to think she might be of interest to him.

Richard drove home later that evening and helped Marjorie up the stairs and into bed. He took off her shoes and removed her dress. He folded the dress carefully peeled off her undergarments and when she was sprawled across the bed snoring softly he stepped back to examine her naked body. Her withered breasts sagged to either side of her pale chest. Each nipple was surrounded by an array of tiny white scars. Along her thighs were other scars. Richard bent over to examine them more closely. He turned away abruptly as he caught the scent of age and decay coming from her. He covered her with a sheet. Her body no longer held any interest for him.

He poured himself a brandy and carried it into his den. He turned on the desk light and pulled a set of keys from his pocket. Unlocking the bottom desk drawer he pulled out a photograph album. On the cover was a picture of a young girl racing across a lush field of sunflowers. A butterfly wafted just out of her reach.

Richard opened the album to the first photograph. He leaned over it, carefully studying each wound in the young girl's body. His breath grew ragged as he turned the pages and intently examined each of the prints on display.

When he closed the album his face was flushed. His hand shook as he picked up his brandy. Sipping, he leaned back in his chair and waited for the moment. He knew it would happen soon.

He reached into the bottom desk drawer again. This time he pulled out a nine-by-twelve manila folder. He laid it on the desk, leaned back and closed his eyes.

When it began, he quickly opened the folder and pulled out the photo inside. He held it in front of his face as he leaned back. The girl in the photograph had been crucified. She was nailed to two cross-beamed two-by-fours. The nails punctured her hands and feet. She was eleven years old. She was naked. Neither of these conditions appeared to bother the man who was pictured masturbating over her face.

Richard groaned as he felt the flood of warmth work its way along his thighs until it concentrated in his groin. He gasped hoarsely, then jerked his hips forward as the meager spurt of hot moisture dampened his stomach.

After showering he climbed into bed. He kept well away from the warm, slightly musty body of his wife. He slept, and his dreams were unspeakably pleasurable.

Twenty-Four

Phillipe Veros was in his second year of internship. His parents had been migrant workers. After the birth of their only child they had settled in Immokalee, a farm community situated forty miles north-east of Siena.

Saving every cent they could manage, they had insured that their son would have more of an opportunity in life than had ever been available for either of them.

Phillipe had been the first Veros to complete high school. He won a scholarship to the University of South Florida and both his parents felt that their years of deprivation had been amply rewarded. When he graduated with honors and was accepted for medical school in Chicago their pride knew no bounds. To have a son that would be a doctor was a possibility beyond all belief.

Rosita Veros died during Phillipe's first year of medical school. After the funeral Phillipe took his father aside and told him that enough was enough. He was going to quit medical school and take a job with a pharmaceutical company. The money, he told his father, would insure that the remainder of his life would be much easier. 'I only regret that I didn't do this earlier. I wish that Mother could have benefited as well,' Phillipe had told him.

José Veros, who had spent his whole life in other people's fields caring for and picking their crops, reached out and cuffed his son across the ear. 'You will do no such thing. It would shame me and the memory of your mother to think that you would even consider such as this. You are to be a doctor, and if you are not to be a doctor then you are not to be my son,' José had said.

Phillipe completed medical school. Of the twenty-two offers he received for internships he applied only to the one in Siena. His application was accepted immediately.

The majority of the general staff considered Phillipe Veros to have the potential to be one of the finest surgeons ever to grace the Siena Hospital's corridors. He had a delicacy of touch and an almost uncanny ability for diagnostics.

Phillipe Veros specialized in trauma-induced injuries.

Stutz located the house off Santa Barbara Drive in The Gate. It was a modest ranch house, contained by a half-acre plot of land. What set it apart from the surrounding ones was the lush garden blooming along each side of the path. Rose bushes, bougainvillaea and pale purple wistaria blossomed brightly across the dark-green lawn.

Stutz paused to admire the garden and walked up to the front door. An elderly Mexican man answered his knock. 'I would like to speak to Phillipe Veros.'

The man examined him warily before finally motioning him inside. 'I will get my son.'

Stutz stood in front of the window and looked out at the profusion of flowers and vines traversing the yard.

'My father did that.'

Stutz turned to the voice. He saw a young man, wearing only a worn pair of shorts, standing before him. 'Phillipe Veros?'

'Yes.' The younger man nodded. 'And who are you?'

'Boland Stutz, I'm with the Siena police force.'

'What can I do for you?' Phillipe motioned for Stutz to be seated. 'Would you like something to drink?'

'No thanks.' Stutz shook his head and asked, 'You were working the emergency room the other night?'

'Yes.'

'Do you remember a young girl being admitted, she'd been in a motorcycle accident?' Stutz asked, and for a brief moment saw something flicker across the younger man's face. It passed too quickly for him to identify.

'Yes, I remember her. She was very young.'

'You admitted her?'

'Yes, I did. Dr Firth handled the case.'

'What condition was she in when you saw her?'

'Why?'

'Just filling in some blanks.'

The other man examined him carefully before responding. 'Minor lacerations and contusions along her right arm and leg. Nothing very serious. The main problem was the head injury. She was disoriented and displayed retinal abbreviation.'

'What does that mean?'

'At the very least a concussion.'

'And at the worst?'

'Possible damage to the skull or brain.' Stutz nodded. 'But as I said, Dr Firth handled the case.' The young man did not meet his eye.

Stutz leaned forward. 'What did you do when you admitted her?'

'This sounds like more than just filling in the blanks,' Phillipe said quietly.

Stutz held the other man's gaze. 'Tell me about Dr Firth.'

'Dr Firth oversees all surgery taking place on the fourth floor.' Noticing Stutz's expression he elaborated. 'Head trauma.'

'He's good, then?'

Phillipe shook his head. 'I can't discuss this with you.'

'I can see that you're forced to.'

Phillipe leaned back and examined the policeman thoughtfully. Slowly he nodded. 'Yes, you probably could, but I don't think you will.' He clasped his hands before him and held Stutz's gaze. Stutz was the first to glance away. 'What is it you're looking for? Maybe if you told me I might be able to help.'

Stutz pushed himself to his feet and walked over to the window. 'Did Firth do anything with the girl that could have caused her death?'

'What are you trying to say?'

Stutz turned to look at the young man. 'I'm not *trying* to say anything, Dr Veros. I'm saying it.'

'That would be impossible.' Phillipe shook his head.

Again, Stutz noticed a hesitation in the doctor's face. 'Why don't you just tell me what caused the girl's death?'

'A blood clot, that's all there was to it. It's always a danger with head injuries. Whenever there is internal damage there's always the possibility of a clot forming and being released.'

'Aren't there ways to insure that this doesn't happen?'

'Yes.'

'Were those precautions taken?' Phillipe met his eye, then looked towards the window. 'Were they taken?' Stutz asked again.

'It was a judgment call,' Phillipe said quietly, turning towards Stutz and meeting his gaze.

'What would your judgement have been?'

'I would have gone on the assumption that there was a possibility of a clot forming. Dr Firth, obviously, did not.'

'Has this ever happened before with Firth?'

'No.'

Stutz eyed the other man carefully. 'Why don't you tell me about Dr Firth.'

'Why should I?' the young doctor challenged.

'I think you already know the answer to that,' Stutz said and waited.

Phillipe nodded reluctantly, leaned forward and began to talk.

Stutz listened carefully, transcribing his words into his notebook.

The apartment block had been built quickly and cheaply in the boom of the early Eighties. The rotting wood and peeling paint attested to the fact that little had been done to it since then. It was a two-storey building with ten units on each floor. The second storey had a rickety aluminum railing that lined the outer walkway. The building was erected in a U-shape. In the center of the U was a picnic table.

When Charlie walked up to the unit three men sat around the table, drinking bottled beer from a case placed beneath the shaded table top. The men watched silently as he took the stairs up to the second floor. He knocked on the door of 206 and heard a flurry of motion from inside. He knocked again.

'What d'you want?' The woman standing in the doorway wore a pair of jean cut-offs and an armless T-shirt. Charlie could see the swell of her sagging breasts through each armhole.

'You're Mrs Cox?'

'Who wants to know?'

'I'm Charlie Benning, I'm with the *Siena News*.'

'So what?' The woman stared back at him impassively.

'I wanted to talk to you about your daughter.'

The woman pushed back a strand of greasy black hair. Charlie noticed a tattoo on the back of her arm.

'What about her?'

'Is she home?'

'No.'

'Do you expect her soon?'

The woman shrugged and sighed in irritation. 'I'm losing all my air.'

'Then why don't I come inside. It *is* kind of hot.' Charlie smiled.

She snorted disdainfully and stepped back from the door.

Charlie entered. A wall air-conditioning unit wheezed asthmatically. It did little more than move the hot air around the room. Below it was a large metal pan, half-filled with rusty water. A frayed couch and two mismatched chairs surrounded an RCA TV set. Of the four pieces of furniture the TV appeared to be the only one purchased within the last five years.

'So what's the little bitch done now?' the woman asked as she sprawled in one of the chairs. She lifted one leg, spotted with dark bruises, and rested it over the arm.

'Nothing, I just wanted to ask you, or her, a few questions.'

'About what?' The woman reached down beside her chair and came up with a bottle of beer.

'School, work,' Charlie shrugged, 'things like that.'

'I thought you said you were with the newspaper. Sounds more like some welfare bullshit to me.' She glared at him suspiciously.

'I am. I just needed to follow up on a story I was working on.'

'And what story might that be?'

'Lailya Conally.'

'Who's that?'

'She was the girl who died the other night. The one in the motor-cycle accident.'

'So what's this got to do with Deb? She know her or something?' The woman lifted the bottle and drank. There was a ring of grime round her neck.

'Yes, she did.'

She shrugged. 'Well, like I said, she ain't home.' She examined Charlie carefully through narrowed eyes. Her leg bent at the knee. The vee of her shorts rode up over her thighs. 'She might be home in a little while. You could wait if you want.'

'Where is she?'

'Working, maybe.'

'Where does she work?'

'Limpy's.' The woman smiled for the first time. Her front teeth were a dark yellow color.

'Maybe I'll try to catch her there.'

'It's up to you.' She shrugged, shifting her leg a little more.

Charlie turned quickly and opened the door. He heard the woman mutter something behind him but kept going.

The men all turned to watch him walk out of the complex. Charlie felt their eyes boring into his back as he went out and climbed into his car.

He drove out to the Limpy's on the south highway. He stepped through the front doors into the cool interior of the franchise, and order a Limpy Burger, fries and a coke. As he waited for his order he examined the girls behind the counter, trying to locate Debbie. After he was sure she wasn't there he carried his burger over to a table and sat down.

He finished his coke and went up to the trash bin by the counter. One of the girls walked over to him as he deposited his refuse. 'May I help you?' She smiled.

Charlie glanced at her and suddenly froze.

'Sir, may I help you?' He couldn't tear his eyes away. 'Sir?'

Charlie turned and quickly left the franchise. He drove back into Siena and out to the other Limpy's on the north highway. In this one he ordered only a coke, carried it over to a table and drank it while he watched the girls behind the counter.

He left ten minutes later and drove down to the newspaper building. He hurried into his office and immediately went to work on the computer. For two hours he worked without let-up and with little success.

He left the newspaper building and drove out to the County Court House. He ignored the information directory and walked quickly down the cool hallway to the last office at the end of the hall.

He spent another two hours pulling up information from the computer. This time his efforts were rewarded.

He drove quickly back to Ryan's motel in Olde Siena, parked and walked down to room 10. The door was open. Charlie walked in and sat down. He glanced at his watch nervously, then forced himself to lean back and wait.

Ryan sat in the front seat of his rental car. He slumped back against the seat and watched the entrance to the office building across the street. Finally, at three thirty, people started to leave.

By four thirty, the steady stream exiting the building had stopped. Ryan climbed out of his car and went in. He took the stairs to the second floor and walked down to the office. He paused outside the door and listened, then quietly opened the door and stepped inside. The lights were off in the outer office, but from one of the offices behind the secretary's desk Ryan could hear the sound of a man's voice. He went over and listened. When he was sure the man was on the phone he moved aside and waited. A few moments later he heard the click of the phone being replaced. Then there was the sound of papers being collected and the squeak of a drawer being closed. When he heard footsteps approaching Ryan pressed himself against the wall.

As the man came through the door Ryan grabbed him by the shoulder and whirled him round.

'What the hell?'

Ryan grinned at the other man.

'You're Neal's brother. Just what do you think you're doing?' the man sputtered.

Ryan shoved him back into his office.

Burdick stumbled and managed to catch himself on the edge of his desk. His briefcase flew out of his hand.

'I want to ask you some questions and this time, my friend, I want some answers.'

'I don't have to put up with this.' Burdick reached for the phone.

Ryan slammed his hand down on the receiver.

Burdick grunted and stepped back. His eyes widened as Ryan closed in on him.

'I want to know what the fuck was going on with Neal, and I want to know now.'

'I don't know anything. I don't know what happened,' Burdick said nervously, backing up until he came against the wall.

Ryan reached out and put a finger to the other man's chest. He

231

pressed him backwards. 'What was Neal doing?'

'Nothing, he wasn't doing anything.'

'What was he doing?' Ryan asked, staring into the other man's face.

'I don't know. Really, I don't.'

'Listen, asshole,' Ryan snarled. 'It's just you and me, no one else. Now what the fuck was going on?'

Burdick's eyes shifted from Ryan's gaze. Ryan slapped him lightly across the face and the blow brought tears to the other man's eyes. 'Talk.'

'I don't . . .'

Ryan slapped the other side of his face.

'I . . .'

Ryan hit him again. Burdick gasped and suddenly reached out to push Ryan away. Ryan used his fist this time. Burdick's nose began to bleed. 'I've got all night, and so do you.' Ryan grinned.

Burdick sobbed and closed his eyes. When he opened them, he shook his head and said, 'I don't know anything.'

'Then you're in for a long night,' Ryan said viciously and hit him again.

'Don't. Please, don't,' Burdick cried. He shook his head and, without looking at Ryan, said, 'I didn't know it meant anything. I didn't. How could I?' he pleaded.

Ryan nodded gently and helped him over to his desk.

Burdick fell into his chair and looked up at Ryan seated on the edge of his desk. 'I just never thought it would be like that. I warned him, I told him he shouldn't get involved, but Neal was . . .' He paused.

'Stubborn,' Ryan supplied.

Burdick quickly agreed and haltingly began to tell him what he wanted to know.

Richard took the call in his den.

'We haven't been able to locate the brother.'

'What about the reporter?'

'Nothing, but we've got someone watching his house.'

Richard nodded thoughtfully.

'You think the brother took off?'

'No, I don't. I think he'll show up eventually. I would prefer it to be as soon as possible. I don't want him complicating the situation.' Richard paused. 'Put someone on Burdick and the girls' parents, and also Neal's house. It's just possible that he might try to question them.'

'I'll get right on it.'

Richard hung up. He went out to the living-room to watch the sun set. As it was just beginning its nocturnal death, the phone called him again.

'We've got problems,' Leonard said without preamble.

'Tell me.'

'I got a call from our security people. A reporter was out at one of the mothers' houses. He wanted to interview her daughter.'

'Did they get a description of the reporter?'

'Yes, it was Benning.'

'They're sure?'

'Positive. What are we going to do about this guy?'

'Don't worry about it. I'll deal with the situation.'

'There's more.'

'What?'

'I called Roland.'

'Why?'

'I couldn't get hold of you and I thought that Roland might be able to help,' Leonard said apologetically.

Richard's hand tightened in disgust. 'What happened?' he forced himself to ask calmly.

'Roland said the reporter was also at the County Clerk's office.' Leonard paused. 'You know what that means, don't you?'

'Yes, Leonard, I do. It will be taken care of immediately.'

'Richard?'

'Yes, Leonard,' Richard answered wearily.

'I'm scared.'

'Don't be. The situation is well in hand. These are just minor complications that we'll soon be able to rectify.'

Richard poured himself a brandy and looked out at the Gulf. The sun had completely disappeared. All that remained was the bloody path of clouds it had left in its wake.

Twenty-Five

Ray, dressed in his street clothes, parked his car a block and a half from the Ryan home. He slouched back against the seat and pulled his newspaper in front of him, peering over the edge at the house. On the seat beside him he had a take-out bag from Limpy's, a thermos filled with coffee and a full pack of cigarettes. The smell of coffee, along with the scent of greasy food and tobacco smoke, filled the car. Ray opened his window and shuffled his newspaper to the front page. He glanced at the headline, smiled and turned to the sports page.

'It's my turn,' Ollie said, glaring up at his sister.

'You got it yesterday.'

'No, I didn't.'

'Yes, you did. Don't you remember, you fell on the porch.'

'Did not, that was Monday.'

'Today is Monday, Ollie,' Lisa explained patiently. Ollie glared at her, then glanced down the street. Lisa followed his gaze. She saw the bicycle turn the corner and heard Ollie's excited squeal beside her. 'It's my turn,' she told him firmly.

Ollie ignored her and began to race crazily round the front yard.

The boy on the bicycle barely slowed his momentum as he came down the block. Without stopping, he would grab a newspaper from the bag hooked round his handlebars and throw it on to the front yards of the houses he passed.

He pulled up to the curb in front of Lisa and Ollie. He balanced his bike on one foot as he reached into his bag and pulled out a newspaper. Ollie rushed in front of his sister, reaching for the paper. The boy smiled at him and shook his head. 'It's your turn,' he said, looking directly at Lisa.

235

Lisa blushed and glanced away as she reached out to take the paper.

'It's my turn,' Ollie maintained.

'No, big guy, you got it yesterday,' the paper-boy told him, 'but I got something else for you.' He glanced at Lisa, reached into his pocket and came out with a Tootsie Roll.

'I hate Toothie Rolls,' Ollie pouted, turned quickly and raced round the front of the house.

Lisa watched him. When she turned back to the paper-boy he was looking at her. She glanced away.

'Well, I got to get on with my route.'

'Thank you,' Lisa responded, risking a peek at him.

He nodded, climbed onto his bike and started down the street. He glanced back at Lisa as he passed the next house. Lisa waved, turned and raced up the steps. She could feel her heart beating wildly in her chest. 'The paper, Mom.' She carried it over to her mother who was seated at the kitchen table.

'Thanks, honey.' She smiled.

Lisa examined the smile carefully. When she was sure it was genuine she returned it.

'Why don't you go out and get Ollie ready for dinner. Okay?'

Lisa nodded and slipped out of the back door.

Maggie flipped the paper over as she rose from her chair. She froze when she saw the front page. Below the headline, set off to the side, was the heading, SUSPECT SOUGHT IN VEHICULAR HOMICIDE; under that was a picture of Eddie.

Maggie read the article carefully. She closed her eyes and, with a disgusted shake of her head, flipped through the pages of the magazine on the table. Without thinking about what she was doing, she retrieved the envelope and opened it. She took out a single piece of notebook paper and read what her husband had written.

When she was done, she replaced the note carefully and resealed the envelope.

Lisa and Ollie, racing into the room, found their mother seated at the kitchen table staring blankly at a seemingly unopened envelope she held in her hand.

Ryan parked in the motel lot. He sat behind the wheel of the car staring out at the motel in front of him. His knuckles tightened on the steering-wheel until each jut of bone stood out whitely against his flesh. He climbed out of the car and went over to room 10.

For a moment he paused at the door as he heard the soft murmur of voices coming from inside. When he walked in the two men immediately grew silent. He tried to catch Charlie's gaze, but his friend refused to meet his eye.

Stutz glared at him. 'I thought I told you not to go anywhere. You're making me sorry I didn't take you in.'

'I got bored just sitting around waiting on you guys,' Ryan responded, going over to the small refrigerator set beneath the sink. He came up with a beer.

'Where d'you go?'

'You first,' Ryan countered.

Stutz shook his head in disgust.

'Let it go, Bo,' Charlie said.

Stutz sighed and waved Ryan over to a chair. 'I went out and talked to the intern who was working the emergency ward that night.' He paused. 'You were right,' he admitted grudgingly. 'Firth isn't looking too good.'

'Tell him all of it,' Charlie prompted.

'Well, according to Veros, Firth didn't prescribe something to control the blood clotting. Veros said it was the first time he could ever recall Firth not doing that.'

'So that proves that Firth's a part of it.'

'No, not necessarily. Veros says it was a judgment call. Could have gone either way.' Stutz shook his head. 'It's circumstantial at best, and even that's questionable.'

'He say anything else?'

'No, not really. Firth came down here about seven years ago. He was some hot-shot surgeon up in Boston.'

'That's about the same time Caldwell came down,' Ryan interrupted.

'Yeah, I noticed that too, but it still doesn't prove anything.'

'Nothing that would stand up in court.'

Stutz glanced over at Ryan sharply. 'What d'you mean by that?'

'Nothing.' Ryan shook his head innocently. 'Just making an observation.'

237

'Well, I found something.' Both men turned to Charlie.

'I talked to Mrs Cox, that's the mother of the other girl we identified in the photographs.' Charlie paused, reached into his breast pocket and pulled out the pictures Ryan had found in the Caldwell house. He passed them to the two other men. The majority of the photos now had an X marked in blue ink at the bottom of the right-hand corner.

'All the girls in the photos marked with the X just happen to work at Limpy's. Either the one on the north or the south highway.'

Both men turned to him.

'The mother told me that Debbie was working at the one on the south highway so I took a ride over there. She wasn't there, so I figured I'd wait a while to see if she showed up. While I was sitting there I suddenly realized that I had seen the girl behind the counter somewhere before. I couldn't figure out where. I mean she looked so different. She looked . . .' Charlie paused and shrugged, 'so young. Once I realized who she was I drove out to the other restaurant on the north highway. I saw three more of the girls in the pictures out there.'

'Where did Lailya work?'

'Limpy's,' Charlie stated. 'I checked into her employment files. She'd been working there almost a year.'

'That's just about how long she said she'd been hooking.'

'Christ, they're recruiting the girls from Limpy's,' Stutz said incredulously.

'It's perfect. That's where every schoolkid goes. They'd have a constant supply of new blood.'

Charlie shook his head wearily. 'There's more. I went out to the courthouse and tried to find out who owns the franchises.'

'What'd you find?' Stutz asked, leaning forward intently.

'They're owned by a local corporation called Group Services Incorporated. They incorporated', Charlie paused to look at each man, 'six years ago.'

'Damn.'

'Yeah.' Charlie nodded. 'I checked into some of their other subsidiaries. They also own the Point Blank Security outfit, along with a couple of other restaurants, a motel and a real estate agency.'

'Who the hell are they?'

Charlie looked over at Ryan.

'Who, Charlie?'

'Firth is one of them.' He turned to Stutz. 'So are Robert Raynor and Roland Wilson.'

Ryan noticed the stunned expression on Stutz's face. 'Who are they?' he asked Charlie.

'Raynor's on the city council and Wilson's a circuit judge. He was the one who issued the warrant for your arrest.'

'Jesus Christ.' Ryan rose and paced the room. 'They've got the whole town locked up.'

'They have their own security force,' Stutz said. 'They can enforce their own laws.'

'Not without someone allowing them to.'

'What d'you mean?'

'C'mon, don't be stupid. They couldn't do this without Rainey being aware of it. At least, he'd have to have an idea of what was going on,' Ryan said impatiently.

'I can't believe that.'

'Believe what you want.' Ryan shrugged. 'The thing we have to figure out now is what we're going to do about it.' He glanced over at Charlie and back at Stutz. Neither man met his gaze. He shook his head and went over to get another beer.

'Where were you?'

Ryan turned and leaned forward on the counter. 'I went over to see Burdick.'

'And?'

Ryan raised his beer and drank. When he spoke he kept his gaze locked on Stutz. 'Guy didn't know anything.' Ryan shrugged. 'He was terrified that what had happened to Neal might happen to him.'

Stutz's eyes bored into him and Ryan looked away and abruptly pushed himself away from the bar. 'What we need to figure out is what we're going to do about this shit.'

Stutz continued to watch him.

'I think we should call in the state police. They're the only ones who can handle it. We can't very well do anything locally, can we?' Charlie asked.

Stutz finally pulled his gaze away from Ryan. 'No,' he said slowly, 'we can't.' He paused. 'But do we know enough?'

'C'mon Stutz. What more do you want?'

'I want something that will stand up in court.'

'Shit, we've got them with the photographs.'

'All the photographs do is link Caldwell.'

'We've got the girls.'

'What do the girls really know? According to you, Lailya never even saw any of their faces. I'm sure it's the same with all of them.'

'What about Point Blank?'

'There's no law that says a private citizen can't own a security service.'

'Goddamn it, are you telling me we're not going to do anything?'

'No, I'm just telling you that we have to have some evidence before we can move.'

'Fuck evidence. These guys are righteous for this shit.'

'We have no proof.'

'Fuck the proof.'

'Hey, take it easy.' Charlie stepped between the two men.

Ryan suddenly sighed and took a pace backwards.

Stutz allowed Charlie to push him back into his chair.

'This isn't going to help any of us. We have to work together on this,' Charlie said reasonably, looking hard at them both.

'What do you suggest?'

'I think we have to keep digging. We're bound to turn up something.'

'Like what?' Ryan snorted in disgust. 'These guys waste everything in their way. Look at what happened to Neal, Caldwell, Lailya and that other fucker that got it today. These guys aren't going to wait around for us to find proof. They're going to take us out. They've already got a warrant out on me. How long do you think it's going to be before they do the same to you?' He glared at both of them.

Neither man would meet his eye.

'Stutz,' Ryan said, turning to the policeman. 'If Rainey's in on this, which I think he has to be, then your ass is sold. The guy's going to come down on you as soon as he figures out what you've been doing.'

Stutz raised his eyes to Ryan's. 'There's nothing we can do. We don't have anything solid yet.'

'Maybe we should get something, then.'

'What do you mean?'

'I mean maybe we're going to have to work for it.'

'Edward,' Charlie cautioned.

'I can still take you in.'

'You can try,' Ryan said defiantly, leveling his gaze at the policeman.

'C'mon, both of you, just calm down. We're not going to get anywhere this way. I say we give it a break. Why don't we sleep on it, and in the morning we can take another look at it.'

After a moment, Ryan shrugged. 'All right. That makes sense to me.'

'Okay,' Stutz agreed. He pushed himself to his feet. 'We'll meet back here tomorrow morning.' He paused to look at Ryan. 'None of us does anything tonight. We'll hold off for a while. Agreed?'

'Yeah.'

Stutz held his eye for a moment longer and turned towards the door. 'Edward, just be cool. Okay?' said Charlie.

Ryan nodded, put his hand on his friend's shoulder and walked him outside. He closed the door and went over to the window. He watched both men climb into their cars and pull out of the lot. He sprawled across the bed, lit a cigarette and stared up at the ceiling. He crossed his arms over his chest and, after a while, closed his eyes and let the darkness take him.

The scent was greasy and had a meaty pungency to it. It was like nothing he'd ever smelled before.

The wind carried it down to the dock where he had been fishing. He turned to see a thunderous black cloud spiraling into the air. For a moment he thought it was a storm, then all at once realized what it actually was. He threw his pole to the ground and raced up along the path to the house.

By the time he got there the fire had completely engulfed the main floor. Smoke poured from the windows and blossomed from the roof. The stilted-bottom structure of the house only added oxygen to the already rapacious flames.

He glanced over his shoulder to see his father's truck parked in the drive. He heard a window shatter and turned back to the blaze. Suddenly he saw Neal stumble out from the mangroves to the side of the house and raced over to his brother's side.

'He's dead.' Neal smiled. Tears, blackened with soot and smoke, streamed from his eyes.

Ryan stared at him, looked at his home and back to Neal.

'He's dead,' Neal said again.

Ryan opened his mouth to say something. What it was he was about to say he never found out, because at that moment both brothers turned to see their mother's car weaving up the driveway.

Neal started forward eagerly, then froze abruptly as he watched his father stagger drunkenly out of the vehicle.

Ryan heard Neal's sob. He moved up beside him and gently reached out. Neal whirled round and glared at him. His gaze held a combination of horror and hate. Ryan wasn't sure where either was directed.

'What've you done?' his father screamed.

Ryan turned.

Before he could defend himself he had grabbed him and thrown him to the ground. He covered his head with his arms, trying to protect himself from his father's boots. He peeked out from between his hands to see Neal gazing down at him with that same expression on his face. He started to call out to him, but a boot crashed into the side of his head.

When he woke up, he was in the city jail awaiting trial for murder.

Ryan abruptly pushed himself out of bed. He walked outside and climbed into his car, pulled out of the lot and drove towards the highway.

Stutz waved Charlie over to the side.

'What is it?' Charlie asked, after rolling down his window.

'Burdick. I think he said something.'

'Why?'

'I don't know.' Stutz shrugged. 'There was just something about the way Ryan answered.' Stutz paused thoughtfully. 'I'm going to go talk to him.'

'You don't trust Edward at all, do you?'

'He hasn't given me any reason to.'

'It was his brother, Bo.'

Stutz shook his head. 'That's not good enough, Charlie. This guy seems to be pretty hard on his relatives.'

Charlie watched the other man's car pull away. He rolled up his window and drove home.

A block from his house he passed an unmarked van. Inside it, two security men watched, as Charlie opened his front door.

The house was on the outskirts of Olde Siena. It was in an area that straddled both the rich and middle-class sections, precariously poised to move in either one or the other direction. Only time would tell which way it would fall.

Burdick answered the door. 'What do you want?' he asked gruffly.

'To talk to you.'

'About what?'

'About Neal Ryan, and maybe his brother Edward.'

Burdick flinched and stepped back.

Stutz followed him inside.

A block down from the house a man climbed out of his car and walked casually to a pay phone.

'A cop's here talking to him,' he reported.

'Keep watching and let me know if anyone else shows up,' the voice commanded.

The man replaced the phone and went back to his car.

'He came to see you today.'

'Yes.' Burdick's eyes shifted nervously around the room.

'What'd you two talk about?'

'I don't have to answer any of these questions.'

'No, you don't. We can go downtown to the station and talk about it there, if you would prefer,' Stutz said politely.

Burdick caved in. His shoulders sagged. 'What do you want?' he mumbled, staring down at his clasped hands.

'What did you talk about today?'

'He wanted to know what Neal was doing,' Burdick said wearily.

'And what did you tell him?'

'I told him I didn't know.'

'That's all you told him?'

'No,' Burdick said softly, shaking his head. 'I also told him that Neal was into something, but I didn't know what it was.'

'What?' Stutz asked sharply.

Burdick shrugged. 'I don't know. I only know that whatever it was, it wasn't right.'

'Why?'

'The money. There was just too much of it for whatever it was he was doing.'

'What exactly was he doing?'

'I'm not sure. He'd managed to pick up a new account. It was something he had done strictly on his own. I didn't have anything to do with it. It was all Neal's,' Burdick pleaded.

'What was all Neal's?'

'I don't know.' Burdick shook his head vehemently. 'All I know is that he started this account. I don't know what or who it was for. After I saw the first month's billing, I knew that whatever it was, it wasn't legal.'

'What'd you do about it?'

'I talked to Neal. I told him that there was just too much money for the amount of work he was doing. And I also told him that I didn't want to get involved with anything illegal.'

'What did he say?'

'He said he was going to drop it.'

'Did he?'

'No, I don't think he did.'

'Why not?'

'The billing stopped, but about two months later one of his personal account slips got mixed up with the business accounts. At first I didn't even think about it, but when I looked at it I realized that Neal must have maintained his relationship with these people.'

'Tell me about the account.'

'It was a deposit slip for twenty thousand dollars.' Burdick glanced up at Stutz. 'It had been deposited into a Caribbean account.'

'What about the people behind the money? Did you know who they were?'

'No.' Burdick shook his head.

'No names? Nothing?' Stutz pressed.

'I didn't know anything about them. I didn't want to know anything.'

Stutz examined the man. 'After what happened, why didn't you tell someone about this?' he asked softly.

Burdick glanced up at him. His hands twisted nervously on his lap. 'I was afraid.'

'And now you're not?' Stutz asked gently.

'Yes, but I'm more afraid of being afraid for the rest of my life,' Burdick said, finally meeting the policeman's gaze.

Stutz drove home. He entered his apartment and grabbed a beer. He turned on the TV, then just as quickly flicked it off. He drank, staring at the empty screen. After his third bottle of beer he climbed into bed.

Twenty-Six

Ryan drove out on the north highway. He pulled into a dirt parking lot and climbed out of his rental car. He stepped round the parked motorcycles to the front door of the bar.

The building was a rectangular structure. Three sides of it were enclosed by a screen that rose from waist height all the way to the ceiling. Storm shutters were hooked above each of the screens. The fourth side housed a small stand-up bar with the beer coolers lined behind it.

Ryan stepped inside. He walked to the bar, ordered a beer and turned to survey the room. Four men stood around a pool table, each of them wore jeans and a black T-shirt. Their arms were liberally tattooed. One man was crouched over the table, leveling his cue stick. His beard brushed against the surface of the stained green felt.

Ryan glanced at the six tables spread out across the small room. Every seat was taken either by a biker or his woman.

Ryan turned back and leaned against the bar. He felt at home.

He drank slowly, listening to the raucous laughter and the clicking of the balls from the pool table.

One of the women walked over and fed the juke-box. Allana Miles screamed 'Black Velvet'. Ryan ordered another beer.

'Any Sinners around?'

The bartender looked up at him sharply.

Ryan shrugged, holding the man's eye.

'Who wants to know?'

'A friend.'

The bartender held his gaze for a moment longer, then stepped away. Ryan watched as he paused in front of a customer at the other

247

end of the bar. Both the bartender and the other man glanced his way.

Ryan nodded to them, tipping his beer bottle in their direction. He turned back to the bar and drank.

The man from the far end of the bar walked down to him. 'What d'you want?' he asked, hunching forward on his elbows.

'To talk.'

The other man examined him closely. 'I know you from somewhere?' Ryan shook his head. 'Then how come you're interested in the Sinners.'

'Rode with Tombstone up around Vegas.'

'Tombstone ain't around any more.'

'I heard that.'

'What else you hear?'

'I heard that Raiford's a bitch.' Ryan met the man's gaze and held it.

The other looked away. He picked up his glass of wine and drank. When he put the glass down red wine streaked the corners of his beard. He wiped the back of his hand across his mouth. 'Who are you?'

'Nobody.' Ryan shrugged.

'Where you from?'

'West.'

'How far west?'

'As far as you can ride.'

'What you do there?'

'I got a bike shop out there.'

'You know Dojo?'

'The Gypsy's.'

'What about Cain?'

'He's down in Arizona.'

'Doing what?'

Ryan smiled. 'Time.'

'What d'you want?'

Ryan turned to him. 'A piece.'

The man shrugged. 'Buy one, man. It's no big thing. You just got to wait three days down here.'

'I want it now.'

'You mean like right now?'

'Yeah.'

'I don't know you, man.' He shook his head and turned back to his wine. 'You know some people, but I don't know who the fuck you are. What makes you think I'd do this?'

Ryan shrugged. 'No reason not to.'

The other man shook his head and laughed. 'Fucking big-time reasons not to do it. Like one solid year of reasons not to do it.'

'Up to you,' Ryan said indifferently and lifted his beer. 'I see Dojo, I'll tell him you said hello.'

'Yeah, and who you going to tell him said hello?'

Ryan turned to him. 'Ice.'

'For someone who doesn't know anything you sure seem to know a lot. Where's your bike?'

'Fucked it up the other night, the cops are holding it for me.'

The man's eyes suddenly narrowed. He nodded thoughtfully. 'I know you.'

'I need a piece,' Ryan said, ignoring his words.

Ice glanced away. He pushed himself away from the bar. Each of his knuckles was tattooed with a blue X.

Ryan watched him walk out of the door. He nursed his beer and waited.

The phone awakened Stutz from a fitful doze. He managed to still it on its fourth ring.

'Did you talk to Burdick?'

'Yeah.'

'Well,' Charlie prompted, 'what did he have to say?'

Stutz ran a hand across his eyes. 'Nothing.'

'That's good then.'

'Yeah, that's just great,' Stutz answered disgustedly. 'I'm going to bed. I'll talk to you in the morning.'

Stutz rolled back into bed. He closed his eyes but sleep eluded him. He went into the kitchen and took out a beer. He carried the bottle into the living-room, sat down and tried to relax. He propped the heel of the bottle on his chest. Cool beads of condensation ran down the glass. He smoothed them into his skin, glancing over thoughtfully at the phone.

'Five twenty.'

Ryan took the gun. It was a .44 magnum. The grips had been removed so that the bare steel was exposed.

'With the handle like that, you got to be careful, 'cause the fucking thing'll kick like a mule.'

Ryan hefted the gun and shoved it into his belt under his T-shirt. He reached into his pocket and counted out the money.

'Shells?'

'Only what's in it. You want to wait, tomorrow I can do something about that.'

Ryan shook his head. He turned and started to walk over to his car.

'Going hunting, my man?'

Ryan glanced over his shoulder at Ice. The bearded man was standing by the entrance way to the bar, smiling at him from across the lot.

Ryan nodded slowly and climbed into his car.

He drove south along the highway, entered the Olde Siena area and drove straight through into Royal Port.

He found Galleon Circle and turned into it. A pair of headlights suddenly flashed in his rear-view mirror. A moment later a Point Blank Security jeep wheeled in front of him. It braked, forcing Ryan to pull over to the side.

'Can I help you with something, sir?' the security guard asked, stepping up to Ryan's window.

'Yeah, maybe you can. I was looking for Dr Firth's house.'

'Any particular reason?'

'Yes.'

The guard looked at him.

Ryan smiled back at the man.

'Would you like to tell me what that reason is?'

'Well,' Ryan said, still smiling, 'I don't think that's any of your fucking business.'

'Sir, I'm afraid that . . .'

Ryan shoved his gun into the man's face.

The guard started to take a step back.

'Don't move,' Ryan hissed and opened his car door. He got out, grabbed the man by the shoulder and whirled him round. He marched him back to his jeep.

'There's no reason for any of this. You're just . . .'

'Shut the fuck up.' Ryan tapped the man lightly on the side of the head with the barrel of the gun. He unhooked the guard's handcuffs from his belt and cuffed him to the passenger seat of the jeep. He climbed into the vehicle and backed it out to the pavement. He drove along the road until he found a dead-end street and parked at the end of it beneath the overhanging roots of a banyan tree.

He took the man's handkerchief and stuffed it in his mouth, then tied it firmly in place with his belt. He found a set of jumper cables in the back seat and used these to tie the guard's legs together. 'Just be cool and everything will pass.' Ryan smiled at him.

He climbed out of the jeep and walked back to his car, driving another four blocks before he found the address.

He cut his lights and parked half a block away. Leaning back, he took a deep breath and steeled himself for what he knew he'd need to do next. A moment later he climbed out of his car and walked back towards the house.

'What if they find out?'

'They can't, Leonard. We've been very careful. There is not one piece of conclusive evidence that would enable them to link any of us to these activities,' Richard said patiently.

'What about the girls?'

'The girls' testimony would only be hearsay. Without a physical identification there's nothing anyone can do.'

'What about the other girls?'

'Those girls, Leonard, will never be found.'

'Are you sure?'

'Leonard, this is the third time you've called me this evening,' Richard said wearily. 'I wish you would please calm down and simply accept the fact that there is nothing anyone can do. We are perfectly safe.'

Leonard sighed. 'All right, I'll try.'

'Just relax. There is nothing to worry about.'

Richard replaced the receiver and began to turn away. It rang before he'd even managed a pace.

'I just got off the phone with Robert,' Roland said. 'He told me the reporter had been out to the County Court House.'

'Yes he has.'

'What's going on, Richard?'

'Roland, I've been through this all evening long with Leonard. Are you going to make me go through it again?'

'Yes.'

Richard sighed and wearily related the day's events.

'You're completely satisfied that nothing can be found?'

'Yes, Roland, I am,' Richard responded impatiently. 'The only way any of us could be put in jeopardy, and even that would be limited at best, would be by our own testimony.' He paused. 'I don't foresee that taking place. All of us are well aware of our positions, and the concomitant advantages those positions accede.'

'I want to be kept apprised of any further developments, Richard.'

'I promise I will call you immediately if anything happens.'

Richard went into his den. He retrieved his photo album from his desk drawer. Without opening it, he carried it into the living-room. He crouched before the fireplace and gently caressed the cover. He glanced down at it fondly, then abruptly threw it into the fire.

He stepped back to watch it burn.

Ryan broke the little finger on Dr Allen Firth's left hand.

The doctor screamed.

Ryan stood over him, watching impassively.

When Firth's sobs had quieted, Ryan grabbed him by the hair and jerked his head back. 'What the fuck did you do to my brother?' he snarled.

Firth cringed.

Ryan slapped the old man across the face. 'What? Tell me,' he shouted, crouching down until he was level with Firth.

The doctor was tied to a kitchen chair. His hands and legs were bound with a sash cord that Ryan had ripped from the Venetian blinds.

The doctor was naked.

'Take a look at this, doc,' Ryan said, rising and reaching into his back pocket. He pulled out the photographs and held them in front of the doctor. 'Which one of these old fuckers is you?'

Firth tried to twist away.

Ryan grabbed the man's head and forced him to look at the pictures as he began slowly to go through them. He examined each print and compared it to the naked man in front of him. 'It's hard to place you. All you old fucks look alike.'

He smiled cruelly.

Firth sobbed and stared down at his left hand. His little finger jutted out crookedly to the side. Already the knuckle and hand had started to swell.

'You feel like talking yet, doc?' Ryan asked casually. He sat on the kitchen table, one leg absently swinging over the edge. 'I've got all night and you've got nine more fingers.'

Firth cried out.

Ryan slapped him. The man's jaw clamped closed with a toothy snap and blood began to dribble from the corner of his mouth. 'You're going to tell me. One way or another, you're going to tell me everything I want to know.' Ryan held the other man's gaze.

The doctor mumbled something.

'What?' Ryan shouted.

'I don't know anything,' Firth screamed, defiantly meeting his eye.

Ryan smiled, then reached over and casually slapped the doctor's broken finger.

Firth wailed.

'I think this one might be you, doc.' Ryan held a picture up in front of the old man. A girl was tied to a toilet. A man stood in front of her, urinating in her face.

'How old you think she is? Eleven, maybe twelve?'

Firth stared down at his lap.

Ryan grabbed him by the chin and forced him to look at the picture. 'You're starting to piss me off,' he said softly.

'I don't know anything,' Firth screamed, shaking his head violently as Ryan crouched over his other hand. 'I don't know. I don't know,' Firth repeated in horror, watching Ryan reach for him.

'Tell me about Lailya.' Ryan gripped the unbroken little finger, tugging it back gently.

Desperately, Firth tried to twist away. He couldn't move. His eyes bulged in horror as Ryan began slowly to pull the finger back. 'Please,' he sobbed.

253

Ryan released the finger. 'Talk to me, old man. Tell me all about it.'

'I can't.'

'You don't have a choice.'

'I can't,' Firth shouted, closing his eyes and shaking his head. Perspiration dripped along his forehead and down his cheeks. It mixed with the tears streaming from his eyes.

Ryan broke his other finger.

Firth screamed and abruptly slumped forward. Only his bound arms and legs held him in place.

Ryan went to the sink. When he returned, he carried a pot filled with water which he threw over the doctor's head.

Firth came back to consciousness, spitting out blood and water. He'd bitten through his lip. Blood wormed its way, in a watery line, from his chin to his chest.

'Eight to go, doc,' Ryan said cheerfully.

Firth screamed.

Stutz hung up after the tenth unanswered ring. He raced into the bedroom and quickly got dressed.

He strapped on his holster, hurriedly pulled on a white shirt and let it hang out over his gun belt.

Stutz paused on his way to the front door. He glanced down at the phone. He started to pick it up, then replaced it when he realized there was no one he could trust. He climbed into his car and drove at speed towards Royal Port.

Maggie stood in the doorway looking at her children. The Mickey Mouse night-light shadowed each sleeping form.

Ollie, as usual, had the sheet twisted between his legs. Maggie straightened it. She kissed the back of his neck and went over to her daughter. Lisa slept soundly and neatly on her back. Her hands were folded across her chest.

Maggie sat down on the edge of her bed and gently reached out to touch her cheek.

Lisa murmured and brushed the hand away.

M×aggie walked down the hallway to her own bedroom. She stepped over to the queen-size bed and paused. Tentatively she reached out to touch it, then pulled her hand away.

She leaned back and closed her eyes tightly. A vague image of Neal came to her. She shook her head, denying the image and opened her eyes.

Maggie sat in the living-room. She sipped a glass of iced tea and listened to the comforting silence of the house. She felt all the questions she had, clamoring for answers at the edges of her thoughts. She sipped her tea, forcing them away, until they grew quiet and slowly faded.

'Come to bed.'

'I can't.'

'There's nothing you can do.' His wife reached out to touch his shoulder.

'There should be.'

'There isn't.'

'There has to be.' He turned to meet her eyes.

'You don't even know.'

'I know,' he answered softly, not meeting her eyes.

'Henry,' his wife pleaded, 'you don't have any choice. They told you what would happen.'

'But what they're doing . . .' He stopped.

'You don't even know for sure that they're doing anything.'

He pushed himself off the bed, walked over to the window and stood there, shadowed against the pale moonlight.

'Please, come to bed. You can't do this to yourself.'

'I knew him,' he said softly, without turning.

'Who?'

'Neal.' He turned.

His wife came to stand beside him. She put her hands on his shoulders and forced him to meet her gaze. 'Henry, there's nothing you can do.' He shook his head. 'Come to bed,' she said softly.

She led him back to the bed and pulled him down beside her. She held him against her chest. 'Go to sleep.'

Captain Rainey closed his eyes and tried to find sleep. It was a long time before he discovered it.

Stutz parked in front of the house. It was the third one he had checked. The first two had been dark. This one was well lit.

He climbed out of his car and raced up to the front door. He was about to knock, when he suddenly noticed the splintered glass hanging from the leaded framework beside the doorway.

He twisted the knob and the door opened. Stutz drew his gun. He entered the house in a crouch.

He paused, listening to the silence around him. It was broken by a single sob coming from the other end of the home. He moved quietly along the hallway towards the noise and the light.

At the doorway he leaned against the wall and listened, hearing the sound of his own heart thudding in his chest. A moment later there was another sob. He crouched and whirled round the door.

Seated in a kitchen chair was an old man. The man was naked. It took a moment for Stutz to realize that he was tied to it. He quickly stepped over to him.

The old man's eyes met his beseechingly. 'Please,' he sobbed.

'Where is he?'

'Who?'

'Ryan.'

The man's eyes tightened in horror.

Stutz glanced down at his hands. Both were swollen and the little finger on each was twisted awkwardly jutting out unnaturally to the side.

He glanced at the man's face and his eyes narrowed as he saw a photograph taped across his chest. It was a picture of a little girl. In the right-hand corner was an X marked in blue ink.

Stutz reached out and tore it off. He found three other photos taped together.

'Untie me, please,' Firth whimpered.

Stutz glanced at him in revulsion. 'Where is he?'

'I don't know.'

Stutz nodded abruptly, turned and started out of the room.

The old man screamed.

'What?' Stutz turned.

'He went to see . . .' The old man stopped. His head drooped to his chest.

Stutz raced back to him and jerked him awake. 'Where did he go?' he screamed.

Haltingly the old man told him. Stutz untied him and headed for the door.

He stopped at the phone and made two calls, then raced off to the address Firth had given him, wondering if he wasn't already too late.

Twenty-Seven

The three of them moved into an apartment in town. Each had his own room. At night Ryan would lie awake in his bed, listening to the noises coming from the other rooms. They were sounds he no longer recognized.

His father quit drinking. He began attending AA meetings with a religiosity that astonished Ryan.

Ryan watched helplessly as his brother, over the year since their mother's death, slowly pulled away from him. The few times Ryan had tried to talk to him, Neal's face had twisted into that same expression he had seen on the day of the fire. Only now had Ryan come to suspect where the horror, as well as the hate, were really directed.

Ryan would wake to an empty apartment. He would find a curt note taped to the refrigerator telling him that his brother and father had gone fishing. They had become inseparable.

Desperate for any paternal affection, and driven by the need to forget what had actually happened that day, Neal had quickly responded to his father's clumsy yet sober overtures.

And his father, Ryan had come grudgingly to realize, was just as desperate in his need to form a bond with his younger son. His older son, Ryan now understood, had become the receptacle for all that had been lost in the fire, and for all the years before the fire.

Ryan became a physical embodiment of all the rage and anger that had haunted each of them for so long.

He would watch the way his brother's face would light up whenever he was in his father's presence. He would see his father reach out warmly for his younger son. And then he would see the despair in his father's eyes when his gaze turned in his direction.

The summer of his fifteenth year, Ryan left home.

He packed a duffle-bag with his few belongings, took his life savings of seventy six dollars and headed west.

No one ever came to look for him.

He lied about his age and worked as a bus boy in restaurants, and took day-labor jobs that no one else was willing to do. In New Mexico, he became a roofer and in New Orleans he was a doorman bouncer.

He took his GED tests in Denver, Colorado, passed them and received his high-school diploma.

He came to Los Angeles, established residency and began to take college courses at night. During the day he worked at a veterinarian school, cleaning out the animals' cages.

He was a semester away from an Associate Degree when he finally worked up the nerve to call home.

Neal refused to talk to him.

He learned about the death of his father, and Neal's marriage to Maggie from Charlie Benning.

Two years later, Ryan fulfilled the requirements for a Bachelor of Arts Degree in the Humanities.

He met Zella the day he graduated. Everything changed. It was as if his life had begun the first moment he saw her.

Six years later she died.

Ryan opened his eyes and glanced over at the house across the street. It fronted the Gulf. He saw a light shining at the back. He lit a cigarette, climbed out of the car and walked across the front lawn. He saw a glimmer of sunlight just beginning to shaft across the eastern horizon as he stepped up to the door.

He knocked, drew out the gun and held it by his side. He heard a shift of movement from the other side of the door.

'Neal,' he whispered softly, then knocked again and waited.

'Where is he?' Gloria asked, following her husband into the kitchen.

Charlie fumbled with the buttons of his white shirt. 'Stutz didn't know.' He paused thoughtfully and added, 'or if he did, he didn't tell me.'

'What are you going to do?'

'What else can I do? I'm going to get over to Firth's place. That's what Stutz told me to do.'

'Charlie, please be careful.'

Charlie glanced over at her.

She stood in the doorway wearing a thin white cotton robe, parted along the front of her body. Brief glimpses of tan flesh, along with the startling contrast of pale skin, peeked out.

Charlie took her in his arms and held her tightly. He felt her body mold to his own. Her arms came round his shoulders and she buried her face in the side of his neck.

'It'll be okay,' he said softly, holding her at arm's length. He smiled and turned toward the door. 'I'll call as soon as I can.'

Gloria stood in the doorway and watched him pull out of the drive. She continued to look at the road long after his lights had disappeared round the corner.

'Yes, may I help you?' the young man in the doorway asked.

Ryan showed him the gun.

The man's expression remained politely impassive.

Ryan grabbed the front of his shirt and shoved him inside. He jammed the gun up beneath his chin. 'Where is he?'

The young man's eyes locked onto Ryan's, who snorted disgustedly and back-handed the man across the head. The servant crumpled to the floor.

Ryan paused to listen, then bent over and dragged him to a closet door. He hauled him inside and quickly tied his hands behind his back. When he stepped out of the closet he heard a voice calling from the back of the house. Ryan smiled and moved quietly down the hall to the room at the end.

The door was partly open. Ryan was surprised by the steady stream of cold air escaping the room. He peered around the edge of the doorframe. A fire blazed, the flames casting eerie reflections along the walls and cathedral ceiling.

Ryan eased himself round the door.

An elderly man stood at one end of the room in front of a wall of glass. The windows looked out at the Gulf. He held a brandy snifter in his hand. He turned and smiled politely at Ryan. 'Ah, you must be the brother,' he said, stepping forward and offering his hand.

Ryan shook his head and snorted in disgust. He pointed the gun at the man.

The man stood perfectly still. Ryan examined him closely. He wore a red cardigan over a white shirt, and a tie. He had on crisply pressed dark pants and black patent-leather shoes. Only his hands, swollen and distorted with arthritis, and face were exposed. His face was criss-crossed with a fine network of tiny wrinkles. 'I have been expecting you, Mr Ryan,' he said politely.

Ryan stared at him.

The old man smiled. 'It would seem my expectations were wrong. I had thought you would come bursting into my house, leveling all sorts of egregious accusations at me.'

'I'm not accusing you of anything.'

'No?' He tilted his head inquisitively.

'We're way past that stage.' Ryan smiled cruelly. 'We're at the judgment stage now.'

'Oh, you're going to kill me, is that it?' Ryan leveled the gun at him. 'Do you mind if I finish my brandy before you shoot me, or would that be too much to request.'

'You're trying to buy time.' Ryan shook his head. 'There's no one here to sell you any.'

For the first time the other's eyes narrowed. He recovered quickly. 'Beautiful view, isn't it?' He turned and waved at the western sheet of windows.

Ryan glanced out at the Gulf, then back again. He shrugged. 'Anybody can look at a sunset, old man. It takes balls to see it rise. And you don't have them.'

The man laughed. He walked over to a chair.

Ryan followed him with the gun.

'Don't you have any questions, Edward? You don't mind if I call you Edward, do you?'

'No, not at all. Not if I can call you Dick,' Ryan said, leaving little doubt about the connotation he put on the word.

Richard regarded Ryan, then thoughtfully swirled his snifter. 'You're young,' he said softly. 'You don't know what it is to grow old. What it is to watch the way others begin to view you as an impediment to their futures, regardless of your value. They see only your age and nothing else.' Richard paused. Ryan stared back at him impassively. 'What is it you want, Edward?'

Ryan shrugged. His eyes never left the face of the man before him.

'Isn't there anything that money could buy you?'

'No.'

The old man smiled. 'Then you're a lucky man.'

'Is that what this is all about? Money?'

'No, not at all. Most of us have more money than we'll ever need.'

'Then what *is* it about?'

'Ah, you do have questions.' Richard smiled happily. 'I'm pleased.' He sipped his brandy. 'That has been one drawback of this whole enterprise. A minor one, I'll admit, but still a nagging problem.' Richard glanced over at Ryan expectantly.

Ryan sighed. 'What problem is that?'

Richard beamed. 'Being able to explain to someone just how successful our activities have been. You see there's no one to tell. No one, at least, whom it would be safe to tell.'

'Neal didn't seem to share that problem.'

Richard glanced at him sharply. 'You think Neal was going to tell someone about our activities?' Richard threw back his head and laughed, his laughter changing abruptly to a cough. He pulled a red handkerchief from his back pocket and held it to his mouth. When he had recovered he refolded the handkerchief neatly and replaced it. 'So you thought Neal was going to talk to the authorities?' Richard said, looking at Ryan sadly. 'I'm sorry to be the one to have to tell you this, but Neal simply wanted a larger percentage.'

'That's bullshit.'

'Now, Edward, I would assume you've acquired a certain amount of information about our activities by now,' Richard said reprovingly. 'Your brother was an integral part of our expansion. He discovered a certain phase of our operation that he mistakenly felt entitled him to a larger slice of the pie, so to speak.'

'What . . . what was this thing he discovered?'

Richard smiled. 'The girls.'

'What about them?'

'He discovered that not all of them were recruited from our operations.'

'Limpy's.'

Richard nodded approvingly. 'We also have agents stationed at some of the local transport facilities.'

Ryan snorted. 'You mean bus stations, old man. You're nothing better than a fucking pimp.' Richard shrugged. 'If, as you say, Neal was in this from the beginning, why would this suddenly start to bother him?'

Richard looked over at him coyly. 'Well, to be perfectly honest with you, Edward, some of the children were strictly cast-offs from our great society. Accepting this fact, we saw no reason to treat them any differently.'

It took a moment for Ryan to comprehend what the man was saying. 'You were snuffing them.'

Richard nodded happily.

'Why? Why would you do this?' Ryan whispered.

Richard shrugged indifferently. 'It was a way to keep young. Youth is a constant array of new experiences. It's only when the experiences are no longer new that the ageing process begins. The girls, the drugs, all of these enterprises were challenging to us. They invigorated us with a youth and power that we hadn't known for decades.'

'You killed Neal.'

'Not personally.'

'You killed Lailya.'

Richard smiled and shook his head. 'I didn't.'

'Firth did.'

'Firth?' Richard asked quickly.

This time, Ryan smiled. 'How do you think I found you? Firth was just sitting there waiting for someone to ask him a question. That's all it's going to take for every one of you fuckers to fall.'

Richard laughed. He reached for his handkerchief.

Ryan watched in disbelief.

'You'll have to forgive me,' he said, patting his handkerchief in place, 'but do you honestly think any of us is going to fall?' He paused, looking at Ryan closely until he saw the slow realization take hold of the other man. 'We're old men, Mr Ryan. What do you think can possibly happen to us? I doubt you have much in the way of direct evidence. I would think circumstantial, at best. We have taken meticulous precautions in that regard. And even if the good Dr Firth were to talk, and it did go to trial, what then? A jury of our peers? They would applaud us for what we've done. And if they didn't, we have enough capital to hire the best lawyers to keep this case tied up in the courts for the rest of our lives. And realistically, Mr Ryan, how long will that actually be? After the trials and the appeals, a judgment might just possibly be rendered in fifteen years.' Richard paused. He looked over at Ryan with contempt. 'No, Mr Ryan. You're no threat. You're merely a troublesome bit of flotsam that will soon pass, as all else has.'

Richard rose and went over to the window. He looked out at the Gulf. Shafts of sunlight had begun to pierce the night and reflect off the dark water. 'See, Mr Ryan,' he said, waving to the window. 'A sunrise. My sunrise. My balls, Mr Ryan.' He sneered and turned to look at the other man. 'You know the way out.' He looked at Ryan disdainfully. 'Take it, before I have you arrested for trespassing.'

Ryan glanced towards the doorway as he heard the sound of a distant siren. He turned back to Richard, who stood at the window smiling at him contemptuously.

Stutz raced down the street. He passed Ryan's rental car a half block from the house, squealed to a stop and jumped out of his car.

The front door was open. Stutz went in, drawing his revolver. He heard a muttered curse coming from a doorway off to the left and flung open the door. A man lay sprawled across the floor. His hands tied behind his back.

Stutz slammed the door and raced down the hallway. He heard voices coming from the room at the end. His grip tightened on his revolver as he ran.

'None of it was my idea.' Firth looked entreatingly up at Charlie.

'I know that, Allen,' Charlie said gently. 'Whose idea was it?'

Firth shook his head and sobbed. 'It was Richard's. It was all his doing,' he gasped.

Charlie solicitously patted the old man on the back. 'Why don't you tell me all about it while we wait for the ambulance to arrive,' Charlie said softly.

Firth glanced up at him gratefully. 'Could I have a glass of water, please?'

Charlie went over to the sink and filled a glass. For a moment he caught sight of his reflection in the dark window. His eyes gazed back at him bleakly. He rearranged his expression and turned back to the doctor. 'Here you go.' He held the glass while the other man drank greedily. 'Tell me about Richard.'

'It was all his fault. He was the one who started it,' Firth began tearfully.

Charlie took notes as the man talked.

He rode with Firth in the ambulance to the emergency ward. Firth didn't stop talking until they wheeled him into an examination room.

Charlie folded his notebook and covered his face with his hands. He slouched forward on the bench, listening to the cries and whimpers of the steady stream of the sick and injured who staggered up to the admissions desk.

'Get out,' Richard commanded. 'You can do nothing to me. If you think you can, then do it. Just leave me in peace until then.' He turned to look out of the window.

Ryan felt the weight of the gun in his hand. He dropped it to his side. He heard a car squeal to a stop in front of the house. The sirens had grown closer. The front door opened and the sound of footsteps came from the hallway.

He closed his eyes.

Neal.

'I won't ever let anything happen to you.'

The stain of soot and smoke darkening his brother's tears.

The bleak imperviousness of his brother's gaze.

His father's rage.

His brother's cries.

Ryan opened his eyes.

Richard glared at him from across the room.

The footsteps came closer.

Ryan slowly raised the gun and shot Richard once in the forehead.

Before Richard's body hit the floor Ryan turned and was out the door.

'What the fuck have you done?' Stutz shouted at him.

Ryan gazed back at him impassively and watched as Stutz hurled himself through the doorway and into the room.

'Shit,' Stutz screamed and stormed back out into the hall.

Ryan stood leaning against a wall. He held the gun out to Stutz.

'You asshole.' Stutz shook his head sadly. 'You poor pathetic son-of-a-bitch. What the fuck do you think's going to happen now?'

Ryan stared back blankly at the policeman.

The sirens grew closer.

Stutz looked at the gun in Ryan's hand and then at Richard's body lying in front of the picture window. The horizon was now hugely splintered by multicolored shafts of sunlight. He turned back to Ryan.

Ryan met his gaze and shrugged wearily. Once more he offered the policeman the gun.

'Asshole,' Stutz muttered in disgust and took it out of his hand.

Twenty-Eight

'I know there are things in your past, things that you won't, or can't, talk to me about. I can accept that,' Zella said. 'Maybe not willingly, but I care enough about you so that I can wait until you're ready to tell me.' Ryan stood by the window, looking out at the alley behind his apartment. 'But I want more than this, Eddie. I want something permanent.' Ryan turned to look at her. 'I need that, Eddie. I really do,' she said solemnly.

'And if I can't give you that?'

Zella shrugged and looked away.

Ryan took a deep breath and moved across the room to her. He put his arms round her and tried to imagine what it would be like never to hold her again.

'Please, Eddie. Please?' she said softly.

Ryan suddenly realized that his decision had been made long since. He touched her chin and gently tilted her face up to his. 'Whatever you want,' he promised, and Zella threw her arms round him and held him tightly.

It was just a house, really nothing extraordinary. It had two bedrooms, a car port and a small back yard. It amazed Ryan how such a simple structure could make him so happy.

Sometimes, in the evening, they would carry their coffee out to the back yard and sit on the grass. Side to side, their backs against the wall, they would watch silently as the stars slowly pierced the dark sky. At these times there was no need for words between them. Just the touch of her beside him, the press of her leg against his, was all that Ryan needed to feel to know that she was a part of him.

That spring Zella planted two apple-trees in the back yard,

promising him an apple pie with their first harvest.

'That'll take years,' Ryan said, shaking his head in amusement.

'So?' Zella answered impishly, meeting his eye. 'You planning on going anywhere?' And Ryan suddenly realized that there was no other place he wanted to be, that this was his place, the place where he belonged and had been looking to find for all those years since leaving Florida.

When he woke, bathed in perspiration, with the greasy scent of the fire in his nostrils, Zella would be there, offering him unquestioning comfort.

Their life together began to supplant the one he had left so long ago, and now, with Zella's help, finally seemed to have put behind him.

Soon even the dreams began to fade, until they were only a disturbing memory.

In October, twenty-three months after they had moved into the house together, Ryan woke up to a scream coming from the kitchen. It took him only a moment to realize it was Zella. The dark rooms of the house fought him as he raced into the kitchen.

'Who the fuck are you?' Zella screamed furiously, then, with a violent shake of her head, attacked him.

Before Ryan could comprehend what was happening Zella had darted across the room and plunged a steak-knife into his shoulder.

'Who are you?' she shouted, stepping back and glaring at him from behind the tangle of her hair.

Ryan reached out for her.

She slashed at him, shredding his hand and chest, then backed away until she came up against the counter.

Ryan watched as she suddenly sagged and crouched over, dropping the knife to the floor. She fell to her knees, covering her face with her hands.

'Eddie,' she sobbed, looking up at him in confusion. She slowly raised her blood-stained hands in front of her and stared at them in horror. 'Oh, Eddie, what's happening?' she cried, as Ryan took her in his arms.

It was called a glioma tumor and it was exerting pressure on the hypothalamus, creating extreme feelings of paranoia and aggression.

An hour after arriving at the hospital, Ryan walked alongside her as they wheeled her into surgery. As he stooped to kiss her she drew back in horror and screamed for help.

Six hours later, with the sun rising over the ridge of the house, Ryan sat alone in the back yard of their home.

Zella had died at five o'eight that morning.

Stunned, Ryan sat, leaning against the wall, unable to tear his eyes away from the branches of the apple-tree.

That night he dreamed, and when he woke, bathed in perspiration with the smell of death all around him, he knew that finally and irrevocably he was alone.

Twenty-Nine

Hal Lundgren had been in charge of the city impound lot for five years. Arriving for work at his usual time he paused at the gate to look over at the rows of confiscated vehicles. He turned to the small gatehouse set to the side of the entrance way. In one hand he carried a cup of steaming coffee, in the other a copy of the morning's edition of the *Miami Herald*. He was looking forward to both.

The sun was just breaking over the eastern horizon. Hal knew he had another hour or so before he would be called upon to begin his working day.

He opened the door of the small office and went in, put his coffee and newspaper on the desk and turned to shut the door.

A man stood by the entrance.

Hal peered through the doorway at him.

'I've got a note here.' The man held out a sheet of paper.

Sighing disgustedly, Hal climbed down the steps and walked over to the gate. He glanced suspiciously at the man on the other side. 'It's a little early for this, isn't it?'

The man shrugged.

Hal took the note and read it carefully. He examined the signature and with a weary sigh unlocked the gate. 'Third row, over that way.' He pointed.

The man nodded and walked across the yard to the third row of confiscated vehicles.

Hal waited impatiently. He glanced longingly at his cup of coffee, then back at the yard.

The quiet morning was suddenly broken by the rumbling sound of an engine. The motor roared and subsided into a steady drone. A moment later the man wheeled out of the aisle towards the gate.

273

Hal stepped back as the motorcycle passed him. He locked up again and looked out through the wire mesh as the man and the motorcycle disappeared round the corner.

'All right, Stutz,' the state policeman said angrily, 'why don't we run through this once more.'

It was the fifth time Stutz had been asked to repeat his story. He couldn't help the weary sigh that escaped him. The sound earned him an angry glare from his questioner.

The state patrol was not happy. They'd showed up on the scene almost an hour ago. They had found only Stutz and the body of Richard Anson in the house.

'Anson had the gun?'

'Yes.'

'He pulled it on you when you accused him of . . .' the man paused to look at his notebook, 'prostitution, is that right?'

'That's right.'

'You fought over the gun and it went off?'

'Yes.'

The man looked at him impatiently. Stutz stared back. The state policeman shook his head in disgust. 'All right, tell me the rest of it. Why didn't you call in the local authorities?'

Stutz began to talk. He started at the beginning and worked his way truthfully almost to the end of his story.

It was only the last ten minutes that he changed. That had been all the time it had taken him to get Ryan out of the house. He'd done it grudgingly. If there had been any other way of handling it he would have gladly taken it. But Stutz had known that Ryan would only complicate an already extremely sensitive situation. His presence would have called into question everything that he, Charlie and Ryan had discovered.

Stutz hadn't wanted those kinds of distractions. He wanted the focus to be completely on Siena and what had been taking place in the town for the last seven years.

After eliciting a promise that he would never, ever see him again, he had written the release note and hurried Ryan towards the back door of the house.

'One thing, Stutz, or I stay and turn this whole thing into a circus,' Ryan had said, stopping at the back door.

'You aren't in much of a bargaining position,' Stutz had reminded him.

Ryan had shrugged and said, 'Neal.'

'What about him?'

'I want him cleared.' Ryan had paused, forcing the policeman to meet his gaze. 'He was all set to break the whole thing wide open, and that's why they killed him. That's the way I want it to read,' Ryan had demanded.

Stutz had glared back at him.

The sirens screamed as they had turned down the street.

'All right,' Stutz had said reluctantly, then watched as Ryan turned and disappeared round the side of the house.

By the time Stutz had returned to the living-room, the state patrol had been at the front door.

'You're saying they're all bad?'

Stutz shook his head. 'No, I'm just saying that I don't know who is and who isn't. There has to be someone on the force who knew about this for it to go on.'

The patrolman examined him closely. 'You realize what you're saying, don't you?'

'Yeah,' Stutz answered, and his sudden smile shocked the state policeman.

Ryan tied his duffle-bag to the back of his bike and climbed on. He drove quickly through town. The morning coolness had almost faded by the time he pulled up in front of Charlie's house. Gloria answered the door. 'Charlie around?'

Gloria shook her head. 'He's down at the office. He just called a little while ago.' She paused to examine him. 'He was worried about you,' she said softly.

Ryan smiled reassuringly. 'I'm fine.'

'Why don't you ride down to the newspaper?'

Ryan glanced away. 'No, I think I'm going to head out.' He turned back to her. 'Why don't you say goodbye for me. Tell him I'll be talking to him.'

'You don't have to go, Edward.' She touched his arm.

'Yeah, I do.' He covered her hand with his.

'You'll call him?'

'I promise,' Ryan said and started down the steps.

'Edward?'

'Yeah.'

'Take care.'

Ryan nodded and swung his leg over his bike. He started it and drove out to the highway.

Maggie answered the door. She stared at him through the screen.

'I'm leaving,' Ryan finally said.

Maggie opened the door and motioned him inside. She poured him a cup of coffee. Ryan stood, leaning against the sink while he drank it. 'Where will you go?'

'West.'

'Los Angeles?'

Ryan shrugged. 'Just west, for the time being.'

Maggie examined him closely. His eyes rose to hers and she glanced away. 'I have something for you,' she said abruptly, then turned and left the room.

Ryan lit a cigarette. He turned as she came back through the doorway.

She held the envelope out to him. It trembled as Ryan took it from her hand. He glanced at his name scrawled across the front, then up at Maggie who wouldn't meet his eye.

Ryan opened the envelope, took out the single piece of notepaper and read it.

I started the fire. It was a long time ago, and no one really gives a shit now. Do whatever the hell you want with this.

Neal

'What does it say?' Maggie asked quietly.

Ryan closed his eyes.

Neal smiling at him.

Ryan's arm round his brother's shoulders.

I won't let anything happen to you.

'What, Eddie? What does it say?' Her words came out tremulously.

276

Ryan opened his eyes and glanced away. 'He said he forgives me,' he said softly and turned to meet her gaze.

Maggie sobbed and slowly raised her arms.

Ryan held her and listened to her crying.

Lisa dreamed that Daddy had come home. He was bending over her to pick her up.

'C'mon, baby,' he said softly, enfolding her in his arms. She went willingly. She curled up against his chest. She buried her face against the side of his neck and was startled by the harsh feel of his beard. She opened her eyes.

'Uncle Eddie,' she whispered softly, looking into the face of the man holding her.

He smiled.

'Daddy,' Ollie said sleepily. They both turned to look at Ollie rising from his bed. He wore his Donald Duck pajamas with the feet. He was rubbing his eyes, staring at the two of them. 'Daddy?' he asked.

Lisa tightened her arms round his neck as he swooped over and picked up Ollie in his other arm.

Her face was only inches away from her brother's. His smile was huge.

As they came out of the bedroom Lisa saw her mother standing beside the doorway. She had an exasperated look on her face, but Lisa could see that it wasn't a real one, it was only a pretend one.

Uncle Eddie carried both of them out to the porch. On the top stair, he slowly bent over and released Lisa. Her bare feet hit the cool wood and she watched as Uncle Eddie carried Ollie down to his motorcycle.

She heard Ollie's excited squeal as Uncle Eddie put him on the front seat. He took a bungi cord from the back of the bike and strapped Ollie round the waist to the front seat, then climbed up behind him.

Lisa saw Ollie glance over at her. His eyes were wide with excitement. His pajamaed feet kicked nervously at the sides of the motorcycle.

She watched as Uncle Eddie started up the bike and slowly rode down the street. The sound of Ollie's delirious scream carried all the way along the block.

He came back and parked in front of the house. Lisa looked on as he gently lifted Ollie from the seat. Uncle Eddie seemed to hold him for a moment longer than necessary before he put him on the ground.

He glanced up at her.

Lisa shook her head nervously and looked over her shoulder.

Her mother smiled and motioned her down the stairs.

Lisa raced down the steps to the side of the motorcycle. She glanced at Ollie, and saw him standing perfectly still in absolute silence as he stared in awe at the motorcycle in front of him.

She felt Uncle Eddie's hands close round her waist, as he lifted her up easily and put her on the seat behind him.

'Hold on tight.'

Lisa wrapped her arms round him and buried her face in his back. The bike throttled forward. She could feel the rush of cool air press along her legs and sides.

The bike shot forward in a sudden burst of speed.

Lisa tightened her grip. She felt the steady beat of her uncle's heart beneath her hands.

It seemed only moments before he slowed and parked in front of the house.

He lifted her, and for a moment she felt his arms tighten round her before he lowered her gently to the ground. She stepped back. She could still feel the steady embrace of his arms.

'Bye, Maggie.'

Lisa glanced back at her mother.

'Goodbye Eddie,' she called, then, brushing at her eyes, quickly turned into the house.

'Later, dude,' Uncle Eddie said to Ollie.

Ollie squealed with delight.

She felt his eyes on hers. He nodded slightly, winked and started his motorcycle.

'Uncle Eddie,' she whispered.

She heard Ollie start up his engine and swiveled to watch him race round the side of the house. His Donald Duck pajamas flapped loosely behind him.

When she turned back to the road Uncle Eddie was gone.

Thirty

Ryan rode seven hundred miles that first day.
   He pulled up to a motel a little south of Mobile, Alabama and took a room.
   He carried his duffle-bag inside and threw it on the floor.
   Exhausted, he slumped across the bed.
   He closed his eyes tightly.
   Zella . . .